1

Kabuki in a G String

M.S. Simpson

3

Round Mountain Press

The characters and events in this book are fictitious. Any similarity real persons, living or dread, is coincidental and not intended by the author.

ISBN: 978-0-9887790-5-1

10 9 8 7 6 5 4 3 2 1

4

Printed in the United States of America

"Travel is fatal to prejudice, bigotry, and narrow-mindedness."

Mark Twain

6

Shrieking, "Take me, sweet Jesus," Roberta Martin's great-grandmother ran into the fiercest tornado in the history of Lubbock County, Texas. She promptly perished in her savior's stormy embrace. Her youngest son Wilson found her naked body – minus the plastic hair curlers and house dress she'd been wearing – naked, wide-eyed and as bald as a bowling ball – out in Orville Covington's cotton field, past the railroad tracks on Avenue 11. Perhaps she was demented; then again, perhaps not. Say what you will, a lot of God exists in a tornado.

Roberta had given up trying to sleep on her Air France flight from New York to Paris. There was too much activity and someone behind her kept belching. She figured on a flight from New York it was best not to say anything to a man who belched, so she just endured it. At the moment, she was thinking about her upcoming reunion with her cousin Chad. More particularly, she was thinking about how other people had momentous meetings, and now it was her turn. Darcie Copely, from upstairs in fines-collections, had met Sylvester Stallone at Universal Citywalk – or so she said (you could never be sure about Darcie's stories). Roberta's parents had a momentous meeting with a freight train one Friday evening on a level crossing down near Sweetwater. They died in the nick of time. Her father had wanted a son and her mother had wanted a real West Texan female, frilly and fluffy. Except for female, Roberta wasn't any of those things, and it had been getting worse not better. Even female was getting iffy. Last winter, during an ice storm – in her defense, she was wearing a flannel jacket and earmuffs – the man at the service station called her 'sir.'

The events that put Roberta on her sleepless Air France flight started two days after she received her termination notice from the library, where she had worked since she was seventeen. Stepping out of the shower and regarding herself in the foggy mirror – foggy mirrors were kind to her – she ran to answer the phone, hoping it was an answer to one of the twenty plus applications she'd put in around town. However, it was neither Fruit Cup nor Eigleman's Bakery, but her Aunt Helen, who'd been the guiding light in Roberta's life since her parents died in their rendezvous with the freight train. Roberta was not surprised to find Helen on the other end of the phone, but she *was* surprised to hear her in tears. One strong woman, Helen never cried, not even at funerals or weepy movies or when they saw a dead dog by the side of road. This tearful Helen announced that she needed to see Roberta – and a request from Helen could not be ignored. So Roberta dressed and sped the several miles to Helen's Tech Terrace mansion, in which cousin Chad and Roberta had spent youthful hours sliding down the banister and playing tennis on the entrance hall floor.

A penciled note advised Roberta to come in without ringing the bell, so Roberta opened the door – only to find the curtains drawn and the house dark. Terrified of what she called "the criminal element," Helen kept lights blazing all night long and slept with a loaded pistol beside her bed, which she intended to use if need be – although, as she put it, "it'll be sure to cause another one of them racial stinks down to Austin." Unless a crime was of a brainy sort, like embezzlement or stock fraud, Helen perceived the criminal element to be of one ethnicity. Roberta called out (fearing that pistol, despite her pale complexion) but there was no response. Moving in darkness toward the kitchen, she called as she went.

At last, a feeble voice came from the den, "I'm in here, Bert."

Roberta made her way as quickly as the darkness allowed. "May I turn on the light, Helen?"

"If you have to."

Flicking on the light, Roberta saw Helen on the sofa in her nightgown, and she rushed across the room and pulled open the drapes along the back windows. "What's the matter? Are you sick?"

"No. I'm shriveling up, like the wicked witch in The Wizard of Oz."

"*What?*"

"Today I went to the doctor and I am suspected of having diabetes." She pronounced it portentously, dah -ah-*beat* -ees.

"Oh, Helen."

"Before long," Helen moaned, closing her eyes in contemplation of the cataclysm, "they're going to cut off my legs. They do that to diabetics. They cut off their legs."

"They *do*? Why?"

"How should I know why? Maybe the disease affects the limbs, they atrophy or something. I told you. I'm shriveling up."

Roberta grasped Helen's hand. "You've always seemed so healthy."

"God is punishing me because I raised up my only son to be a Godless sinner."

"Chad's not a godless sinner."

"*Pooh*. He turned his back on his kith and kin, said so many cruel things, after he'd been living like a wanton heathen — which you don't know the half of — and now God has chosen to show me how bad a mama I really was."

Roberta could not allow diabetes to stand as divine punishment. "You're a good woman, Helen," she said firmly.

"If I were such a good woman, my son would be here by my side, wouldn't he?"

"When you tell him about your illness, I'm sure he'll come right home."

"Tell him? How? When I write him letters he sends them back with my address scratched on top of his. Two months ago, I had a total stranger at the supermarket write down his address on an envelope, and then I put my letter in it and sent that envelope to my friend Elaine, the one who moved out there to California (why, I have *no* idea) and

I had *her* address a new envelope and put the one the stranger wrote on inside of it – and the damn thing still came back to me unopened. If I try to phone him he hangs up on me. When Loreen found me his email address at that fancy school of his school in Paris, on that Google thingy, he damn well put a block on me. It's hopeless." After an eloquent silence, Helen spat out, "*And* his life is sordid. I know all about his antics. I never told you, Roberta, but I had me a report done by a private detective up to Amarillo – Annabel York recommended him. You know, he helped her find that no-account daughter of hers, the one who ran off with her chemistry teacher, and when I confronted Chad – as God is my witness, the sinner admitted everything. And for Chad's sins I'm being punished. Just look at me. Oh, Roberta, what *am* I to do?"

"Would you like me to write to him?" After all, Roberta sent Chad a Christmas and birthday card every year and they never once came back. She even sent him photographs through email and bits and pieces of her news, such as it was, and he clearly didn't have a block on her. "Or I could send him a cheery email; he doesn't block my emails."

"He'd know I'd put you up to it, you blockhead. Once I told him to come home because his father was dying."

"And he *didn't*?"

"Well, Mack wasn't actually dying then. That came later, and it was only in the crush of becoming a widow and all that I forgot to send word about his *real* death – see, that's what comes from living way over there. But anyway, back to my point: Mack was sick, I could tell it, even if the doctors couldn't, and Chad ignored me. It wouldn't be any different now."

"I could disguise my handwriting," Roberta said. "I can pretend to be a concerned third party."

"Didn't you listen to my supermarket story? He's clever. His kind always is. He'd no doubt enjoy the thought of me lying here legless, shooting myself up with drugs. He'd make some quip about not being able to answer the door for the Avon lady – and we both know that I haven't bought an Avon product for ten years or more. Do they even still sell door-to-door? I don't think they do that door-to-door stuff anymore, do they? The way things are these days they'd all get raped or serial killed."

Roberta had a decanter of rose-scented perfume on the back of her toilet that said other-wise about Helen's Avon purchases, but she held her tongue.

"Roberta. I want you to move in here with me and I want to adopt you. I want to make you my legal daughter. My heir."

Roberta flushed. *"Helen."*

"But first I need you to go over there to Paris and bring back my son."

"You want me to go to Paris? *France*?"

"All expenses paid. We'll see if that tramp can evade Roberta Martin. When you're on your game, Missy, you might quail even Satan."

"You mean," Roberta wondered, still flabbergasted, "that I'm going over there all by myself?"

"Yes. For your dear, dying, almost legless aunt, who has given you the best years of her life and never denied you a thing."

Roberta nodded slowly. In her present emotional state Helen was clearly forgetting that she point-blank refused to help Roberta buy a nicer car because, as she put it, "poor people and luxury make bad company." Of course, Helen's refusal had been morally instructive, not exactly denying. "But what if he doesn't come home even then?"

"He will. You'll make him see the evil of his present life. God and Roberta Martin will bring back my boy to me."

For a brief moment Roberta wondered if she was being drawn into something unethical. But when she looked into her mentor's eye she said, "I'll do my best, Helen."

"Thank our dear Lord Jesus for you, Roberta." Helen kissed Roberta's hand. "Perhaps they'll be able to rig me out in artificial legs and we'll get us a dog and the three of us will go for walks. No, no, better *still*, we'll get us a big old comfy wheelchair and Chad can push me, while you take the dog on a leash."

At this moment the front door opened and Loreen K. Albrighton flounced into the house. Loreen K. Albrighton had been Helen's friend since childhood, and she'd never accepted Roberta's presence in Helen's life. In return, Roberta detested Loreen. When they were young, she spent hours entertaining Chad by mimicking Loreen, who had a particularly odious way of introducing herself as, 'Loreen K. Albrighton, the K. stands for Karlie.' Why didn't she just introduce herself as Loreen Karlie Albrighton and be done with it, Roberta had always wondered?

"Oh, hey," Loreen said, "you here *again*, Roberta girl."

No, Roberta thought, I'm not here; this is one of those holograms. "Hey, Loreen."

"I got me a new hairdresser," Loreen said, "just come up from the place, in that new mall thingy – you know, down to Quaker and 98th?"

"The new strip mall," Roberta said.

"Our preacher said not to call them that no more," Loreen said stiffly, "on account of what it might do to kids to be hearing the word strip all the time."

"So he recommended mall thingy instead?"

"Your hair looks just the same," Helen said, observing the ringlets piled on Loreen's head.

"I didn't want my hair different, I just wanted to find me a new girl to do it. That last girl – remember? She kept saying how she liked my things, first my purse, and then my shoes, well, don't tell me she wasn't fixin' to steal something."

"Maybe she was just admiring," Roberta said.

"Wanted me to tell her what they were worth."

"Roberta and I are working on some family business here, Loreen," Helen said with a knowing look. "You want to rustle us up some fresh coffee?"

"Sure thing," Loreen said. "By the way, Roberta, you got them stripes going the wrong way."

"No, I don't, this is the way they go."

"I mean, for big women they's supposed to go up and down, not sideways. Sideways makes you look even bigger."

"Well, I didn't design it, I just bought it – down there to the outlet place," Roberta added, on the chance Helen might think she'd been extravagant.

"Ain't nothing but tacky old stuff nobody else wanted down there," Loreen sniffed, "you ought to buy yourself something decent over to Wal-Mart. Wal-Mart's got all kinds of nice things in big girl sizes." She turned toward the kitchen. "Coffee's a comin'."

With Loreen out of the room, Helen turned her attention back to Roberta. "Oh please, Roberta, bring that boy back home to Texas."

"Yes. All right. I'll go and get him – if I can."

"That's my girl."

And so it was that Roberta turned up on her flight to Paris, with too much money, an American Express card off Helen's account, a suitcase stuffed with new clothes, and a mandate from God and Helen Newsome to fetch the wayward son from exile.

Chad reached the balcony through the open *porte-fenetre*. Below, on *rue des Bernardins*, a woman on a bicycle negotiated the narrow space between stacks of paper goods in the process of being delivered to the corner stationery store. Her bell tinkled up the street. So many things had once seemed certain to Chad. There'd been an illusion of solidity, and even if he'd known it was illusory, it had been there. Now, his life quivered, boneless as jelly. He couldn't retrieve the solidifying lies of the past. Stepping to the rail Chad noticed, on the balcony two floors below, one of the Norwegians who shared that apartment.

"*Salut*, Aksel."

"*Salut*. We missed you."

Chad peered down at him.

"At Galsworthy's," Aksel said. "Simon taught me to spit grape seeds – he can spit the farthest, of course. He thinks of organizing a seed-spitting competition."

"That Simon."

After a moment of reflection, Aksel said, "The students at your school worship him."

"And you know this – ?"

"Galsworthy tells me stories. According to him, ninety percent of the boys want to be him and ten percent want him to – well, it has to do with this theory of ten percent gay people."

"I get the idea."

"He had a poetry reading – Galsworthy, I mean, not Simon. Croatian boys with bad teeth."

"I'm a stickler for good teeth."

"I know. Very American of you."

"We're a sadly superficial culture."

Over the roof of the adjoining youth hostel Chad watched clouds roil above the Left Bank and smelled the heavy odor of an approaching storm. Back home in Texas, they'd call this tornado weather. Chad had family history where tornadoes were concerned.

"Where's Imad?"

"Here somewhere." In fact, behind him, Chad heard Imad on the telephone, filling someone in on his recent trip to Barcelona. "Later," Chad said.

Aksel returned his sunglasses to the bridge of his nose. "Later," he echoed.

Chad stepped through the *porte-fenetre* and looked back across the street, to where Paris City workers repaired broken pavement. Then, for a long while, he stared at the wall, where a series of Imad's framed photographs galloped toward the window.

"Hello." Imad said, from where he stood now in the doorway. "What are you doing?"

"Nothing, really. I just stepped out for a look at the clouds and got distracted."

"I meant, what are you doing staring at the wall?" Imad walked over, joining him at the *porte-fenetre* and looking up at the sky. "And how does one become distracted by clouds, if I might ask?"

"Not so much clouds as a fake blond delivering boxes and Aksel's white chest on the balcony."

"If you're noticing Aksel's chest then you're not decrepit yet, even if you do have that 'my god I'm nearly forty' look again."

"What look's that?"

"Like a hare in headlights. Or someone who stares at walls."

"I wish it would stay sunny awhile."

"No you don't, you hate a *canicule* in Paris. Heat waves scare you." Imad adjusted his dirty glasses. He smelled of vanilla.

"Do I really look worried?" Chad asked.

"Always," Imad said.

"Always?"

"Well — recently always."

"Who phoned?"

"Simon."

"And how's Simon?"

"Simon is Simon."

They stood quietly, and looking at his lover Chad felt Imad's propinquity acutely. Not beautiful, if one were being unbiased, but at thirty-six Imad had presence. Imad walked into a room, people noticed. He exuded something. He stood out from the crowd.

"You seem anxious to get started on the Barcelona work."

"Anxious?" Imad thought about that. "No. I want to try some experiments next week, while the memories are fresh. I did love the trip."

"I know you did," Chad said.

Imad looked at him.

Chad returned the look, thinking that although he wanted something from Imad, needed something in fact, he couldn't figure out what it might be. "You're right. I'm melancholy today."

"Melancholy?"

"Pensive," Chad offered.

Imad peered up at the cloud-bound sky, woolly with the misty beginnings of rain. "I'm sorry."

"It's not – disagreeable." Chad wished Imad would look at him. He wondered why they never quite fulfilled their mutual needs for intimacy, despite their deep, even deepening, love. "Somehow it's – productive. The thoughts we think on the eve of the big four-oh."

"Galsworthy wants to throw a birthday party for you."

"Yikes."

"Galsworthy's parties are brilliant," Imad said.

"So are oil slicks."

"Chad."

"Somebody asked me last week where he's from – and all I could say was presumably he's American. What does that tell you?"

"That presumably he's American?"

"Do *you* know where he's from?" Chad wondered.

"I've heard California. He seems Californian."

"You've *heard*. See? I'll admit I like the guy's apartment as a party venue – who wouldn't? – but I didn't like retrieving our coats from under copulating science teachers."

Imad thought a moment. "Oh, right. Those two. Paul and Hélène. They've broken up now."

"I didn't know – that they'd broken up, I mean."

"According to Galsworthy, Paul found out that Hélène and the delivery boy from the *Bon Marché* food hall were going at it like gibbons. The delivery guy with the tattoos? He brought the party platters that time."

"Oh, *him* – cute guy. From Chile, I think."

"That's the one. And it was an Empire sofa, which Galsworthy claims he found in an antique shop in St. Tropez."

"I wouldn't have thought St. Tropez had antique shops," Chad said, "just wrinkled up Brigitte Bardot clones and other relics."

"Like Empire sofas?"

"This is why the Galsworthy's of this world get all the priceless sofas – and 60's retro sunglasses. If it's really so valuable, let's hope they were careful."

"They had our jackets as mops," Imad said.

Chad made a sour face and then shrugged. "A party will be all right, I guess. But guide him toward the afternoon if you can."

"If you want fun: Galsworthy is fun."

"I'm nearly forty," Chad told him. "I've gone off fun."

Imad turned suddenly and, leaning against Chad's shoulder, kissed his neck. "But I love you."

Stunned, Chad looked at the slant of Imad's forehead and the tilt of his glasses. "I love you too," he said softly. Then, "I think I'll take a nap."

"You shouldn't nap. You have nightmares when you nap and you don't sleep at night and then you complain because you're tired – and then you take another nap and have another nightmare and well –"

'I'm not that bad – am I?"

"Yes. You are."

Just then the storm broke with a vengeance. Rain basted the windows, water puddling through the crack in the *porte-fenetre*, spreading in a river along the skirting boards.

"Come into the kitchen with me," Imad said, "I'm in the middle of something."

"Okay." Chad followed him out to the kitchen, and halted in the doorframe.

Imad busied himself once again with a mixing bowl and flour. "We should go somewhere warm this year, for winter break."

"Isn't it a bit early to be thinking about winter break?"

"Book early," Imad said, "that's rule number two for traveling."

"What's rule number one?"

"Treat a plane like a flying bar."

"I thought the airlines had done away with that 'drink 'em while you can' mentality."

"Good luck to them. They shouldn't have started charging for everything. It's probably their biggest money earner. My God, they thunder up down the aisles on their cloven hooves and out-of-fashion uniforms, trying to spot terrorists while dispensing miniature five Euro cans of Stella Artois. It's disgraceful and, yes, I *shall* treat their under-maintenanced aircraft as a flying bar – and yes I do detest being stared at as if I have a bomb hidden in my bifocal frames just because I'm brown and named Imad."

"Nice speech," Chad said. "Though speaking of alcohol, I don't suppose I should mention that our liquor is still in hiding from your parents' last visit. They can't really think you're – whatever – practicing? Do they think you go to the mosque? They know we're lovers."

Imad shrugged. He had long ago given up any worries about religion, the rules of which he once described as sillier than the politics of the UMP political party and neither of his parents would think of mentioning the matter. Breaking rules he found silly seemed always to please Imad. In fact he took particular pride in having once eaten ham on an Icelandair flight.

"What are you making?" Chad wondered, peeking into the mixing bowl.

"Crumb cake, new recipe from Galsworthy." Imad shrugged his shoulders, as if to say 'we do talk.'

Chad poured a glass of wine and went to where he could just touch his lips against the back of Imad's neck. "Something has altered," he said.

"What?" Imad said, looking up from his mixing bowl.

"I don't know," Chad said, and his eyes filled with tears. When he turned and looked out the window, his sense of ripening crisis only loomed larger. He seemed to see his life stretched out before him like flat plains, and though he glimpsed the horizon, it was without discernible landmarks. His mouth tasted cottony with anxiety. He was at the same time stunned and empty. He watched a pair of birds, framed against the trees and the gray sky, and his life seemed positively pathetic.

Imad put his hands on Chad's shoulders. "We'll get over your fortieth, same as everyone else does, and – well, everything will be right as rain. And you're off to London tonight with your rich brats. You love going to London on school trips, you always come back full of tales and smiles and blood pudding."

"I've never once eaten blood pudding, for God's sake."

"But I made you smile."

Chad caressed Imad's cheek. "Yes. You did."

Somehow, the moment seemed consequential. Chad understood something, though he could hardly have articulated what that 'something' was. Like a sea anemone when you touch it, he shrank back into himself, but the consequentiality was still there – wherever *there* was.

Aksel and Imad encountered one another in the lobby.

"Hello," Imad said.

Aksel scrutinized him. "Everything is all right with you and Chad?"

"Why do you ask me that?"

"We saw him leaving."

"Oh. He's just off to London on a school trip." Then, "could everything possibly be all right with anyone?"

"An intriguing and one might think unnecessary equivocation," Aksel said.

"Things with Chad are — well, the same, I suppose — fine, I should say. Yes, emphatically fine."

"Rather like emphatically abstaining," Aksel said. "You want to get a coffee? You can flirt with Jean Claude. That always cheers you up."

"*Aksel.*"

"You pronounce my name as if it is a metal rod connecting two automobile tires."

"Because I don't know how to pronounce Norwegian."

"When I first learned English I was told by a girl from San Diego that I spoke like a Muppet."

"That would be the Swedish chef. You don't look like him though. All right," Imad smiled, "a coffee and a small flirtation might be just the ticket."

They walked together out the door and down to the corner.

But they had no sooner ordered — as luck would have it, Jean-Claude was not working this afternoon, thus confounding Aksel's 'flirtation will set you free' design —

when Galsworthy and his two long-haired Dachshunds, Alcazar and Alhambra, came round the corner.

"Darlings," he rhapsodized to Aksel and Imad.

"Hello, Alcazar," Aksel said to his favorite, who sat upright on her hind legs.

"*Arrêtes ce sottise tout de suite*," Galsworthy snapped. The dog fell flat on the floor. "She looks like a huge wiener dog row of tits when she does that. Like an undignified circus hound."

"Imad is refusing to discuss Chad," Aksel said.

Galsworthy shrugged. "A sensible domestic activity. I permanently refuse to discuss any man with whom I've cohabited, it improves my opinion of them tremendously. I love them oodles more when I ignore them than I ever did when one of them was actually bonking me. Which, come to think of it, was never that often."

"I'm not refusing to talk about Chad," Imad said.

"The big birthday?" Galsworthy asked.

A moment of loyal hesitation, then, "possibly," Imad said, "he's a bit cranky about it."

Peremptorily tossing the dog leashes to the waiter — who caught them in mid-throw, cartoon-like, with outstretched forefingers — Galsworthy enveloped a chair at their table. Like the perennial pebble in the pond, undulating waves of fragrance washed over them, perfume, hairspray, and cigarettes.

"I've been working on my party," Galsworthy said, "I talked to Roger about the banjo."

Aksel and Imad made confused faces.

"Remember," Galsworthy said, "he played that dueling banjos thing — I can't remember where now? At Isabelle's, I think. That evening in Neuilly?"

"Short bald man?" Imad said.

"Yes."

"The one Chad called the 'chia troll?'" Aksel asked.

"*Pardon?*"

"His orange hair looked like it was sprouting from wet terracotta."

"Sun bed and hair dye," Imad said. "A bad combination."

"Chad does not share his catty nicknames with me," Galsworthy said, "You two are clearly more privileged. At any rate, Roger has agreed to play for my party."

"It takes two people to make a duel," Aksel said.

Galsworthy stared at him. "This dueling banjos thing is a musical piece. Is it not, Imad? Everyone knows that."

"Chad says day time, please, for your party," Imad told him, ignoring the dueling banjos.

"Day time? Absolutely not. Good freaking whatever. I mean, I certainly know *I* always look my best in bright sunlight. You've forgotten that, *most* discommoding, as Rupert and I told Antoine when he bought it for me, my apartment faces west. There's not even the occasional kindly shadow until after midnight in the summer." He waved a hand dismissively. "No, it will not be 'day time, please.' You may tell Chad that Galsworthy says 'night time, please.'"

"Well," Imad said, "I've passed on the request."

"Conveniently, then, let's say I have not heard you." Galsworthy reflected a moment. "Or better yet, you can say you mentioned it but I appeared distracted. I was − *what*? Looking to see if the dogs were being watered − or not, as appears to be the case. I will claim to remember nothing about any request for a daytime party. That is a lovely chemise, by the way."

"Thank you," Aksel said, "From Spontini."

"Then it will shrink."

"No it won't."

"Yes, it will." Galsworthy leaned over and took Imad's hand. "So, what's up, sunshine?"

"I don't know."

"Which is Queen's English for−?"

"For I don't know."

They eyeballed one another a moment.

Then, shrugging at Aksel, Galsworthy said, "we are playing at being inscrutable today."

"I mean to say that I don't know what's bothering me – not exactly."

"Is it important to know exactly? Bother is an imprecise thing, that's part of what's so bothering about it." Galsworthy received his cappuccino from the waiter. "The fortieth birthday of your lover is always a threat, to every couple – always."

"A threat to what?" Imad asked.

"Read Henry James."

'No one can actually read Henry James," Aksel said.

"Do tell," Galsworthy snorted.

He and Aksel glared at each other.

"His sentences are two pages long," Aksel said.

"And this from someone whose native tongue has twelve different ways to say fish fillet."

"That is a complete lie."

"There's no such thing as a complete lie, my pet, not even to Italians, and they are the acknowledged experts in this field. I've married two of them, Giuseppe and Paolo – though not at the same time, of course, they were separated by Helmut, who was German and rather brutal in bed, though honest to a fault – so I ought to know. *Si non e vero, e bon travato.* The fortieth birthday awakens everything dormant, and these awakened things stumble around eating flesh, like the zombies in *Night of the Living Dead.*"

"*Night of the Living Dead*?" Imad said.

"It's a cult classic; don't pretend you don't know it. Of course he might just up and run off to somewhere new and glamorous – California, perhaps, where he would never be accused of being a girlie-man, not even by that Neanderthal with a head the size of a tennis ball – the one who's married to the whippet-like television lady with lizard skin – Chad is far too butch to be a girlie-man."

"I really don't think Chad's birthday is what's bothering me — I've just come up against one of those moments."

"And which moments might those be?" Galsworthy asked.

"A moment, moment."

"Articulately put, my dear, you ought to be a teacher. Imad, my darling, fortieth birthday equals threat. Grasp that, *mon petit*, and you've got it."

2

They came into the city while she slept in the back seat. In fact, she only awoke as the driver pulled up sharply in front of a building on a narrow street. He leaned across, opened the door, and said brightly, "Here we are. Forty-two Euros, please." She dug in her purse, found forty-five and gave it to him. She was too tired to try and calculate fifteen percent for a tip, and she could hear Helen's voice in her ear saying something like, 'only *you'd* think you have to tip a damned taxi driver anyway, Roberta.' "Thanks so much," Roberta said, stepping out on to the warm pavement and taking her suitcase from the backseat. The driver sped off. With a heave, she lifted up her things and, after staring for a few minutes at the door frame, pressed a button that had Chad's name on it. When the door buzzed (which wasn't quite what she expected) she pushed it open and walked into a cool, high-ceilinged, marble-tiled lobby. It smelled of something old and not quite clean, but had a chandelier and columns beside the staircase.

An elderly man said something to her in French from the shadowy inside of what looked like a closet.

"I'm sorry," she said, startled.

"*Qu'est-ce que vous cherchez?*" he repeated, much louder, as if perhaps she were hard of hearing.

"Oh dear. Well, here's the thing – my name's Roberta Martin, and I'm looking for my cousin, Chad Newsome. I hope I haven't come to the wrong place. Somebody let me in – I mean, when I pressed the button, the door buzzed."

The man looked at her warily. Then, relenting, "Mr. Newsome? Okay," the man said. "4th floor, you go on left."

"Thanks," she said.

"*On va trouver l'ascenseur par là,*" he said, pointing.

"I'm sorry, what?"

"The elevator." He pointed again, jabbing with his finger. "Over there."

"Oh, okay – I see. Thank you kindly, sir." She found the elevator and went up to the 4th floor, which she realized was really the fifth floor. The floor she entered on was listed as O, which made no sense. Why would you want a Floor O? Coming off the elevator she saw an apartment in the corner with the name Newsome on it. She pressed another buzzer.

When the door opened after a minute or two, it revealed a man with soft brown skin, tortoise shell glasses, and a tight, navy blue collared shirt.

"Hello," he said in surprise, clearly expecting someone else.

"*Oh,*" she said, clearly expecting someone else. "I sure do hope this is my cousin Chad's place, because if it's not –" she lacked words for what might happen to her if it were not, so she simply shrugged her conclusion.

There was an uncomfortably long pause. "Chad lives here and he does have a cousin. I know who you are. You haven't come to the wrong apartment. Come in, come in."

"Oh, praise the *Lord*. Thanks."

"But he isn't home, I'm afraid." He showed her into a large foyer, expensively decorated. "He's gone to London. He should be back tomorrow night."

"Oh, poop."

"Poop?"

"I mean I'm disappointed."

"I don't believe he knew you were coming – did he?"

"I'm a stinker," she admitted. "I've just kind of dropped in unexpectedly."

He regarded her a moment or two before he said, "Excuse my suspicious nature, but how can you just have dropped in unexpectedly to Paris?" He actually glanced up a moment through the windows, as if he searched for the hot-air balloon or helicopter that had dropped her on the crowded Paris streets. "I really don't understand."

"The truth is I didn't exactly plan it, it just kind of – happened, that's what I mean. And so now I've come to stay for awhile – with my cousin." She peered into a spacious living room, with tall door-like windows overlooking blocks of stylish apartments across a narrow street.

"Like it?" Imad asked.

"I'll say. What a wonderful view. I hope it's okay."

"Yes, it's perhaps a bit uncomfortable at first to watch your neighbors showering, one of the things I never do get used to about Paris, but it really is okay and quite a lot of fun once you allow yourself the liberty."

"I meant I hope it's okay if I stay with Chad."

"I knew what you meant," Imad said, "I was teasing you. And we'll let Chad speak for himself, shall we? I suspect he'll be glad to see you. He's spoken of you often enough."

"*Really*?" She found the man's accent intriguing. "Do you live here too?"

"Yes. My name's Imad, I'm a photographer and teacher. I teach at Chad's school."

"Is that one yours?" she gestured toward a photograph on the wall.

"Yes. Do you like it?"

She stepped closer. "How beautiful she is. Who is she?"

"My sister."

"Yes, I do like it. What's she wearing – on her head?"

"A scarf – of sorts. Have you come alone, Miss Martin?"

"You may as well call me Roberta. And, yes, I have."

"You drove from the airport?"

"*Drove*? Are you kidding? The way everybody here whips around like crazy people? No, sir, this nice taxi driver gave me a ride, he's originally from some place in Africa, but I forget the whole story he was telling me, it was kind of complicated and sad, and anyway I fell asleep about halfway through." She touched her blouse nervously. "You know, well – this seems a little bit stupider now that I've done it than it did before – I did it. If that makes sense. See, basically, I was afraid Chad might not answer my email. There have been a few problems with him answering letters and all, I mean. So it seemed best just to come, without any fanfare."

"You avoided fanfare, that's true. But you knew he'd welcome you once you arrived?"

27

"I knew he wouldn't put me out in the cold. Chad and I were best friends once."

"It's warm enough this time of the year, but we won't put you out in any case. You're tired," he announced. "Come on in, I'll make some coffee."

She crossed her arms on her chest, stepped just inside the living room, and surveyed it with appreciative eyes. "Does he look the same? Chad?"

"How would the same be?"

"Handsome, rugged – bighearted?"

"I don't know how bighearted looks. But he's still handsome and rugged. How long has it been since you've seen him?"

"I don't rightly know. A long time, that's for sure. Too long." She turned to Imad. "We've all missed him."

"Of course you have. Come into the kitchen, I'll get the coffee. I suppose you're hungry?"

Hunger had made her feel faint. She could not even pretend to delicacy. "Absolutely starving. That's a pretty song," She said, gesturing toward the sound system.

"Le premier amour,'" he said, "Anaïs? Dated and a bit silly, though she's one of those young artists one likes to like."

This description baffled her. "Well, whatever – it's pretty, which is all that matters with music, isn't it?" But reflecting on the nature of his description, she felt outclassed and said, "About that something to eat, I'm famished."

"I'll find something." He brought her with him into a surprisingly modern kitchen. As he busied himself making the coffee and putting together some sandwiches, he looked over at her. "And you're right, of course – ultimately, music is about the way it sounds. You know, somehow I'd pictured you differently."

"More attractive?"

"No," he said honestly, "plainer."

"Oh." She thought about that. "Thanks for the compliment, then – I guess."

He carried the sandwiches to where she sat at the table, staring into the neighboring building and stroking a cat, which had suddenly appeared in her lap. "Vegetarian pâté and goat's cheese," Imad said, "it's all we've got. Hope it satisfies."

Vegetarian pâté and goat's cheese sounded as repulsive to her as motor oil and sawdust. However, good guest that she was she knew she had to force it down.

He swung his long legs around, sitting back to front on one of the cane chairs. He stared at her a moment before he asked, "So, has Chad's mother sent you here?"

"*Gosh*. You're so direct." No answer at all must serve her, Roberta thought. If it were in spirit a lie, she asked the Lord for forgiveness. Strictly speaking, Helen's faith did not much agree with the concept of forgiveness – forgiveness was one of those suspicion Catholic things, like playing with beads and wearing outlandish headgear and sitting in cubbyholes and touching up little boys. "I got laid off from the library where I worked, and this beats cooling my heels in Lubbock."

"No doubt. I'm sorry to hear it," he said, smiling at her diplomacy. He appeared to know full well that she'd evaded his question. "Had you worked there a long time?"

"Since forever. They told me that the library had to make economies. It still puzzles the heck out of me. I mean, my aunt practically keeps the library propped up. I can't believe they'd even *dare* lay off any relative of hers. But, never mind, they did. I'm one of her more dispensable relatives, I guess. And times change, don't you know. Better me than a subscription to the *Knitting Gazette* and inserts for the *Encyclopedia of Hunting*. No old lady or college professor is going to picket city hall on my account."

"Terrible to be expendable."

"It is," she agreed. "You said Chad will be home tomorrow night?"

"Yes. Though it depends partly on what Gemma has on his schedule."

"Gemma?"

"Gemma."

"Oh."

The name Gemma sounded sexy. Helen had made it clear that there was a cheap and sordid side to Chad's life. A woman named Gemma might definitely fit the bill. Although nothing in the room gave away the presence of a cohabiting slut, Roberta wondered, as she bit into her remaining piece of ghastly sandwich, just how she would face up to a sluttish woman of the world. Attractive sluts – like Connie Sue, one of the check-out ladies at the library – were always the first to use Roberta's weight against her. The battle for the soul of her beloved cousin, once it commenced, might be bloodier warfare than even Helen had anticipated.

When she finished eating, Imad took her plate to the sink. "If you'd like to have a bath and a nap, the two of us can plan a dinner tonight. Would you like that?"

"Sure. Thanks." She eyed the man named Imad carefully, gulped down the last of her milk, and went back with him into the hall.

Roberta sat bolt upright from a deep sleep.

A warbling fire engine siren blared, like from out of a James Bond movie. For several horrifying moments she had no idea where she was. The room and its radiator – Roberta had never seen a radiator before – were unspeakably alien. Then, she remembered everything and glanced at her watch. She had slept too long. It was nearing nine o'clock, although the sun still filled the room. The fire engine warbled again. She climbed from bed and went to the window. Pulling it open, she stuck her head out. Below, she saw a fire station, the trucks moving into traffic and the firemen running out of the station. She leaned further out.

Behind her she heard, with a laugh, "they *are* worth watching. We call them 'the boys.' Some people think it's terrible living next to a *caserne*. But we love it. Have a nice sleep?"

"I must have," she yawned. "I've ruined everything, I suppose."

He came toward her. "No one ever ruins anything around here. All plans are flexible. It's a house rule."

"How civilized."

"We can still walk out for dinner, if you'd like."

"Okay. Is there some way I can call Chad? To let him know I'm here?"

"You could ring him at his hotel in London. But since, in any event, you'll surprise the hell out of him; maybe you'd better do that in person."

She thought a moment, planning her strategy. "Will she be coming back with him?"

"Who?"

"That woman you mentioned?"

"Gemma? Of course. She lives here in Paris, just off the Boulevard – *ah*. You didn't think they – ?" He laughed. "I'm quite sure he'll come back alone, in the sense you mean. Gemma is the Upper School Principal at our school."

"Oh. The Principal at his school. Okay, then." She'd never have imagined a Principal named Gemma (it was not at all the right name for a Principal), although she supposed she believed him. "I'll be ready in a minute," she said.

Notre Dame loomed in front of them, an intimidating tourist sighting.

"Oh, my word," Roberta exclaimed, as she and Imad came up to the parapet above the Seine.

"Not so shabby?"

"Like a – well," she looked at him, then back at Notre Dame, "it's just exactly the way you imagine it, isn't it? Just so incredibly pretty and everything." She turned back almost giddily to Imad, "I see why this is a city people talk about – you know, about it being a place where people fall in love. Mind you, people always fall in love on trips no matter where they go, don't they? Though I don't know if it counts as falling in love if y'all just have *sex* with a bartender down to Cancun in Mexico. That's what Rhonda Lynn Rasmussen from next door did, but I guess she *thought* it was love or she wouldn't have done it. I mean, Rhonda Lynn's pretty prissy, and that bartender was some college kid from Seattle who was just working there during summer. I saw the pictures, so I know for a fact that he was gorgeous. He was a wrestler – or maybe he was on the baseball team. Sorry," she said, "I tend to blabber on a bit, don't I? It's one of my many failings. There's a word for it."

"For what?"

"Talking like I do – I mean, something other than blabbering."

"I shouldn't worry about it. Your stories are amusing."

"Really?" She leaned against the wall, and looked at the trees. "How long have you known Chad?"

"Does it matter?"

"Somehow it seems to," Roberta said.

"A long time – we met at a party here in Paris. I found him sitting by himself in the *sejour* – the living room – and I told him I ought to take his photograph, because he reminded me of Mrs. Siddons as the tragic muse." He smiled at the memory and then turned quickly to Roberta, "Gainsborough, an English painter. We went for a drink and talked the night away. It seemed he was suffering from a recent break-up. Anyway, we found we liked each other and we had much in common. And there we are. I'll tell you more about all that someday." He looked at his watch. "But we'd better be getting back now."

This confirmation of entanglements in Chad's life – like break-ups and drink – fell in Helen's favor, yet she could not but envy someone who had come into contact with the live wire of passion – and here, in a place so beautiful. Imad inclined his head, and they began walking back up the narrow street, distorted and somewhat greenish from the streetlight. Roberta paused to catch her breath and looked back at Notre Dame. Lights painted the surfaces of the church, windows, arches, and roof. The shadows of trees made contrasting patches on the stone. People walked hand-in-hand or in groups along the walled bank of the river.

Watching her, Imad said, "What would happen to Helen Newsome's well-laid plans, if you decided to escape too?"

"What well-laid plans?"

He laughed.

She looked at him crossly.

But he only laughed louder.

Roberta awoke slowly.

Her body clung to the last torpid vestiges of sleep. She tasted her last dream, a dream set on the airplane and Chad was there and Imad had been the pilot – or had he been a flight attendant? The uniform looked good on him, in any case. She turned over on her back and thought about the dream, and about having arrived in Paris, and about the sun which streamed in through the slightly open window. Birds twittered frenetically in the trees and she thought she heard a bicycle on the street. Had she ever awakened in such a room and beheld such a day and place? She felt exhilarated. Her toes stretched out under the duvet, and then she forced herself up and into her robe. The apartment was as silent as if it had been abandoned. She walked slowly across the main hall and dining room, through to the kitchen.

She found no coffee maker, only an electric kettle, the interior thickly furred with lime. After examining it for awhile, she filled it with water, plugged it in, and waited for it to boil. Her hand drifted against the window pane and caressed the warmth. When she was twelve she'd stayed with her father's sisters in Fort Worth, and she'd risen early and sat alone then too. At the time she'd not imagined anything could be stranger than that – they'd all called her 'honeybunch,' in that weird Fort Worth accent, and one of them stole a sweater from out of her suitcase and never gave it back – but this was stranger than that by a long shot.

The kettle rocked back and forth, grunted, and shot forth steam. She wasn't sure how to turn it off, so she simply yanked the cord out from the wall. Helen had imbued her with a fear of electricity; on account of the fact that Uncle Ray nearly electrocuted himself once while rigging up lights out in his chicken coop. Actually, Roberta chiefly remembered Helen forcing her to sit dutifully by Uncle Ray's hospital bed while he snored. They assigned the task to Roberta because Roberta was all he deserved, since everybody knew he'd been out in the chicken coop – *again* – drunk as a skunk. Roberta filled her mug with instant coffee and boiled water. As she stirred her coffee she sat at one of the chairs and half pretended to read yesterday's International Herald Tribune, which she found on the sideboard. Gurgles came from the wall behind her head. Imad must be up.

She sipped her coffee, stared out the window, and *understood*. Cars passed on the road now. She felt truly at peace, more even than being in church. Well, that was a bad comparison – because she never felt at peace in church, always wondering if her bra strap was showing or if she'd put on too much perfume – Helen frowned on perfume. Come to think of it, why did people back in Lubbock act like going to church was like being at 'home,' when it was always so darned stressful? Who in the be-jeepers sat around at home in tummy smoothers, up-lifter bras and tight shoes? Not even Helen, who wore panty hose under her bathrobe, and who always looked positively gloomy in slacks. Roberta felt at home here and – yes – peaceful.

She turned as Imad came into the room, wearing a cotton pullover and corduroy pants. His hair was mussed. "You managed coffee, I see."

"Any West Texan gal worth her salt can make coffee on a moment's notice," she smiled at him.

He laughed and went to the window. "Welcome again, Roberta."

"It doesn't even sound like my own name when y'all say it."

"What does it sound like?"

She peered at him over her coffee and tried to imitate him, "Ruh-bair-tuh."

He laughed again. "At least I don't make you sound like a character from the Muppets."

"What?"

"Sit. I'll make you some better coffee — we've got a cone and filters here in the cupboard, you didn't have to use that dinosaur — and a breakfast of savories and delights."

"Savories and delights," she echoed, imitating his accent. "Now that sounds — " she was about to say 'promising,' but she couldn't forget yesterday's motor oil and sawdust sandwich, so she said "kind of you."

"You look pretty this morning. Rested. I'm glad."

"Pretty?"

"Yes," he said, as if surprised by her question.

After the better part of a bottle of Gewurztraminer one Thanksgiving, Helen said to Roberta, 'excuse my French, Roberta, but you're too butt ugly ever to get a real man, but you can cook a turkey to die for. If you're ever going to get into the sack, you're going to have to feed the poor sucker first.' Helen had never wanted Roberta to harbor illusions; she was against illusions of any kind. Helen did not, for instance, believe that the Russians had changed their spots. For someone who'd once led a boycott of a supermarket that sold canned Polish sardines, this 'end of the nasty Russians business' was too great a leap of faith. It was illusion.

"If I could sing I'd do it," Roberta said.

"Name a song, I'll accompany you."

35

"*Nearer My God to Thee*? But with a fast tempo, which is really how it's meant to be sung – it's not supposed to be all slow and everything."

"What are we, rearranging the deck chairs on the *Titanic*?"

"Oh, you know it. I didn't think you would. It's my favorite hymn."

"I'm a rather surprising Muslim, you'll find."

"*Oh*," she said with a hot intake of breath. This had not crossed her mind. But it explained the scarf his sister was wearing in the photograph, didn't it? She'd never known a Muslim.

He laughed, watching her face. "You actually have a favorite hymn?"

"Of course."

"I'll have to think about that."

"Why?"

"Because it is strange to the point of being *bizarre*, I am afraid."

She wrinkled her nose at him. It wasn't clear if he was teasing her or being serious, but in either case she thought it ranked as poor taste of him to say it. But she liked him so much, and there was such a glint in his eyes, that he easily won her back. She'd have to be lenient in this brave new world of vegetarian pâté and Muslims. Even Helen Newsome was forced, from time to time, to give lip service to acceptance. On the other hand, Helen often chastised Roberta for giving in too easily on matters of principle. Helen took matters of principle so seriously that she once refused to speak to her sister Elizabeth Ann for an entire year, after Aunt Lizzie left a coffee ring on Helen's second floor bookcase, the one on the landing with the Billy Graham biography. Roberta looked up at the neighboring building. There was a trail of puffy cloud over the rooftops.

"People must already be missing you back home," Imad said.

"Oh, good gravy, they definitely are not. Back in Lubbock, everybody thinks I'm only good for babysitting and helping pick the zucchini out of Aunt Edna's foul garden. She throws all kinds of dog-do and stuff out there on her plants, cat turds from her cat box and rotten watermelon rinds, and once I found a whole uneaten pop tart underneath her pumpkin plants. Nobody else in the family will even go over there – and they all throw her vegetables away in the alley when they get any of 'em. I'm the only one ever ate anything of Aunt Edna's. I made some zucchini bread once, but I boiled that zucchini so long it looked like play dough and I drained the water off it three whole times."

He smiled at her. "From what Chad's said there's worse than cat shit and rinds out there"

"You know about Edna's garden?"

"Yes."

She thought about that. "You must be Chad's very best friend, if he's told you that sort of thing."

Imad smiled. "He's told me quite a few things actually. He told me you were self-sacrificing. He's told me that a number of times.

"What does he mean, when he says I'm self-sacrificing?"

"Well," Imad said, "you gave away all of your Christmas presents once. That's self-sacrificing."

"I didn't give them away exactly. I took them back to the store and got the money and sent all the money to help an orphan baby named Diego in some Latin American place or another. I still remember his name. They sent me a little card thingy with his face on it." She looked at Imad. "I reckon they probably sent that same card to everybody, don't you? Though I believed it at first, and I kept that card tucked in my bathroom mirror for a whole year, until I knocked it one morning with my robe and it fell in the toilet and I just went ahead and flushed it, 'cause I was fed up with sending money to some fake kid named Diego."

"There aren't many people who'd do that."

"Not many people that stupid, you mean."

"No. *Self-sacrificing*. I admire that trait more than I can say."

"So when Chad says I'm self-sacrificing," she said, closing her eyes a moment, "he means it as a compliment?"

"Oh yes." Imad reached over and took her hand. "It must have been hard on you, losing your parents and having to move in with another family. It's tragic to lose even one parent when you're young, let alone both. I can't imagine what that must have been like for you, Roberta. You were an only child?"

"Only me. Though I can't say mama ever doted on me, not like you imagine people do when you hear they've got an only child. Maybe mama thought she doted, but I doubt it. I reckon she prided herself on *not* doting. They were hard people, my parents. See, daddy's family lost everything way back when, so he grew up dirt poor, and growing up poor makes you hard, but mama always had – *aspirations*, and when you don't get your aspirations in life, well that makes you hard too and in a worse way. Mama was from Midland," Roberta told him, as if it were common knowledge that people in Midland were troubled by aspirations.

"Is Midland a city?"

"Midland's a city all right, oil money and all. I think mama wanted me to be, well, you know, a little bit more *Texan*. More like all my Cooper girl cousins from Midland." She turned to him with a fake smile. "Can I twirl my baton for y'all? One Thanksgiving, Celeste and Nadine, those were my cousins on mama's Midland side, the Coopers, they had themselves a baton twirl-off in Uncle Earl's backyard. Celeste won, of course, she was always winning everything, beauty pageants all over everywhere from Oklahoma City to El Paso. She twirled to a record of '*The Eyes of Texas are Upon You*,' and she could even twirl on her knees. The baton, I mean. Mama just loved that stuff. Now, to her credit, Aunt Helen always looked down on the Midland relatives. Thank God in heaven I didn't have to go and live with Celeste and Nadine after my parents died." She was quiet a moment, and then said, "I never could get the hang of baton twirling."

"Moving in with Chad – well, honestly, I adored him; he was so good to me. And you've no idea how handsome he was.

He was just about to *die for*. I used to try and sneak looks at him with his shirt off in the bathroom. His chest kind of shimmied, you know, when he moved his arm to shave? He was hairy-chested in the right kind of way, like somebody did him up for a movie. I thought I'd like to die. *Die*. With Chad around, I didn't feel sad. Just numb sometimes, but not sad."

They looked at one another a moment or two.

"Sometimes," Roberta continued, "I wonder just how much I really loved my parents, though I shouldn't be saying that, should I? I'll go to hell for that if, according to the good book, I weren't already going there for having touched snails. I don't think I've touched a ferret yet, unless you count my cousin Dwight who — well, never *mind* about Cousin Dwight, he's gone now anyway, and getting caught up in a hay-bailer isn't a pretty way to go, even if he *did* deserve it, the pervert." She shuddered at the memory of the hay-bailer and cousin Dwight. "Things like losing your parents, they're just sort of meant to be — they happen, you don't have any control over it. Leastwise, that's what I've always thought. Chad used to tell me that you can't change what can't be changed. He told me that a lot — and it was true. And sometimes it was nice living there at Aunt Helen's, I mean, there were always cakes and things to eat, Little Debbie snacks, Swiss rolls and stuff. I'd never have gotten junk food like that from mama; mama disapproved of store bought stuff, she baked everything from scratch, she even made chess pie now and then. Once I ate a whole one of her chess pies at Christmas and barfed."

"Chess pie?"

"Butter, sugar and eggs. More or less. There might be some vanilla in it."

"*You are joking.*"

She winced at his shriek, but feeling kindly toward him demurred with, "That's probably why he was so athletic. He was burning off all that sugar."

Imad seemed about to say something. He looked directly into her face, and his mouth seemed to form the word

'Chad'. But then he thought better of whatever it was he was going to say and shrugged.

"I'm an intrusion, aren't I?" she asked.

"Not a terrible one." He took her hand a moment and squeezed it reassuringly. "Don't worry. To tell the truth, you're a pleasant change, Roberta. And I'm beginning to think that the issues you're forcing are all – necessary." He turned away from and walked a step or two toward the window. Far away the noise of an airplane came through from the living room, and the sounds of someone shouting down on *rue des Bernadins*. They seemed lost in their own thoughts for a long while, until Imad said, "Did you ever see Chad's apartment? The one he had after he moved out of his mom's house? Before he left to go to university in England?"

"Once," she said, startled. "Why?"

"Because it was the first place he ever had of his own. Have him tell you about why it meant so much to him, Roberta. It'll give you insight."

"But that apartment was nasty – it had silverfishes and smelled like dog pee. I think it was in The Wagon Wheel, that vile old brown thing up by the North Loop, an ugly barn of a building."

"That I wouldn't know, since he doesn't have any photographs. But he talks about trying to make almond cookies and writing until three in the morning and taking care of the neighbor's dog. The one that was hit and killed by a package delivery van?"

"A *what*? Oh, you mean by a UPS Truck. I do remember him telling me about that. It was a German shepherd mix, which is generally speaking a pretty good dog. I mean, they don't run away like that, not usually. You ask me, there's more to that story." She stopped a moment, and then wondered aloud about the drift of their conversation, "Are you trying to say you're afraid of me taking him away to Texas?"

"You'll make him relive all the memories, the bad ones he remembers on his own – but the good ones – that's what you'll make him think about."

40

"That can't be so wrong? To think about good memories? It sure as heck isn't anything to be afraid of. Why, y'all could come to Lubbock too. You'd be as welcome as welcome could be."

Imad turned to her with a gentle smile. "Really? Do you think so? Can you imagine how your Aunt Helen would react to me? A Muslim boy with a taste for couscous? And that's not the half of what I have a taste for."

"What's couscous?"

"Something you eat, and it sounds like maybe it's in short supply in Lubbock. I don't think you'll take him away, Roberta, not *physically*. But once he starts remembering – oh, I don't know. We always need some closing of the past, even if we don't resolve all our inner conflicts. So, come to think of it, that's why it's probably good that you're here." He looked at her. "You'll bring some closure."

Thinking about what he'd said, she began to feel a little guilty, and she said, "Do you mind if I have a shower now? And I need to wash out my underwear."

3

Roberta was washing her underwear in the bathtub when she heard the front door open and close. It had to be Chad. This was, of course, why she'd been sent these many thousands of miles. Yet she waited in the bathroom, anxious and afraid, her hands full of sudsy panty. Why didn't she hurry to see him? Somehow, for those long moments of waiting, she felt ridiculous. And then, realizing what she had to do, but without overcoming her fears, she crept out to the hallway — leaving her panties behind, of course, and drying her hands.

Chad stood in the hallway, startled — and then gaping at her — and then exploding with, "oh my God. *Roberta*? Is it really you? I hadn't any idea at all. Imad didn't say a word. How long have you been here?"

"Since yesterday afternoon. Imad has been entertaining me. I hope you don't mind? About me coming over?"

"I don't mind at all," he waved, "come and give me a hug."

"Let me finish something and I'll be right there."

Roberta hurried into the bathroom, tossed her still sudsy panties into a plastic bag, returned them to her room, then rushed out to the living room — and into Chad's waiting arms. He felt so good to her, so real and familial and loving, that she experienced something nearly sexual. In the whole world as she understood it, this man was her family, more than Helen, more than Aunt Edna or Aunt Lorraine, more than any of the rest of them.

"Roberta, my God, how really *good* it is to see you."

"You too, Chad. Wow, you're better looking than ever." She whistled at him, hugged him again, and kissed his neck. He smelled like travel and just slightly of the soap he'd showered with that morning. Once, when he'd won some game, he'd come home to the house and hugged her, and he'd smelled the same. She'd loved him then, too. "It should be illegal to be so handsome, you rascal."

"So you've put Imad to work, then?"

"He's made me feel right at home."

"He's good at that." He held her at arm's length and regarded her. "So mama finally got you to come over here and try to bring me back to the land of dust devils and tarantulas?" he asked, releasing her from his grip. "I knew she would sooner or later."

"Yes." Face to face with Chad, calculations and plans came to nothing, for Roberta had never been able to lie to him and she should have remembered that before accepting her mission. "She did it – and here I am."

At two in the morning Roberta awoke abruptly, dry-mouthed and famished. She'd fallen asleep with the light on and her book now lay bent-spined on the floor. She looked at it a moment. On the cover, a woman cradled herself in a field. People talked in the apartments across the street. *Rue des Bernardins*, she'd noticed, grew narrower as it stretched away from the Seine. At this point, at its terminus near the Pantheon, you could almost reach across from balcony to balcony. In the distance, one of those exotic French sirens warbled. The apartment itself seemed peaceful. She got up, put her robe around her shoulders, and went to the *porte-fenetre*. Activity swirled on the *Rue Monge*, where students congregated in the square near the church. She could almost smell their cigarettes. Thirsty, she went out to the kitchen, where she saw that Imad had left a note on the refrigerator and a light burning on the counter. Orange juice if she desired; cookies in the jar; cake in the box. She filled a glass with tap water, drank it quickly, filled it again, and walked through the living room, to another *porte-fenetre*. Here it was quieter; here she felt that people actually did sleep in Paris. Although a light shone next door, she saw darkened windows behind which people did not stir.

She would never have gone walking at night in Lubbock, but here with people on the streets and a thousand ears within screaming distance, she felt safe. So finding the key Chad had given her and looking carefully at the paper which had the digi-code for the front door written on it, she dressed and left the apartment. She went straight down *rue des Bernardins*, as she had that morning with Imad, came to the quay, crossed it, and was suddenly looking at the rounded back of Notre Dame and the deep left hand channel of the Seine. A breeze played in her hair and she leaned against the stone balustrade, looking west down the river along the side of the cathedral. Her hands were chilled by the wind and she placed them in her jacket pocket.

It was there, unexpected under her fingers: a once-red lift ticket from a ski vacation in Ruidoso with Aunt Helen, mangled from living for two years in the crook of a jacket pocket. Her cold hand held it out, as if offering it again to the chairlift man, and then she held it against her jacket, where once it had been joyfully clipped, as she and Helen frolicked up and down the runs. She'd been wrong about Helen not doing nice things for her and not being generous. Of course Helen had been generous. Again Roberta looked at the ticket, trying hard in the wan light to read what was written there, to see how much it had cost. Then carefully she put it back in her jacket pocket, that lift ticket from Ruidoso, and she kept her hand on it, warming it with unexpected memory.

Notre Dame glimmered beneath lights, Catholic and yet secular, touristy, and the way in which this great church had changed over the centuries made Roberta's thoughts drift toward the biblical view of religion, which her thoughts seemed to do a lot these days. Sometimes the bible didn't seem helpful to her at all, just confusing and old fashioned, which she could admit to herself, standing there looking at Notre Dame, a place that seemed somehow to feel the same way. She'd made a fleeting reference to these confusions in a conversation with Imad, when she'd mentioned snails and ferrets. And while Roberta would never have breathed a word of her worries, she wondered sometimes – all alone, for example, driving in her car down 98th Street — well, she wondered if the bible hadn't actually been written by some kind of lunatic.

She and her friend Becky got hung up once on *Leviticus*, the evening after Debby Saunder's swim party. They had pulled out Debby's grandma's big painted up bible, which had been around for years, having originally come in a covered wagon during the Oklahoma land rush or something like that. Anyway, the two of them had tried unsuccessfully to interpret such oddities as not growing things in the fiftieth year and all of the pages (yes, *pages*) on how to tell who's a leper and who's just bald. Who the heck cares about that and why was it a part of their religion? Was it necessary for being a Christian that you know who's a leper and who's only bald? Clearly the bible hadn't anticipated chemotherapy, which Becky's aunt had gone through the year before, because the poor woman met every single one of the biblical criteria for leprosy.

"It says here she might be one of them *lepers*," Becky screamed, "and we should shun her — or would she be one of the ones where y'all have to throw stones at her and kill her?"

Quite frankly that afternoon put Roberta off the bible for a long time, despite what Aunt Helen said about her believing it all, and despite her pretty pretense at Sunday school and beyond. In fact, Roberta didn't much believe the bible at all, not after that day. This probably counted as the biggest secret in her entire life: she was a big old hypocrite. After that day with Becky, Roberta suspected the bible was just plain weird, what with saying things like, "and the ferret, and the chameleon, and the lizard, and the snail, and the mole. These are unclean to you among all that creep: whosoever doth touch them, when they be dead, shall be unclean until the even." Did that mean you were supposed to leave all the dead snails out on the geraniums, since you couldn't touch them and be morally pure?

Weird. Face it.

Holding on to that ski-trip ticket, and with a last wistful look at the bastion of Notre Dame, Roberta made her way back up the street thinking as she walked that she was already

46

starting to change. The Roberta who had arrived in Paris was already somebody else.

Chad awoke with a start. A light was on in the living room. Collecting himself, he rose, put on a T-shirt, and went out to where Roberta sat at the *porte-fenetre*.

She turned to him. "A man in boxer shorts just walked into the room."

"Couldn't sleep?" he asked.

She nodded. "I don't know if it's jet lag or I'm just unbelievably excited. I feel like I did that time I drank too much coffee over at Edna's. I liked to stay awake for three nights – you know how she grinds her own beans and it's like drinking roofing tar?"

"I'll take your word on it. Sounds like jet lag to me."

"I went out for a walk – and it was beautiful and I felt real safe and everything – but it didn't make me any sleepier."

"We can take another walk if you want."

"No." She shook her head. "But thanks." They were quiet together for awhile, then she said, "I suppose you ought to hear me say it straight – Helen did make me come, although I wasn't supposed to do it like this, I mean, give things all away. Aunt Helen has some good reasons for you to come home, Chad."

"I am home, Roberta."

They looked at one another.

"Ah, Bertie, smile. It's all right. You're supposed to make me want to go back there. And I can imagine your extensive training. I know how mama's mind works. She'll have told you to be ready for the fact that I'll claim to be happy here, and that I won't want to go back – so, she'll have given you instructions on how to break my chains and set me free from – well, from whatever mama's pea-brain thinks is holding me here."

She looked at him, afraid to say anything.

"It's a plot, Bert. She chose you as her accomplice. You're a good choice, I give her that. So – how'd you become available for the covert mission? Are you using up all your vacation time from the library?"

"Vacation time? No. They fired me, if you can believe it, though they called it something else. Reduction in force, something like that – laying me off. After all that time. I can't imagine why, when I was the hardest darned worker they ever had, and you know full well your mama just about props up the Lubbock County library."

"They fired you because Mama made them."

"*What*?"

"Sure. They had to fire you so that you'd be free to do her dirty work over here."

With sudden, truthful pain, Roberta saw that this had to be right. Helen, the library's main source of outside funding, gave them an edict: fire that idiot niece of mine so that I can send her off to Paris. But despite her sinking feeling of betrayal Roberta said dutifully, "y'all are just being silly."

"I'm not. But it doesn't matter, I'm glad as hell you're here, whatever the reason and however many were the duplicities that caused it.

Roberta played with a skein of her hair, thinking about the way Chad talked, looking him over and seeing now a sophisticated, older, more cosmopolitan version of her beloved cousin. "I think my whole world's going to be changed by coming here," she said.

"Mama won't like that," he said. "She'll make you come back home again postie j. toastie."

"Our old expression," she exclaimed.

"You think I'd forget that?"

"Aunt Helen wouldn't notice any change in me. She doesn't notice things about me, you know that."

"Never underestimate her, Roberta."

Roberta thought that was sound advice. The mayor's ex-wife underestimated Helen's spite once and ended up sitting next to the men's bathroom at the civic center holiday hoedown. Men pee a lot when they've been square-dancing and drinking Miller Lite, and coming out of the bathroom while still zipping up tended to give them ideas once they laid eyes on her red hair and big boobs.

"So, let me guess. Mama promised to adopt you, if you bring me back?"

"Wow." She whistled. "How the heck did you guess *that*?"

"It's always been her trump card, hasn't it? She should have adopted you years ago, the only reason she didn't was so that she could hold it over your head when the time came she needed something from you. I guess that time finally came."

"I don't think it's like that," she told him, though what he said had a perturbing ring of honesty to it, "in fact, it was *real* kind of her to promise it and – okay, it was the thing that made me feel like I had to come, I admit it. But if this is what it takes – well, don't you want me to be your legal sister?"

"I've thought of you as my sister for years, Bertie. I don't need papers to confirm it. I for damn sure wouldn't want to have to go back to Lubbock, Texas to prove my feelings for you. You're as much a sister to me as anyone ever could be."

"But I live way over there in Lubbock, Chad. Oh, I'd love to have you back home again, even if only for a little while. I'd like to show you all of the changes, what they've done out to Lake Ransom and the Ranching Heritage Center and how they've done up the mall like brand new – well, and all of it. If you'd come back to Lubbock, just for a little visit, you'd make me the happiest person in the whole world. Honest."

"Can't you see how much I like Paris? Look around. Isn't this worth staying away from Lubbock?"

She met his eyes. "Liking Paris wouldn't hardly be enough reason for Aunt Helen, that's for sure. I mean, if *that's* all that's the problem –"

"The problem?" He sighed with irritation. "I wasn't aware there was a problem, Roberta. By the way, just so Imad and I know, how often are you supposed to report in to her? We might need to subscribe to one of those special telephone rates."

"Oh – lots. I mean, not so often that it costs you an arm and a leg – but, yes sir, I'm supposed to talk to her pretty often." She took a measured breath. "Okay. I really didn't want to talk about all this just yet – this is all too fast for me, Chad. But here it is:" She took a gulp of air for the fight, paused, and said with every ounce of gravitas she could muster, "your mama is ill. *Very ill.* In fact, they're fixin' to cut her legs off."

"*What?*"

"They're putting her in a wheelchair – one of them electric ones I hope, because I sure as heck don't relish the thought of having to be the chief pusher-arounder, which is what she's got planned. Though I guess it would be a good way to lose weight, come to think of it."

"What the Hell are you talking about? Has there been an accident?"

"Yes," Roberta said. "Diabetes."

"Diabetes?"

"Diabetes."

"Okay, wait a minute. Tell me exactly what you know."

"The doctor told her that she might have diabetes, and if she does, then Helen says they'll have to cut off her legs. She wants you to come back and take care of her. Spell me off in pushing her in her wheelchair while we walk some sort of a dog – but Helen doesn't have a dog, so I don't reckon that's really part of it, though she keeps mentioning it, so she must be planning to buy one. I hope she gets a Labrador, a golden one."

"But she's not in a wheelchair now?"

"No. She's just lying there on her couch, in the dark, if you can believe it."

"Roberta," Chad burst out laughing. "You've been had. The old bag has set you up."

"She hasn't."

"She has."

Roberta shook her head vehemently. For attacks upon Helen's integrity Roberta had prepared herself. Even handsome Chad couldn't melt all that resolve. "She hasn't, Chad. I saw her. I know. She's sick and she misses you. She needs you. Trust me."

"There's not even anything definite about this diagnosis of diabetes, you admit that."

"It hasn't been definitely confirmed, at least not that I know of. But the doctor wouldn't have any reason to lie about it."

"But my mother would."

"*Chad.*"

He turned to her with a smile. "You know full well that my mother is a liar. Everyone from Houston to Denver knows that."

"Chad, please, don't."

"We'll have to declare a truce, then. Declare mama off limits. But then where does that leave you and your mission? You might as well go home tomorrow, Roberta."

"No, no, let's not set limits." This turn of events was making Roberta feel despondent. "Let's just drop it all until tomorrow. We can talk about it then. All right? I couldn't possibly go home so soon, Chad, not after Aunt Helen spent all this money and everything. Dear me, she'd skin me alive, you know that."

"Yes. I do know that. Fair enough. Until tomorrow then."

They looked at one another in wary silence.

"So tell me about *you*?" Chad said. "You must have some good-looking guy on a string back there. Tell me all about him."

"Nobody's on any string of mine. I haven't even had a date since Aunt Helen set me up with that policeman from Tulia, the very one who showed up later on *Sixty Minutes* because he shot some black kids dead in a grain elevator, and I'm not kidding you. I liked to die when I saw him there on the television, the big old racist, and there he'd been trying to touch me up in the front seat of his Pontiac not two weeks before."

"You make yourself sound desperate."

"I am desperate. You don't need to feel sorry for me or anything, but I am for sure hard up in the man department. Last year, at the Post Rodeo, I thought one of the clowns had a good build. *Yup.* I mean, hello — he had on these huge old red shoes with blue bows, gigantic purple pants and green suspenders and there I was *lusting* after his big shoulders and hairy chest. I could see this black hair there where his polka-dot shirt was opened at the neck. You know how I am about hairy chests. Those clowns get a lot of exercise, running after those bulls. Anyway, it's reached that point — I'm lusting after *clowns.*"

He laughed. "I can't believe someone hasn't married you long ago."

"Fat women have long shelf lives where dating is concerned. We get used to sitting home alone and fantasizing about how to get some clown out of his suspenders and baggy pants."

"You're not fat and you've never been fat, Bert."

"Thanks. But I am — sort of."

Chad laughed. "Have it your way."

She looked at him, and though blurred by exhaustion her eyes seemed to see something. "You know, I think a lot these days about our great grandma — how she killed herself in the tornado?"

"How funny that you say that, Bert. I think about her a lot too. Poor old thing. Seems like a terrible way to go — and yet she was having a vision, so who knows? Maybe it wasn't so bad after all. Maybe I'll be looking for my own tornado before too long."

She thought about that, rubbing her eyes and looking back at him, but with less clarity now and more exhaustion. "We don't get tornados on command — nor avoid them neither."

"True."

"When you left Texas, was this what you wanted, Chad?"

"I don't know."

"Remember when you used to talk about getting a motorcycle? I can still imagine you like that," she said, "Easy Rider, coursing across that big old Painted Desert. Of course, that always has been the way I think of you — it still makes more sense to me than fabric-covered walls and marble fireplaces."

"it's a nice word, coursing. I like that. On a Harley?"

"Sure thing." She reached out a hand, as if to catch hold of something, dropped it. "Sorry about you not being able to sleep."

"Don't be," He said. "I'm used to wandering the floors at night."

Imad heard Chad and Roberta chatting in the living room. Listening to them, his stomach ached. Finally, he got up, put on his robe, and went into the living room.

Roberta and Chad both turned as he came in.

Imad went over to Chad and gently ruffled his hair. "Still here, are you? I thought she'd have you on the next plane back to Texas."

"Apparently my mama will soon be legless. Double amputations all around. Maybe we could have them stuffed and use them as hearth ornaments. That would get peoples' attention. Patent leather pumps and net stockings?"

"Can I choose the stockings?"

Chad looked over at Roberta's mortified face. "Actually, Imad, I forgot — we're not supposed to talk about my mother until tomorrow. We've declared a moratorium. That would include her legs too, stuffed or unstuffed."

"*Ah*. My apologies." Imad winked at Roberta.

"Everybody's just tired, I reckon," Roberta said. "Me, I'm going back to bed now. I think I can finally sleep. So, good night," she said, getting up.

"Good night, my beautiful Renaissance Venus of a cousin."

"*Huh?*"

"I mean it. You have a Botticelli beauty, Bertie. A plenitude of beauty. You know, I love you very much."

For a moment longer she looked at him – and then at an equally startled Imad – and then her hand came up and rested upon the blush that now burned her cheek. She knew that Renaissance Venus' were on the plump side, but it was a compliment nonetheless. Maybe it was the best compliment she'd ever received. There were ways like this – at times like this – in which he had never been and could never be Helen Newsome's son.

"I love you too, Chad." Then she smiled at both of them, left the room, and went to bed.

4

Coming down the stairs, Roberta encountered Galsworthy and Aksel in the lobby, where they examined a half-dead potted ficus. Aksel had pulled it into the light streaming through the windows to the courtyard.

"Aha, *la cousine*," Galsworthy said, looking straight into Roberta's face and holding out a ringed hand attached to a braceleted arm.

"Hello," Roberta said.

"Galsworthy."

Roberta took his hand. "Hi."

"Torvald Aksel. But I am known as Aksel."

"Hi."

"I'm your party maven," Galsworthy said, running the same hand through his springy curls of highlighted hair.

"*Party*?"

"Maven."

"What? Oh, goodness, what does that mean?"

"Maven — as in *maven*? I thought we were playing a game. You know, hello — *dolly*, soup — *salad*." They stared at one another, and with a sigh through his nose Galsworthy said, "I'm the Galsworthy whose party you're attending."

Still they stared at one another.

"Aha. They haven't told you."

"I don't mean to be rude, but I haven't the tiniest notion of what y'all are talking about."

"Classic. You see, they think that if they ignore me, I shall go away. But I shan't, I'm like Emily Dickinson's poetry, I will remain — a continual if occasionally ignorable presence. By the way, I see now that you've killed it with fertilizer," he said to Aksel.

"How? I never fertilized it. Not even once."

"*Voila, mon petit*. Those are clearly fertilizer burns. And you are definitely expected to come to Chad's birthday party," he said to Roberta, "I will have to invite you myself, I see that."

"Oh. Thank you. When is it exactly?"

"Exactly? Well — I don't know, I mean, I can't remember which night I finally settled on. Do you remember which night I finally chose?" he asked Aksel.

"Was I invited?"

"Don't be daft. Are your evenings already booked up?" Galsworthy asked Roberta.

"No, no, of course not," she said. "Do you work with Chad and Imad?"

"It is work of a sort," Galsworthy said.

"Not I. I merely live here," Aksel said.

"Blithely murdering plants," Galsworthy said.

"I have done nothing to it, I swear."

"'I'm not quite ready yet to hear someone swear in Norwegian. What do you do when swearing in Norwegian, compare people's privates to misshapen herrings?"

Aksel glared at him.

"However, if you've done nothing, as you *say*, then, that might also be the problem. Or it's possible that what's-his-name, your little boyfriend, might have fertilized it," Galsworthy said, looking carefully again at the brown leaves.

"No, he has not fertilized. And he is not little."

"We will have to take your word on that, I've no independent source as to his endowments. They may in fact be little for all I know and you're just being loyal. Are Norwegians particularly loyal? *Damn*. The boys are straying." Galsworthy opened the door, growled a command, and the two dachshunds crabwalked across the lobby floor, one after the other, nails clicking like castanets on the tiles. "You are not as I imagined," Galsworthy told Roberta.

"I'm not?" she asked, recalling how Imad had said a similar thing.

"You're a sharper piece of work than I conjured up after talking to Imad. I expected that vacuous look we see on — what is that program's name?" he asked Aksel, "that one from Los Angeles."

"I don't know. They are all from Los Angeles or New York. It has a post code in it."

"Set – where is it set?"

"The beach," Aksel said.

"Of course the beach, that's my point. Otherwise it would be New York." Galsworthy sighed with pained exasperation. "But you don't look like that, you look – *wholesome*," he said, as if wholesome were something to be feared, like a disease, something about which Imad should have warned him so that he could take precautions.

"Maybe the radiator burned it," Aksel said.

"Do you drape damp towels on your radiators as I told you to do?"

"Once."

"*Once*? Then," Galsworthy threw his hands up theatrically, "we have found the culprit. The radiators. Coffee?" he asked Roberta.

"Thanks, but I can't. We've already got plans for today and everything, and right now, you know, I was just sneaking out for some air – a little walk."

"*Sneaking*?"

"It's only an expression."

"But expressions express, sweetness, that's what expressions do." He took Roberta's hand. "I bet you keep a daily journal. What do they call it? A blink."

"A what? Oh, y'all mean one of them on-line thingies? Those are called blogs, and no, sir, I wouldn't never do that, so that everybody and his sister can read what you're writing down." Roberta took back her hand from him. "I keep a plain old fashioned diary – well, at least hit and miss I do. It's got a picture of the state capitol down to Austin on it, which is kind of pretty – but I forget now who gave it to me. Aunt Edna I think, so she must have re-gifted it, because she never would have found something that nice for me on her own."

"I have no idea what you're talking about, darling – do *you*?" Galsworthy asked. Then he snapped his fingers at the dogs, who were preparing to relieve themselves on Aksel's ficus.

"None of that now boys, though such a hideous botanical specimen is indeed worthy of your disdain. Alcazar and Alhambra," he told Roberta.

"What pretty names."

"Yes, that's why I chose them." Galsworthy looked at her with real scrutiny. "Has his work cut out for him, poor old Imad, doesn't he?"

"Pardon me?"

"You should be pardoning me, to be honest, I am far too plain-spoken. It is both my charm and my heel."

"Your what?" Roberta asked.

"Charm."

"No, the other part."

"Oh. Heel. As in Achilles?"

"Of course. Heel. I see." But she didn't see at all, in fact her head swam.

"Roberta," Chad said from the landing upstairs, "is that you down there?"

"Yes, I'm talking with your neighbors," she called up.

"*Neighbor*?" Galsworthy snorted, "I've cut people for years for less provocation than that. I do not live within spitting distance of this arrondissement, let alone in this plant-destroying relic of a building."

"Ah," Chad said, peering down at them, "I see you've met the Galsworthy."

"Are we to be amused by the '*the*'?" Galsworthy asked.

"Warned, I believe, was my intent."

"And me," Aksel said, "I'm here."

"Hello, Aksel," Chad said, "Imad is wondering if you want some *crêpes*, Roberta?"

"I'd love some," she said, beginning to retrace her steps up the staircase. "Nice to have met you both."

"You can write all about us in your blink," Galsworthy said.

"I'll look forward to that party y'all are having. Do Chad and Imad know the date and time?"

"I don't invite people without telling them the particulars, my dear."

"You didn't tell *me* any particulars," Aksel said, "I shall have to ask Sebastian about it. Perhaps he knows." Aksel gave an abbreviated wave to Roberta. "Until later."

"Until later," Roberta said, fleeing toward the safety of Chad.

"I am not one dimensional," Galsworthy said.

Roberta turned back. "Excuse me?"

"I am not one dimensional. Even I can see myself that way at times, so it's understandable that others do, that they dismiss me as a crackpot. But I am not – be forewarned. *Arrêtes cette bêtise*," he said, snapping his fingers again. One of the dachshunds collapsed, whining, on the floor.

"You want people to think you're a crackpot," Chad said down the stairwell, "but you're the love child of Lucretia Borgia and Eleanor Roosevelt."

"Thank you all the same, Chad, but I don't compare well to Lesbians. Boys," Galsworthy said to the dachshunds, "we're off." He opened the door. "Throw the damn thing out," he advised Aksel, "it's just about the ugliest excuse for a house plant I've ever seen – and don't keep house plants unless you're prepared to drape your radiators with wet towels."

He and the dachshunds disappeared; Roberta continued back up the stairs.

Imad, Chad, and Roberta were chatting in the living room when the phone rang.

Chad looked across at Roberta. "That'll be mama for you," he said. "I'm clairvoyant. "Go on, answer it."

"You sure?" Roberta asked.

"Oh, yes," Chad told her.

At that, Roberta ran into the foyer and snatched the receiver off the hook. "Hello?"

"International telegrams by phone, I have an urgent message for – "

"Helen? Is that you?"

"Thank goodness, Roberta. That's one excellent strategy to answer the phone yourself. But you were supposed to have checked in by now, what the blazes is the matter with you? I can't be expected to call you now, can I? Not in my condition and considering he's like to hang up on me. You've got to follow the rules, girl. Anyway, it was quick thinking for you to answer, I give you that much. And I don't even know if they have telegrams these days, do they? I think they've done away with them. But I couldn't think what else to say. Where is he?"

"In the living room."

"Can he hear you?"

"No, I don't think so."

"Excellent. Just tell him I was some little old friend from the library or something. Is he coming round?"

"I've hardly had a chance to talk to him. He was in London."

"London? Why was he in London? He's like to get himself blown up over there."

"I think he was on a school trip or something."

"Roberta, you meathead, you've got to find out everything. *Everything*. What's his living environment like?"

"It's not an environment, Aunt Helen, unless, oh – I get it, you mean – "

"Oh, good Lord, get to the point, Roberta. You needn't spare me."

"Okay. Well, he's got this huge old apartment that has a view of this real pretty street that goes down toward a boulevard – Boulevard St. Germain, that's it – and then all the way down to Notre Dame, if you can believe it, and it's been all decorated up and everything, the apartment, I mean. There's this one lamp, it's about six feet tall, that's got three legs on it and looks like a Greek Olympic torch kind of a thing. I've never seen a lamp like it before, Aunt Helen, except maybe in movies. Oh, you know, one of those apartments on L.A. Law had furniture like this. Anyway, the balcony's full of these huge old flowers. It's just gorgeous – "

"Don't tell me about the flowers, I didn't pay good money to send you over there to talk like a Jap gardener. Does he live alone?"

"No. He has a tenant."

"I knew it. A fancy word for something else, I say."

"Well, it's not his word, it's my word. And his tenant isn't a woman, it's a man, a very nice man, he's – French." Just plain French seemed the safest approach for the moment. The time didn't seem ripe for introducing the Muslim and Moroccan component, since Roberta hoped to have Imad invited out to Lubbock for a visit. Simply being French would make that hard enough where Helen was concerned.

"Get a clue, Roberta."

"About what?"

"Oh, for heaven's sake, never mind, you numbskull, I can't raise your I.Q. fifty points or I'd have done it for you before now. Listen," Helen said, "have you told him about my illness?"

"Yes."

"What'd he say?"

"Not much."

"I can just see the saws now, hacking, hacking. Oh, Roberta. I need him here, here to hold my hand. I wish you'd become a nurse. *Please*? Couldn't you do a training course or something? They've got this great new program over to Methodist Hospital, Aylene Berkshire told me all about it, her little niece Wendy, the one who got into trouble with that oil field trash up in Brownfield who deceived her something awful, she's looking into it for next year after – well, anyway, she's going to need a profession now, isn't she? And it's a good program."

Roberta experienced a true frisson of horror. She'd always hated hospitals and couldn't bear the thought of bed pans, catheters and dead bodies. And what she felt about

Wendy Berkshire — who had not been deceived about much, Roberta didn't think — was not worth saying. "I don't want to be a nurse, Aunt Helen," she said, with as much conviction as she dared, "And I think Wendy Berkshire is just an uttermost — you know what."

"And she probably thinks you're a fat old blimp who plays with herself. So what? And what do you know about what you want to do? Huh? You'd gladly sit there at the library and enter junk into a computer your whole life and think that celebrating some other fat lady's birthday over to the Spiral Staircase at Dillard's was the be all and the end all. I worry about you, Roberta. And you'll have to do something to make a proper living, whether you like the idea or not. But we'll discuss our plans when you get home. *Now*. Tell him about my legs. Tell him I'll have huge hypodermic needles and drug addicts will attack me for my stash and I'll get that drug-resistant AIDS. Poor legless thing, they'll break into my house and steal my dope."

"Oh, Aunt Helen, really."

"It's true. I've seen it on TV. Diabetics use hypodermics and dope. You think I'm kidding? I'm not kidding."

"They use insulin, Helen, not dope."

"Don't be a know-it-all, Roberta. Remember when the preacher talked about — well, I can't be expected to remember what part of the bible it came from just now, but God doesn't look kindly on know-it-alls, does he? Listen, if Chad wants to see me alive again he'd better come home soon. Tell him."

"Right now?"

"No, numbskull. When we get off the phone."

"That's what I meant."

"Bless you, Roberta. Bless you. I'll go now. Rendezvous again day after tomorrow. And this time you call me like you're supposed to. Keep working on him. Bye, now, honey."

"Bye."

The line went dead. Roberta had not at all liked this conversation with Helen. It had been like talking to some demented stranger. No, she thought: it had been like talking to Helen Newsome.

Imad came around the corner with his calm voice. "We're wondering what happened to you."

"*I'm* wondering what's happened to me."

He seemed to scrutinize her. "Are you all right?"

"Yes and no. Can I say I don't know?"

"But of course."

"Okay, then. I don't know. Why do you ask, anyway?"

"Because you're staring at the ceiling," he said.

"That was Chad's mother on the phone."

"We guessed it was – remember?"

She looked at him and then suddenly she burst forth with a shriek of laughter. "I am all right. Dang it. I really am."

He laughed with her. "Okay. I believe you."

They were gathered around Imad as he fried broccoli and tofu in a wok. He patiently explained his seasonings and showed Roberta how to slice the tofu (which she thought looked revolting, though she didn't say so), and just when to throw in the ginger. Despite her disgust with the rubbery-looking tofu, Roberta was mesmerized. She'd only recently mastered a decent chicken fried steak with sausage gravy, so the intricacies of cooking in a wok astounded her. She remembered how Isabelle, one of the security people at the library, told her how she'd used a wok and it spattered grease all over her ceiling and burned her mushrooms to a crisp. They looked like bacon bits, she said. Inasmuch as Roberta trusted Isabelle – she lived in a trailer out by the airport surrounded by chrysanthemums, which Roberta associated with domesticity and kindness – she'd thought that woks were potentially lethal.

"Karl and cousin Jamie broke up," she told Chad.

"I didn't even know cousin Jamie was married. Why'd they break up?"

"It happened at the Culbert wedding reception. I went with them — remember Graham Culbert, from Tahoka? You played football with his brother Tyler? Anyway, the reception was out in one of those rank motels by the old traffic circle? It's all highway now, of course," she looked at Imad, "but we still say out by the old traffic circle. Makes it confusing, I know. Anyway, we went there together and they got in this big old fight. She told him that he looked like a mannequin — he kind of did, I have to be honest. He had on this styling gel stuff, he gets his hair cut at the Bijou, same place you used to go to, and he looked like he could survive a hit with a sledgehammer — and he told her to shut up. It went from bad to worse. She spent an hour locked in one of the stalls of the bathroom and on the other side there was a real pretty girl from California, who had the stomach flu — or else she drank too much — so I kind of took care of both of them. After that, well, Karl and Jamie never did make up proper. He filed for divorce and now he's dating some girl from Ropesville. Darla something or another. Jamie's gone back to Tech to get her a degree. In P.E., I think."

64

"Supper's on," Imad announced.

They followed him out to the dining room and allowed him to fill their plates.

"I'm glad I've lost touch with all of that nonsense," Chad told her.

She smarted a moment, shrugged. "Sounds pretty small town?" she asked.

"That's putting it nicely. I'd say it sounds ignorant."

She thought about that and then she turned to Imad. "There are probably more ignorant people in the world than the other way around, if you think about it."

"Did you just put me in my place, Roberta?" Chad laughed.

She simply shrugged again.

"Do you and mama sit around and talk about me?" Chad asked.

"I don't think Aunt Helen and I have ever once done anything that could be called sitting around together. But when we talk, you come up. I don't really think of it as us talking about you so much as Helen talking and me listening. She uses you a lot for value lesson stuff, like 'that's where I went wrong with Chad' or 'that's how come I sit home alone every night.' You know, that kind of thing. But here we are talking about Aunt Helen again," Roberta told them. "She tends to dominate things even when she's not in the room. These potatoes are delicious, Imad."

"Are you big potato eaters out in West Texas?" he asked her.

"Potatoes? Well – I don't know for sure about that." His question made her think of the Mr. Potato Head toy she'd played with as a girl. You stuck hard plastic eyes, lips, eyebrows, ears and mouth into a cleaned potato. Suddenly, she felt homesick and tired. "I guess we eat potato salad a lot in the summer, don't we, Chad?"

He caught something in her voice. "Yeah. Plenty of potato salad, Roberta." He leaned toward her and planted a noisy kiss on her forehead. "So much of that goddamned potato salad I could scream – it tastes like mucous," he told Imad.

"You're not homesick ever, are you?" she asked, but more as a statement than a question.

"I miss diarrhea and George Bush more, to be perfectly honest."

She looked at her cousin and attempted a smile, though she could feel the heat on her cheeks. "And right now," she told him, "I'd give anything to be walking with you down 98th Street close to Quaker. And we'd look up at the stars – they burn just like phosphorus, and you can make out the big dipper and everything – and if we saw a shooting star, like I sometimes do, we'd make a wish. And then we'd go for a drive to Gardski's and eat a big basket of special fries – oh yeah, that's also how we eat potatoes, Imad – and giggle over an iced tea."

"Do you really turn your headlights on in dust storms?" Imad asked.

"Yup, but lights don't help much when you're trying to look through dirt, but at least they make you feel like you're not about to drive into a telephone pole," Roberta said. "That's my home, God love it, mucous-tasting potato salad and dust storms, and I love it all to pieces."

5

Roberta awoke from a nightmare. She had been repeating lines from *The Lord's Prayer* out of order, and everybody in church was watching her, including Loreen K. Albrighton and her friend Lucille Vernon from Muleshoe. The two of them had been giggling at her. Roberta turned on the light and sat up. But even in the light, this dream of jumbled prayer bewildered her (longstanding suspicions about the Bible notwithstanding). She felt that something in her dream endangered her relationship with God. Roberta had never before felt that her relationship to God could be endangered. Her relationship to Him was so personal, so unrelated to Bible and Sunday School and the rest of that. So the effect of her dream was shocking – as shocking as the time she saw sexually aroused Carl Heims, Junior – from next door but one – buck naked through the window of his family's pool cabana. Seeing her first erect penis (she hadn't reckoned on an erect penis being so big, she'd imagined it more like an old-fashioned ballpoint pen), had shaken her. It shook her still.

Roberta had been reared on the idea that God had a plan for her. This divine omniscience and – *planning* – was the cornerstone of her faith. When things went wrong, or occasionally right, she chalked it up to God's plan. Too many times Roberta had chirped in the face of adversity, "I just know God has a plan for me." And she meant it. Or rather, she *had* meant it. Because tonight, in Paris, unable to pray – she doubted. She didn't doubt God's love for her – or hers for him – or her belief in good and evil, but she doubted the whole plan thing, which essentially meant she doubted her faith. Sitting there thinking, she became only more doubtful. Who in the heck came up with that plan idea anyway? Why would God need to have plans? What did he do, store them up alphabetized in filing cabinets, waiting for the right occasion?

And did these plans only start when Jesus was born? Didn't God make plans before that? If not, why not? It seemed weird to have all those filing cabinets sitting empty up there in Heaven, and then suddenly need to fill them all up with plans.

She wanted to come close to God through effort, pleasing Him with her devotion. But what could her devotion really mean if he knew about everything in advance or had even planned it? Had he *planned* her devotion to Him? That scared the heck out of her. Since none of what she'd always believed seemed to make sense to her just then, she got out of bed and put on her robe. Helen had given her a phone calling card, and she considered phoning home to the safety of Lubbock, Texas. But if she called Helen, she'd only want to plot strategy about Chad. If she called their Preacher, he'd pass her off on his gossipy wife Marlene (whose brother had married the daughter of a judge down in Waco, which always seemed to come up in conversations with Marlene), and then Marlene would make Roberta sound ludicrous once she told everybody at the Tuesday evening Bible class about their conversation. Marlene couldn't keep secrets.

So, instead, Roberta got dressed and went out to the living room. It was delightful there, surrounded by the sophisticated riches of Chad and Imad's apartment. It felt like one of those big antique stores out by Tech, near the Loop. She loved those stores; they had a similar old smell. Wonderfully, but also a little disconcertingly, once she had nestled in an armchair, her theological battles faded away.

"You okay?" Chad asked from the doorway.

"*Oh*, did I wake you up? *Again*? I tried as hard as I could to be quiet."

He came and sat opposite her, on the sofa. "I was already awake."

"I probably shook the building. Something bovine this way comes."

"Roberta."

She admired him in his boxer shorts, as she done the night before. "Aren't you cold?"

"No. What're you doing out here? You're not reading."

"Kind of praying."

"Kind of?"

"Well, worrying about praying." She met his puzzled look. "Chad, do you think God has a plan for us?"

"I'm not even sure I *believe* in God anymore, Roberta, let alone his plans."

This didn't surprise her, though it did surprise her that it didn't surprise her. How could so much in her be changing so fast? "I do believe in God, and in Jesus Christ, our Lord and Savior," she told him, "but I don't know if there's a plan for me, or if it's up to me to prove my love for God by coming up with one on my own – you know, one that rejects evil and chooses good and makes it – you know, worthwhile that I end up on God's side because I had to find my own way over there?"

He thought about what she said. "How can you possibly be thinking about *that* in the middle of the night?"

Again they looked at each other.

"I don't know – but I am. Chad," Roberta asked, "is there or is there not a woman in this all? And you know what I mean, so pretty please don't be skipping around the subject, like you were before. Can't you just answer me plain and simple? Is there a woman – with all kinds of complications – making you stay here in Paris?"

"Roberta," Chad smiled. "There is no woman in this. Promise. Okay?"

She nodded, but committed nothing to words.

"And I think you may have stumbled upon something, you know, in all this consideration of God's plan – or lack of a plan."

"All right," she nodded again. "That's me – always stumbling upon things. But just so's I'm clear: there's *no* woman."

"You're clear. There's *no* woman."

They lolled amid the smell of flowers on metal chairs in the Luxembourg gardens, full of food and wine. Traffic noise sieved through chestnut trees; flags snapped from the roof of Catherine de Medici's palace, now the French Senate. Listening to the voices around her, Roberta wondered what they were saying —so intently, so magically. The inchoate sensation of it electrified her, these words like fogged visions, *étampes, crevettes, cette, la*. Now and then, she snuck a look at the Australian, Simon, who'd taken his shirt off and slept in the sunshine like a catalog model, hairy-chested and flat-stomached, legs extended across an empty chair. He'd joined their group when they discovered him consuming coffee and croissants in their favorite café. Roberta thought Simon was the manliest man she'd ever seen, and she liked his quirkiness. It was almost West Texan. Maybe Australians and West Texans had something in common? Chad and Imad spoke quietly together.

She stood up, held a finger to her lips, pointed in the direction of the toilets, and walked off down the path. Arriving at the terrace, she passed to the left and continued toward the *Orangerie*, remembering something she had read that morning in Chad's *Michelin Guide* about a monument to Delacroix. She didn't know who Delacroix was (actually, she'd read that he was a painter), but she supposed she ought to see his monument — in case somebody asked her about it. The sun pursued her along the open path. Through the trees, above the *Orangerie*, she saw the irregular towers of St. Sulpice. Delacroix's statue came upon her easily enough, and she admired it a moment or two (she wasn't sure what you were meant to do with a statue exactly), before strolling along the dirt path that ran parallel to Rue Guynemer. Suddenly she came face to face with Imad.

"I guessed you'd come back up this way," he said.

She held her hair away from her face. "Were you looking for me?"

"Catching you up."

"Catching me up?"

"Yes."

They stood quietly opposite the tennis courts, before he gestured toward a bench and they sat down. Bits of hair held fast to her neck.

"Paris is an oven in summer," Imad said, guessing her thoughts on the heat, "these paving stones and rooftops. Anyone who can, leaves – and even those who can't afford to leave, somehow manage to do it in August. August in Paris is worse than Death Valley. We usually go to La Rochelle, we take a flat there – the same one every year."

"Where's that?"

"On the coast, Charente Maritime."

"Oh, right, of course. The Shar – whatever you said. *That* helps." She was quiet a moment. "I'm sorry, I didn't mean to be sarcastic. It's just that I don't know a darned thing about any of this. I'm a flat out ignoramous where Europe is concerned." For what felt like a long time, she gazed through the leaves of a chestnut tree, trying to find a focus for the conversation, then she turned back to him and asked, "So why were you catching me up? Are we bonding? Like we did when I was first here?"

"When people say that I always imagine they're implying bondage."

She smiled again, imagining herself as the dominatrix she'd seen once in an episode of *CSI*, with a whip, wearing leather and dark lipstick. Wouldn't that picture of Roberta Martin just curl Aunt Helen's hair? She wouldn't need her monthly perm for at least a year. A pair of skinny American girls passed by with a bouquet of soap and hair products, talking about the boys who were staying upstairs from them in their hotel. Roberta and Imad watched them drift off chattering down the steps toward the fountain.

"Something's changed," Roberta said, "I can sense it. You're not happy about me being here, that's what I think. At first you were okay with me, but –"

He looked at his fingers, saying obliquely, "you and Chad have a lot of past together."

"I'd like to think so. People do – they have their pasts, don't they? But you shouldn't be jealous of it."

"I'm not jealous. It's just – "

She looked at him, but what she saw was hard for her to decipher.

"It's not that I don't know he has to go back eventually. He can't hide out in Paris forever. After all, it's one of life's immutable laws: sooner or later they go back to the place from whence they came, then they remember, then they make amends – "

"Then they stay?" she asked, thinking that when Imad said "from whence," he sounded just like the visiting preacher they had down from Little Rock last Thanksgiving. He used expressions like that. She wondered how that visiting preacher from Arkansas would take it, if he knew she was comparing him to a Moslem?

"Yes. That's the immutable law. Then they stay. People can and do go home again; in fact, they almost *always* go home again."

She took his hand, comfortable now with the heat, him, the conversation. Somehow, it all fell into place. But he looked down distrustfully at his hand in hers. Glancing off through the trees again she said, "*is* he hiding out?"

"We both know he is."

"From?"

"Yes, from that and more," Imad said. "But you didn't think about Chad's life here when you came over as Helen Newsome's ambassador. I mean, you didn't think about the people in Chad's life here. You were only thinking about what *you'd* lost, not about what he might have found – and what others might lose if he were to go away."

She nodded at the embarrassing truthfulness of that.

His look remained fixed on their linked hands. "You're the past. You live where he grew up. You're at least a menace to his equilibrium, if you weren't then Helen Fucking Newsome would never have sent you on her errand, would she?"

"A *menace*?" she asked, recoiling from the word itself as well as the Helen Fucking Newsome remark.

Taking back his hand, he pointed toward the tennis courts, visible through the trees, "yes, to all of this, to his Paris world."

"I don't want to be a menace." She tried to think of herself as someone reckless and destructive, but the image didn't coalesce. Of course, her intent in coming was to lure Chad back into their lives. So she had to be dangerous to Chad's Parisian equilibrium. On the other hand, wasn't luring him back into her life encoded in her DNA? They were family; that's how it worked. "You know, I think this city," she said, looking at the park, the trees, the dome of the Pantheon, "is just about everything Chad's ever wanted. I can see it real clear, even if he can't. This is – well, this is Chad."

"If you're going to hide out, Paris is the place to do it. A tradition, of sorts, I suppose."

"He must be happy here."

"Happy? Hard to say."

She felt a long quiet grow around them. A man in a gray T-shirt, sitting on one of the benches, slowly took off his sunglasses, adjusted the fit, and cleaned the lenses. He had muscular arms, and a strong nose in the middle of a handsome face. When he put the glasses back on he leaned into the bench and rotated his face into the sun. And where is *he* from, she wondered? And how has Paris affected him?

"I really don't want to threaten Chad's life in Paris, Imad. I'm not that kind of a person. It's – you know – Aunt Helen being sick and all and her wanting me to do something good for her – and then me getting laid off – or vice versa. And of course I love Chad, I really do love him. He's – gosh, he's Chad."

"It's clear you've missed him."

She puzzled that remark. Was it wrong to miss him?

"And Chad has missed you."

"Does he ever talk about coming home?"

"*Home*. You see. There's the word."

She shrugged then, also meaningfully.

"He knows he'll go back someday."

"For a funeral, you mean?"

"Odd way to put it, but yes, I suppose that's it."

"He didn't come home for his daddy's funeral, though I understand he might not have gotten the word in time. Apparently there was some confusion about when Uncle Mack was actually dying. All I can say right now – and I would never, ever have thought I'd be saying this – and not, you know, in the first couple days that I was here. But I'm kind of sorry that I came over like this."

Imad stood up. Looking a long while in the direction of the *Observatoire*, which clumped at the top of the Park like a miniature palace, looking elegant and oblivious to the fact that it was no longer an observatory and that the people who built it had long ago been eradicated by revolution and time, he said, "it must be hard always being apart from him, Roberta, because I know you love Chad and I know you've missed him."

"Thanks, it is."

"It's not as if Chad hasn't thought about all of this a thousand times, someone appearing here like you've done, or needing to go home for a funeral. After all, people grow old and die, that's what they do."

She stood up and joined him in the middle of the path. "No matter what I say or how hard I try, well – you know – the truth of it is that he doesn't *have* to come back."

"But he does," Imad said, "that's the thing. He does."

"It gets pulled fifteen feet out of plumb every day," Imad said.

"*Mercy.*" Roberta peered cautiously down from the windows of the Eiffel Tower observation deck. "How's that possible?"

"It's iron, it expands in the heat. When the sun hits one side of it, well, there you have it."

"How can it possibly be safe?" she asked.

"It probably isn't."

"Don't worry," Chad said, "it won't fall down today."

"Quite right," Simon told them. "And you're wrong about the sway, Imad. It's never been recorded at more than 12 centimeters, which is about 4 and a bit inches, right? And in height, I think you got your fifteen from that, mate, because it's fifteen centimeters it changes in height, given the temperature. Six inches?"

"I'm sure I read about the sway on one side," Imad said weakly, outgunned.

Simon shrugged, a fair winner. "It's safe as houses, anyway."

"So *you* say," Roberta whispered. She looked off over the Seine, into the rooftop refrigerator magnet view. Sun glinted on windows; clouds foamed in the background. Moving around the deck, Roberta looked down on expanses of lawn, trees, cars, streets. She gazed a long while at the glittering Dome of the *Invalides*. "Beautiful," she said softly, "utterly beautiful."

"They wanted to pull it down," Simon told her.

"What?"

"The Eiffel Tower."

"No, I mean what like – *hello*. That kind of what. Why would they tear it down, for goodness' sake?"

"Thought it was ugly as sin. 1909, I think it was. Turns out they needed it, so they couldn't."

"Needed it?"

"For telegraph, then wireless radio transmission, finally for television. Technology saving technology."

"I'm glad they left it."

His eyes seemed to alter somewhat, as if he now regarded her differently.

"So am I," he said.

"I was thinking about lunch in the Latin Quarter." Chad caught Imad's upper arm. "Your Moroccan place."

Imad pulled free. "It's not *my* Moroccan place and it's generic Maghreb food anyway – it really makes me crazy that you can't get the difference right."

"Whichever it is, it's an interesting place to eat."

"We'd have to take the metro. Why don't we find some place closer, off the Champs des Mars. *La Tour Maubourg*?"

"Too many tourists."

"As if you'd miss them anywhere you went this summer," Simon said.

"I don't mind," Roberta said, "anywhere will be fine." And she pressed up toward the view again, breathing in the vista, the distance, the irreality of space and time.

They stood together, Roberta and Simon, observing the *Arc de Triomphe* by night, as traffic blasted down the *Champs-Elysees*.

When Simon, while putting on his shirt after basking in the sun, suddenly asked her if she wanted to have dinner with him she'd been – actually, she didn't have the words for what she'd been. Surprised hardly began to describe it. But she could tell his invitation was serious, and despite the fact that there couldn't really – not *really* – be any hope that a man like Simon would be interested in a woman like her, she'd said yes so fast her tongue smoked. She'd seen the eye contact between Imad and Chad and, of course, Chad later said a few off-putting things about Simon's problems with depression – but with that chest and face and arms, Roberta wouldn't have cared if he were Jack the Ripper.

He'd taken her for dinner at a restaurant called *The Hippo*, which was part of a nationwide chain — not stylish and not at all French. Simon, however, assured her that it was *more* French, since it wasn't a Parisian Disneyland-esque tourist bistro. The French liked to think of themselves as modern people. But this couldn't possibly be what the French thought of as modern, could it, Roberta wondered? In some ways the restaurant reminded her of the *Bob's Big Boy* out by the airport (which had excellent fries, so she wasn't complaining about that part of the comparison), though she judiciously didn't say so to him. Now, as they walked, they passed those Disney cafés crowded with foreigners, as well as apartments with ornate facades and curtained windows, stores with recognizable names (some of them the same ones she could find in the South Plains Mall, in Lubbock), and narrow shopping arcades that looked like movie sets.

After dinner, he'd offered in his casual manner to take her sight-seeing, as if it were a stray thought, as if he just as much thought she'd say no as yes. Casualness, the opposite of the glad-handling vivacity of the men she'd chiefly dated, including her murderous policeman, seemed particularly attractive to her. So did Simon himself tonight, truth be told. She admired not just the way he was dressed, in a baggy white shirt and dark corduroys, but the way he held himself. Intensely masculine, he stood as if disconnected from the hurly-burly around him, unconcerned with the scurrying masses of people. They kept on walking beneath trees, past cafés and apartments, more stores, another arcade. Traffic thrummed next to them.

"How long have y'all lived in Paris?" she asked him.

"A long time."

"Years?"

"Seven to be exact," he said.

"How'd you end up here?"

"A long way from the antipodes?"

"The anti-*whats*?"

He laughed. "Australia, New Zealand — Australia, in my case. I was working in Melbourne, at a grammar school, I'd been living with Marlene for a couple of years and we finished. Seemed like a good time to get out of Australia. I ended up here."

Roberta thought about what he had said, reconciling herself to the fact that a man this handsome would have had his fair share of women by now. So the Marlene news was no surprise though – embarrassingly – it made her jealous. That might have been what made her blurt out, "was she pregnant?"

"Why do you ask that?"

She was in too deep now. "Something about that clear out of Australia part of the story."

He shrugged. "No. She wasn't pregnant, not that I knew of and not by me. You like it, do you?" He waved at the pandemonium of traffic and people.

She would have preferred to follow up on the "if pregnant not by me" aspect of his story, but she said, "oh, Simon – you know – it's awesome."

"I thought so too when I first arrived."

"You don't think so now?"

"Oh, off and on I still do, sure. More often, though, it just seems like a big, dirty city. Cliché, I suspect, you get used to anything, don't you? People, places, things."

"Sad."

"Just the way it is."

"Can't things stay fresh?" she wondered.

"No," he said, "that's why fresh is fresh and stale is stale. They can't be the same thing now, can they?"

"I guess not."

They walked toward the *Place Clemenceau*.

"I want to ask you something personal, Simon. If you don't mind."

"I won't know if I mind until after you've asked, will I?" he said sensibly.

Then having second thoughts, and wondering why in heaven's name she needed to ask him about his mental state, she said vaguely, "oh, you know," she said, "I've wanted to ask you what your last name is."

"Matthews," he said,

She twirled the name off her tongue, "Simon Matthews. We take a lot of pride in names back home. They mean a lot, names do."

"Yes, they do – and that's not a personal question, Roberta, that's public knowledge."

She looked at him, with his masculine five o'clock shadow and quizzical face. "I wanted to ask – well, it's not all that big a deal and anyway I know full well that Julie Riggs, my supervisor at the library, she had herself a real terrible bout of something and nearly drowned a whole litter of those prize Afghan pups of hers until they got her fixed up with some kind of – oh *heck*, I think it was called Paxa-something and then she was right as rain and she even gave me a birthday card, which shocked the be-jeepers out of me, I hope to tell you. Anyway, that's what I wanted to asked – if it's true that you're depressed?"

They stood at the edge of a chaotic traffic circle with noisy exhaust smuts.

"It's called a *rond-point* in French," he said.

"What is?"

"This." He pointed at the whirling circus of cars. "You aren't meant to ask people about depression, you know."

"I bet not." She nodded. "But I wanted to know and my social skills are not up to par, just ask my Aunt Helen. She tried to make me take some sort of etiquette class at the Y, but I put down the wrong phone number by pretend-accident on the application form – by the time it got sorted out it was too late, *thank goodness*. Can you imagine taking a class like that?"

He laughed a long time. "No, I can't. All right, then. You want to know if I'm *depressed* depressed? I don't take any tablets. Not now. Not anymore. I still have my moments, I suppose. Chad and Imad obviously think I'm loopy, since that's obviously where this is coming from. So – who knows?" He shrugged. "I could be a complete nutter – I could be a cured nutter – or I could just be someone who had a bad patch and was never a nutter. Which of them told you, by the by?"

"I'm not sure I should tell."

"Imad or Chad?" he pursued.

Looking into his narrowing eyes, she relented almost immediately. "Chad."

"Good old Imad. He's a friend you can trust."

"Isn't Chad your friend?"

"No, he's an acquaintance. Imad is a friend."

She thought about the difference between a friend and an acquaintance, and about how honest he was to say it. She liked his honesty almost as much as his five o'clock shadow – though she liked the five o'clock shadow better, if *she* were being honest. "I have lots of friends I can't trust," she told him.

He face flashed astonishment. "If you do, then they're not friends."

"Of course they're my friends. Just kind of – unreliable. People aren't perfect, and you've got to cut them lots of slack – *lordy*, some of the worst things that ever happened to me, happened on account of my friends. I mean, they were my friends at the time," she hedged, because she had been known to cut people who commented about her weight. She was sensitive in that area.

"No," he said, "they're not friends if you can't trust them. It's the way life is, Roberta. Anything else is deception. Mind you, people deceive themselves a great deal on the subject of friendship."

"Something real bad must have happened to you to make you feel this way."

"If you mean have I been burned, then you bet, I've been burned."

"I'm sorry about that," she said. "And Chad – he just told me in passing, Simon. Honestly."

"Right. Just a little something you needed to know – in *passing*."

"It's not like that," she said, though it had been exactly like that.

"Of course it is. It's the way we talk — we turn other people into objects, we give them labels. Simon's depressed. That's clearly my label with Chad. It works. It made you worry, made you ask me. Wouldn't want to be walking around Paris with a head case, would you? Of course, some labels are 'in' and some labels are 'out,' so it's quite a game, really. I have these Canadian acquaintances here in Paris, don't like to live among African immigrants and yet they don't want to appear racist, God forbid, they're Canadian after all and this is the Obama era, so they say 'new neighbors.' It's a code. 'Look, a few of our new neighbors,' or 'our new neighbors would like that.' Clever and yet ugly at the same time."

She nodded. "I'm not sure I got issued the handbook for all that stuff."

"Nor I," he agreed with a sharp laugh.

They turned the corner, continued between the *Grand* and *Petit Palais*.

"Oh, look. It's our county courthouse," she told him, pointing at the *Petit Palais*.

"Come again?"

"They copied it. Rich old bunch of cotton growers. I'd know that thing anywhere, I really would. It's a good story, you know, how it caught some rich man's eye, so they copied it for our courthouse in — oh, I can't remember the exact date. Nineteen something, real early anyway."

"Amazed you remember."

"It's a story everybody knows."

"I doubt that." He looked at her in the light from the *Grand Palais* courtyard. "A person gets depressed sometimes," he said, "I, for one, think that's about as normal to the human condition as needing to eat or take a whiz, if you'll excuse my French."

She smiled. "I've often thought that's kind of true for myself, more normal, I mean, than we make out — I can't hardly say I've ever been happy with myself, Simon — always wanting to be thinner or prettier or — gosh, if I had a penny for every time I was sad or went to bed crying — I'd be a millionaire for sure. But I couldn't hardly get help back home, could I? I don't have the right kind of insurance to get them paxa-whatevers – heck, my insurance won't keep my out of a pauper's grave, it's that pitiful." Then she felt profoundly startled by what she had said, this admission of weakness to a man she hardly knew – a man so handsome that he was causing her to experience something akin to heart palpitations. She took a deep breath. Glancing at the stenciled light on the confectionary roof of the *Grand Palais* she was struck by a kind of – what was the word for it? She knew there was a word for it, like the opposite of *déjà vu*. This evening with Simon, this walk, this city, it was such a contrast to the rest of her life. She was at the same time cannily aware of herself, her feelings, her history, her past and future and yet assiduously self-exotic, unrecognizable, a stranger in Roberta Martin's skin.

"What kinds of things do you like to do?" Simon asked.

"*Pardon me?*"

"I was thinking of a jazz club, that's what I was thinking," he laughed, "if you're up to it, not mad love-making or snogging."

"That's good, then," she said, wishing that it had been mad lovemaking or snogging (which sounded blissful, whatever it was) that he was after. Again they looked at one another; again she looked away. Could she, Roberta Martin, possibly pin any romantic hopes on this hairy-chested god who looked like he stepped out of a magazine? Or was she being drawn into something that would ultimately embarrass her and cause everybody back home to giggle once Aunt Helen got wind of it. "What time is it?" she asked him.

He looked at his watch. "About eleven thirty."

"I'd better call it a night," she said, "I'm feeling those time zones a smidgen."

Running a hand lazily over the contours of his hairy chest, he asked, "How about we do something day after tomorrow, then? I'm free. Maybe we could go out to Versailles? I could show you around?"

"Okay, sure," she said, unable to keep the surprise from her voice, because this time there was no aloofness in him, none of the offhandedness she'd noticed before. This time she saw that he desired her – and, of course, she desired him as well. She felt her cheeks sizzle. "Day after tomorrow then, Simon."

"Right, then," he said, "there we are."

Contemplating his evening's adventure and Roberta's keen interest in him (and his in her), Simon felt he might as well have been back in Melbourne, still a young man, only dreaming of a Europe far away from madness and Australia. Throughout their first months together, Marlene had looked at him the way Roberta had tonight – but not at the end. He recalled that last afternoon with Marlene in Melbourne, recalled how his reflection gazed back at him from the windows Marlene spent hours cleaning, one of her many insinuating offerings. He'd stood with his back against the garden wall, framed against clematis, shirtless, hairy-chested, strong forearms hanging ape-like along the side of his torso, left thumb curled over the top of his jeans. Feeling posed, he cocked his head at his image, as if to say, this is Simon Matthews and this is precisely the thing from which I am fleeing. He'd just told Marlene he was leaving Australia for good.

Earlier that same day, he'd come through the hospital gate and blinked in the December glare of a Melbourne summer sky. Marlene waited for him, red vinyl purse in hand, under a willow on the bristly grass in the park that led down toward the Yarra River. There was no traffic. The Melbourne cityscape rumbled into itself along the margin of his vision, but did not impede his view of Marlene and sanity; and his sudden knowledge that he must leave all of this, Marlene and Melbourne, behind. Yet he walked to her and took her in his arms, deceitfully reassuring her with the strong, hard kisses of a man restored to life from the brink of some cheerless crevasse.

"All right, then?" she asked.

"Oh yeah, right as rain," he said back, and he took her hand, leading her across the grass toward the bus stop.

A hesitant silence sifted round them, the awkwardness of remembered intimacies and his attempted suicide, and he felt as if even to recognize that silence was to confirm his need for flight.

"What's new, Marlene?" he asked, refuting the silence.

"Tess had them kittens."

"Was she preggers, then?"

"Yeah, you knew it," she said.

He said nothing to that. Looking both ways as they crossed the street, they made their way into the meager shade of the bus stop. Hours later he stood full of beer, shirtless in the summer garden. The hours of awkwardness had become the undiscovered country of their wary domestic exile, and they were embroiled in battle.

From the shadows, her voice sounded closer to defeat. "You don't know what you want, just what you *don't* want, that's what hurts."

"I do know what I want," he said, purposefully turning away from the shirtless pornography of his own reflected charms, "and that's what hurts you – or should."

That comment, a successful salvo, won the battle.

She rushed headlong, sobbing, into the lounge and the phone and the cradled embrace of those sustaining conversations, which she'd no doubt relied upon while he was dining on his metallic-tasting pills. After all, Marlene had found him on the bathroom floor, she'd called the aid car, signed the forms, visited him with patient resignation, shared his triumphs and shortfalls, and known all along that he'd come back cured. And, he thought suddenly, he had. He had come back cured, without the phantom outriders and without the desire to succumb to the depression that had haunted his family for generations.

He went to the door of the lounge and hung in the entrance, watching her.

"Go on, then." She sniffled at him. "If you're going, go."

"I'm going," he said, but he hung a moment longer in the doorframe.

They stared at one another.

"Bloody send me your address this time."

"This isn't like the last time," he warned her.

She shrugged.

He released the doorframe and walked to the bedroom, turning from the doorway, and looking out across the sparse landscape of their time together, toward the clematis they'd planted, the furniture they'd collected, the dreams they'd claimed to dream. Going to the wardrobe, he packed quickly and then, his backpack pulled over his T-shirt, he left her.

True to his word, he never did go back.

It wasn't a bedroom at all, but a room filled with large photographs.

She had thought it was Imad's bedroom, into which he disappeared at night to sleep – which was precisely what he did at night: disappear. One moment he would be sitting in the living room reading or banging around in the kitchen, the next moment she would notice that he had vanished. Her curiosity about what an 'Imad bedroom' would look like caused her finally to peek in. But this room had no bed, not even a sofa. Clearly, no one slept here. Moving along the line of large, dusty-rimmed frames, Roberta stopped and turned one around. A good-looking man sat naked on the edge of a disheveled bed. Startled, she placed it back the way she had found it and turned around another. The same man looked out at her, this time standing naked at the top of a staircase. She lingered longer over this one (it was kind of like an anatomy lesson, really) before turning it back around. She soon discovered that all of the photographs in the dusty corner were of the same man.

"Roberta?"

"*Imad.*"

Imad stood in the doorway, frowning at her. "What are you doing?" he asked.

"Chad said you'd gone shopping and I was kind of curious – you know, I was thinking how you must have such a pretty comforter or something nice, like you do – have nice things, I mean. You're so stylish. Nice curtains, maybe. So I decided to have a peek."

"Nice curtains? A comforter?" he asked in genuine confusion. "What are you talking about?"

"For your bed. Or your window, if you mean the curtains. But there's no bed. Though there is a window," and she pointed at it, as if that might help her out of the situation, "right there."

"You thought – ah, right, I *see*. Okay. This is where you thought I slept?"

"But it isn't, is it?" She stood guilty in discovery.

He went to the window and looked out on the street. "No, Roberta, it isn't." Finally he turned to her. "So, what do you think?" he asked.

"About – ?"

"My photographs."

Their eyes locked. "You know I don't know about art."

"How would I know that?"

"Because you're not stupid," she said.

"I'm not so sure about that. I feel thick as a brick at times. And it isn't right to look at them and not tell me what you think."

She literally felt sweat dribble down from her underarms. Her face was red. Having violated his space, and clearly having upset him – she knew she had to say something about the photographs. She didn't think she should mention that the man had rather prominent testicles. Not that she was an expert on testicles, but they were what she noticed most of all. One seemed to hang much lower than the other, and they were shaped like goose eggs. "I think they are, oh heck, I mean the pictures in general – *powerful* and, well, human." Human definitely worked; testicles were human, weren't they? They helped make new humans. "Yes. I like their human side the best, although I have to confess that I don't do too well with naked man pictures."

He sat down on a stool, gesturing, more agreeably now, toward the dusty photographs. "He's someone I lived with, shortly after I moved to Paris."

"He must have been a real good friend to pose buck naked like that."

"His name's Julien."

"Has Chad seen these?"

"These particular ones? I don't know. Possibly. I've never shown them to him. He might have snooped in here too, just like you."

"Are you saving them instead of selling them? It's that why they're stored away like this?"

"I don't sell much of my work. These? Well, I've thought of destroying them, more than I've thought of selling them. I can't live with them and I can't live without them."

"But you sell some of your work, I know — Chad told me."

"Yes. I do."

She thought about this turn of events. "I'm really sorry I snooped, Imad, it was a dumb thing to do."

"Roberta." His face was suddenly wreathed in a smile. "Who could reject an apology like that?" He held out his hand to her. "Friends?"

"Friends," she said.

Chad stood motionless in the shower, water pirouetting over his shoulders. He turned off the water, stepped out, toweled dry, tucked the towel around his waist and marched down the hall to Roberta's room. He'd heard her go in while he was drying.

He knocked.

"Yes?" she asked through the door.

She'd been standing at her window, reflecting in the middle of removing her make-up, on her encounter with Imad. She didn't like feeling as if she'd done something wrong. Once, while repeating a story to Charlene Cantrell upstairs in bookbinding, a story that Helen had told her at Loreen K. Albrighton's Fourth of July barbecue (at which everybody but Roberta got drunk as skunks), and which involved a racially insensitive word, *well* right when she got to that particular word, Lawanda Burnside came around the corner and heard her. Roberta just about died. Even telling somebody else's story (and since Helen's stories were peppered with these sorts of words, it was hard to root them all out), she knew better than to use them. And, of course, no amount of explaining made Lawanda forgive her. She felt that way now, standing there watching birds play in an enormous tree.

"Roberta, it's me. I need to tell you something."

Roberta opened the door, staring at Chad above a face full of cleansing cream. She could see that the medicated odor stung his nostrils. "I don't usually wear as much make-up as I've done the last day or two," she explained, "and it's like getting out from under fly paper. I've been scrubbing all evening."

"Roberta," he said, "I'm gay."

There was a vast silence.

"Pardon me?"

"Gay."

"Gay as in homosexual?"

"Yes."

She felt lightheaded. "Oh – well." She sat down hard on the couch. Why hadn't she guessed this? Thelma, in the church choir, had a homosexual brother out in San Francisco – though that was one *big* old secret and the only other person who knew it beside Roberta was some Methodist over in Plainview who'd dated Thelma for a couple of months – and Thelma told Roberta that you couldn't hardly ever tell who's 'homo' and who isn't out in San Francisco. It must be the same in Paris. "And Imad – ?" Roberta asked.

"Imad is my lover. I'm his lover. We're lovers. He thinks you've guessed we're gay by snooping at some photographs today. He thinks he gave it all away to you in his studio."

"No." Her eyes met his, widening as she took it all in. "I mean, no he didn't give it away. I didn't know until just this minute."

"*Ah.* Okay."

"Does Helen know?"

"Of course."

Roberta absorbed this information before asking. "Then how come she didn't she tell me, Chad?"

"Would it have mattered?"

"I sure as shootin' wouldn't have come tromping in here like – like – like Rebecca of Sunnybrook farm."

"Haven't heard that reference in awhile," he said. "Out of curiosity, how would you have come in, Roberta?"

"More like, well, with more tact." She looked at him a moment, his hairy chest well-defined, his towel slung casually around his waist, a strong and masculine man. "Are you only telling me this because Imad thinks he let it slip?"

"No," he said, "not only for that. I'm telling you because it's time you knew. In fact, I'm sorry I didn't tell you years ago."

"Is being gay why you left Lubbock?"

"Partly," he said, then, "mostly, I suppose."

"And it's why you and Aunt Helen had such a big bust up?"

"Oh no, I think that was just meant to be. But I can't say she made it easy for me, especially when I tried to explain myself to her. And you might as well know, she had a private detective track me around for awhile."

"She told me something about a private detective, just not – " She closed her eyes, opened them, and then closed them yet again. "As I live and breathe," she said. "As I live and breathe."

Roberta had been walking for the better part of two hours, aimlessly circling the Pantheon, looping down to Boulevard St. Germain, then back up again through the Latin Quarter. She now feared being considered a loiterer. 'No loitering' was an important concept for Roberta, and somehow she thought loitering might mean trouble in Paris, where there seemed to be police on every block. However, she was running out of pretend initiative and finding her emotions no less calm – and her vision of the next turn in her life's path no clearer. In some desperation, she had turned to the bible about half an hour ago. 'Judge not, lest ye be judged,' that's what it said in Matthew and that was *new testament*, which was supposed to be more important than old testament. Though that increasingly didn't seem to be the case back home, which confused Roberta and she even said so once to their Preacher, who couldn't have cared less.

Of course, it didn't seem right to her that a Christ who forgave hookers and thieves and tax collectors (it said so right there in the bible, didn't it?) couldn't bring Himself to take the side of people who – well, who did what Chad and Imad did. How could it be better to be a thief? Could it be right to kill men who had sex with other men but leave all the thieves unmolested? Actually, Roberta didn't really have a problem with either hookers or tax collectors, especially with hookers, although she wasn't keen on the people she imagined used them and abused them. She guessed that if somebody wanted to sell the use of her privates, that was her own business – but she'd certainly continue to keep that opinion a secret.

After the time she'd spent in the company of Imad and Chad, Roberta was having trouble maintaining her life-long conviction that homosexuality was a sin. Perhaps her conviction worked using those once-a-year images of ear-ringed men in sequins and go-go boots, shaking their rear-ends on a tacky float during Gay Pride down to Houston. Channel 11 always made a big deal out of those floats, and pictures are worth a thousand words, aren't they? But this imagery did not work with her handsome and sophisticated cousin – and Imad. 'Judge not, lest ye be judged' seemed crucial to Roberta. She was, of course, prepared to believe that being gay was wrong, perhaps even sinful. But for crying out loud, thinking lustful thoughts of any sort was sinful and – *face it* – who the Hades didn't do that? It was sinful to cheat, lie, steal and touch yourself, and yet she once looked at Priscilla James' English test and copied the answers, and she once lied straight to Aunt Helen's face about Uncle Earl.

Actually, she'd lied a lot more than once, but the time she was thinking of was when she told Helen that she hadn't seen Uncle Earl all day – when she'd seen him hiding from Aunt Edna out in the pump house, after Edna found him drinking from a bottle of Jack Daniels in the bathroom. Who in his right mind wouldn't hide from Edna when she was riled up? Roberta always felt protective of Uncle Earl, who sported a black eye one Monday morning that they all knew Edna had given him. He'd been on a bender Saturday night, apparently. Roberta once took an unopened pack of panty hose from a suitcase she found abandoned by the road out to the airport (which certainly counted as stealing), and she touched herself all the time. Stealing an unopened pack of panty hose was not murder; and neither was Chad doing whatever he did to Imad – or vice versa. What did they do exactly? She didn't want to think about that part just yet. It made her feel woozy with anxiety.

She only realized she'd fainted when she looked up and saw overcast sky and faces looming over her. As it dawned on her what had happened, she had simultaneous thoughts. Had she shrieked? Had her collapse been an embarrassing stumble in which she'd crushed someone? She didn't feel anything (or anyone) underneath her. She also felt that she had to explain herself, which she did by saying (to no one in particular), "I've been dieting." Then, thinking further about the fact that she seemed to be lying on her back on a Paris sidewalk, she spoke aloud her other thought, "I need a shower."

"Hang on here, please, Roberta," a voice from the crowd said to her in Scandinavian-accented English, a voice presumably attached to the man who now knelt beside her, "I think somebody has called the *pompiers*."

She recognized him as the Norwegian man named Aksel whom she'd met in Chad's lobby.

"This is worse than when the heel broke off my shoe at the senior midwinter ball," Roberta said, and she knew she sounded groggy, like someone who'd just woken up, the words mushed in her mouth, "and everybody thought it was because I bought shoes too high-heelie for a fat girl. Carleen Middleditch said it right to me, she said "y'all are too fat for them heels,' but it wasn't true. There was a gopher hole by the sidewalk and I stepped down hard in it. Of course, Carleen always was hateful, served her right about having to live over there to Guam with that no-account husband of hers."

"She does not sound nice at all, this Carleen woman," the voice said.

A siren could be heard warbling its way toward them from the fire station Roberta had been watching from her window – the one she'd learn to call a *caserne*. Well, of course, it wasn't the station she'd been watching, it was the firemen. She'd even picked out her favorites and given them make-believe names, and rated them all as boyfriend prospects, on a one to ten scale, with a courtesy upgrade just for being firemen. From the vantage point of Chad's apartment, they all seemed handsome and available – the latter because you couldn't see wedding rings from her distance, not even with binoculars. She knew because she'd tried with the pair she found in the closet. What were they there for anyway? She liked the firemen better when she wasn't looking at them through binoculars. The binoculars showed too much (like one of the cutest ones smoking and another one giving some kind of mean-spirited lecture to an old lady, who started crying) and thus ruined the romances she created for Pierre and Philippe. Those were two of the French names she'd come up with. She didn't know many French names yet, unfortunately.

Roberta imagined the crackling French voices of her boys over the air, saying (however you said it in French), 'fat lady down, repeat fat lady down, corner of Boulevard St. Germain and rue des Bernardins.'

"At least you're smiling," Aksel said from beside her.

Was she, Roberta wondered? If so, that seemed completely wrong, she'd end up in the loony bin like Brett whatever his name was from high school. Aunt Helen, who told Roberta about Brett's mental illness, said that it had to do with drugs. But Roberta thought that maybe he just moved to Oklahoma and never *was* in a loony bin. Aunt Helen tended to think of Oklahoma as one big loony bin. She said things like, 'she belongs in Oklahoma, that woman, you could put mooring lights on her hips and use her in one of those lame-brained artificial lakes they're so proud of up there,' or 'I swear that family of clodhoppers just moved here from Oklahoma with granny in the back on a rocking chair.' Roberta knew Helen had taken that image from reruns of *The Beverly Hillbillies*, which they sometimes watched together on a cable station, but the Beverly Hillbillies weren't from Oklahoma.

"Can you help me get up?" Roberta asked. "I'd rather not lie here any longer than I have to."

"Oh, yes, of course. Here, lean upon me."

And Aksel helped her up and then to a seat at the corner café, just beside where she'd fallen. Someone brought a glass of water.

"You just dropped," Aksel told her. "I have never seen anything like this. Although it was rather graceful, almost like the dying swan."

Having no idea what it meant to be almost like the dying swan, which didn't sound at all graceful to her (what sorts of things did swans die of, anyway? Bird flu?), Roberta said, "I didn't have a clue. I sure was thinking about some strange stuff though, so that probably *was* a clue, wasn't it? Only I didn't know it at the time, that it was a clue, I mean. I was thinking something about my Aunt Vivian having a baby, and she's sixty something, never been married, and all crippled up with arthritis. She's not really my aunt, by the way, we just call her that. She and my Aunt Helen, that's my real aunt, they grew up together. Sweet Jesus, I *hope* Aunt Viv isn't having any babies. Anyway, then I was looking up at y'all."

Aksel shook his head.

Just then three firemen came over to where Roberta and Aksel, and a group of curious hangers-on, had located themselves. Thank goodness, Roberta thought, only one of them was recognizable to her and cute in the way firemen were supposed to be cute — and neither make-believe Pierre nor Philippe was among them. Except for the cute one, the other two were complete strangers and it was one of the strangers who spoke to her, not the cute one, who seemed far more interested in the waiter. He and the waiter chatted away on Roberta's periphery. Of course the waiter, like the fireman, was also cute. All the waiters in their neighborhood were cute, as if it were a requirement. Perhaps it was in France? She didn't mind this turn of events, however, since she wouldn't want a cute fireman seeing her in a state like this, all sweaty and gross with her hair catawampus. In truth, Roberta found these firemen disturbingly perfunctory. They didn't give her anything like the kind of service you'd expect back home. They asked her a couple of almost smart-alecky questions, took her blood pressure, not quite listened to her admittedly too complicated story that Aksel had to translate for them (she felt she had to add in the part about Aunt Vivian and the time one of her cousins fainted during Great Uncle Leroy's funeral), pronounced her *stabilisé*, told her to go see a doctor (they had a list of English speakers on a thin paper sheet) and then they were off.

The cute fireman never even looked in her direction. He was still focused on the waiter, even as the men drifted out in laughter toward their fire truck, surrounded now by a small crowd.

"Feeling reassured?" Aksel asked.

"Not really. But I know why I fainted. I've been starving myself since yesterday. It works; you know, my no food diet. I've lost ten pounds so far by fasting. I met this guy named Simon and I'm doing it for him. We have a date tonight – I mean, he asked me out to dinner again tonight. I don't know if it's exactly a date or not. I suppose that sounds weird? I guess it does. Y'all are going to think I'm some kind of freak."

"Why will I be thinking that you are a freak?"

"Fainting on street corners, I guess, and not eating, or maybe the other way around."

"Normality is a myth," Aksel smiled. "We are all freaks in our own way."

Roberta found this a strange response, and she stared a moment too long into Aksel's eyes. Roberta blinked first.

"Have a coffee with me?" Aksel asked.

"Okay," Roberta said.

"And maybe we can share something to eat?"

"It's a good idea, the eating part. Otherwise, I'll faint again on the way home." She turned in her chair, asking, "There isn't anything nasty on my back, is there? Can you check for me?"

Aksel looked her over. "I cannot see anything."

"I'm probably crawling with tuberculosis bacilli and things I don't even know the name for."

Aksel laughed out loud, just as the waiter came over. Aksel ordered for them. Then turning his attention back to Roberta he asked, "where are you from in America?"

"Lubbock, Texas."

"I have never heard of this place. Well, I have never heard of the Lubbock part. I'm sad to say that I *have* heard of Texas."

"*Sad*? You don't like Texas?"

"It produces some strange people. I have a friend named Gordon from New York and he makes me laugh when he says that Texas produces people who should be rotating the tires on their grandpappy's trailer but are instead rotating troops around the globe. It seems like a scary place, Texas. Grandpappy, that is a word?"

Despite herself Roberta laughed, because she couldn't help thinking how furious Aksel's question would make Aunt Helen, especially coming from a foreigner. Helen would be fuming for days and making sarcastic remarks about illegal immigration and how Houston had become as bad as New York (in terms of all sorts living down there at any rate). Paris, being French, was vastly worse than Oklahoma in the Aunt Helen lexicon. Paris trumped everywhere for evil incarnate, which was part of Roberta's mission here, needless to say. "I don't think many people say grandpappy anymore. It's kind of old fashioned. But Texas isn't scary," Roberta said. "It's just like any other place, if you think about it. You probably get the same proportion of nice people and bad people anywhere. It doesn't matter where, it doesn't matter what kind of people live there, rich or poor. I guess I'm learning that."

Aksel nodded. "I suppose this is true." Then after a moment, "Are you enjoying Paris?"

"Yes, but I didn't come here for sight seeing. I'm staying with my cousin Chad because his mama's real sick – and I'm hoping he'll come back home with me. You know? To help take care of his mama, the way you're supposed to."

'I would *never* be taking care of *my* mother," Aksel said, "she is too demanding and she calls me always by my brother's name, Olaf – which sounds nothing like Aksel, so how can she be confusing them? I think she does it with purpose. And we have the good homes in Norway for old people, so she belongs in there. You are Chad's cousin?"

"I have the honor."

"I did not know that Chad came originally from this place in Texas."

"Lubbock. We grew up together."

Water and cokes arrived on their table. Roberta guzzled the coke.

"What do you make for a profession? For a *living*, I mean to say?" Aksel asked.

"Nothing really," Roberta told him. "I worked in the library until I got laid off. But I wasn't a real librarian or anything. Sounds funny to say out loud, you know, but I don't think I actually *have* a profession. Does that make me weird?"

"You seem to worry a lot of about appearing to be weird."

"I do, I worry about it a lot."

"We let ourselves become victims," Aksel said. "I don't know the exact quote, but Hannah Arendt is the one who said it brilliantly, something about no victim without his acquiescence. You know, how we acquiesce in our own oppression?"

Roberta had not the vaguest notion of who Hannah Arendt might be (or a hundred percent sure what *acquiesce* meant), but she figured this woman must be a self-help person, like that loud-mouthed bald guy Oprah helped make famous. "I always get confused over philosophical stuff," Roberta said. "For people like me, on the day-to-day, in the here and now –

people care a heck of a lot about pleasing their oppressors. You know something, I've never actually used the word *oppressor* in a sentence before. Now, no offense, but using oppressor in a sentence sounds weird. Anyway, we always make accommodations, don't we? That's how we survive. And I've always worried about being weird. When I was little, after my parents died, my cousin Chad was just about the only person who didn't make me feel like I was a weirdo. I don't ever think I'm the same as anybody else, because for one thing I'm not and for another thing they don't let me forget it."

"Like Carleen and the high heels."

"How do you know about Carleen?" Roberta asked, stunned.

"You told me, when you were lying on the sidewalk."

"I did? Oh, gosh. What else did I say?"

"You are worrying again," Aksel said.

"You bet I am. I hope I didn't say too much. Why was I telling you about Carleen?"

"Because lying on the sidewalk was worse than the time you broke the heel on your shoe," Aksel said, with a 'this is logical' tone to his voice.

"Oh, that. I didn't think that was so bad. You mean the senior midwinter ball? Heck, that's small potatoes. Why would I be telling you that?" Roberta shook her head, sincerely puzzled. "I stand out for miles in West Texas, let me tell you. Single at my age and a big girl on top of it *is* weird where I come from."

"You are not a big girl," Aksel said, "although it is obvious to me that you have body issues. And you shouldn't be losing weight because of a man; I think that is retrograde bullshit. But not having a profession? That probably makes you normal."

Roberta pondered the notion of 'retrograde bullshit,' which she wasn't sure she understood but was too embarrassed to have clarified for her. In Paris you were evidently supposed to know expressions like that and be familiar with words like acquiesce. She needed some sort of dictionary of eggheadedness. She remembered when Bob Haskell showed her the little laminated card he bought to go to Europe, with sayings on the back and translations of things like 'that there's the cheese I want' and 'the train leaves in thirty minutes.' Roberta had wanted one, but she'd lacked the nerve to ask Aunt Helen, since she was already being so generous. She needed a laminated egghead card.

"Your English is really good," Roberta said.

"We would be in dire straits if we depended upon the quality of your Norwegian."

"Did y'all learn English in school?"

"Yes, we all do. We have no choice. A small country." He lifted his palms up. "Beats learning Swedish, huh? Or German during the occupation. That's what my grandparents had to do. Norwegians have always had to learn somebody else's language. We are used to it, I suppose."

"Like the Dutch. I saw Hans Brinker and the Silver Skates about five times, after it was repeated for a special event on the Hallmark Hall of Fame and my Aunt Helen recorded it. They had this real good explanation part to it, you know, all about modern Holland and everything."

"We are wholly different from the Dutch," Aksel said with quick indignation, "the Dutch are a most unusual people, as you should know if you saw this Hans Brinker program. But in this one matter of languages – yes, all right, we are similar enough."

She looked at the passing crowds. "I don't know who knows what around here – but –Aksel, do you know about Chad and Imad?"

"*Know* about them?"

"Do you know that they're – oh, gosh – I'm not trying to gossip, I'm just trying to figure everything out, and y'all are so nice and everything. Aksel, did you know that they're gay? Homosexual?"

"Oh, but of course I know – and they know that Sebastian and I are gay as well. Sebastian is my husband. We were married legally in Brussels last year."

Roberta felt her face flush hot and, once again, a woozy faintfulness came over her.

"You are still fainting?" he asked.

"I don't know."

He looked at her a long while. "You didn't know this before you came to Paris? About your cousin?"

"Nobody told me a thing."

"Does it matter to you?"

She shrugged. "I just flat out can't answer that right now, because I don't know – well, I don't even know who *I am* this very minute. Like everything I've been doing in my life has been some kind of playacting, some kind of thing I've been doing out of necessity and – I don't know the '*and*' part yet, but wouldn't it be nice to think there's something else I am but I just don't know it, or I haven't quite figured it out? Sorry, I'm blabbing something awful."

"If blabbing means talking too much, I think perhaps you are doing this thing," Aksel said, "however, I don't mind. It is good to listen to you. I enjoy it."

Their food arrived, chicken fingers with dipping sauce.

Aksel pointed. "Can your diet stand the bread crumbs?"

"My diet could stand me eating the menu and table top right now." In fact, she'd already dived into the chicken.

Aksel shook his head and then she said, rather softly, "Hippolyte Taine."

"Pardon me?"

"Hippolyte Taine. He was a Frenchman who made a science out of the idea of types in fiction. You are a type, Roberta, this is for sure."

Roberta thought about that, reflecting on the positive as well as the negative ways in which this remark could be taken. "But I'm not in fiction."

"True."

"A type of what?" she finally asked, expecting the answer to be woman or girl or at worst some polite form of trailer trash.

Instead, Aksel said, "a clean living American from the heartland of North America."

She met his eyes and he stared back.

"I guess we do come from different places," Roberta said, which was certainly an understatement, considering that in this place she was talking quite normally to a gay Norwegian with an ear ring, after she'd fainted on a public street in a city where her cousin was living in a homosexual relationship with a Muslim. Aunt Helen once said that the devil was a Black Muslim, she even knew which one he was by name, and claimed that their preacher had confirmed it for them in one of their special Thursday night once-a-month bible classes where you have to reserve space in advance. Aunt Helen always liked the Thursday night class because she thought that having paid-for reservations stopped riff-raff from showing up. "But are we types because of where we come from?"

"In some ways," Aksel said. "The way we speak, sometimes the way we think, certainly the way we have learned to, you know, be polite, discuss politics, all of these things. And if you are thinking that you will take Chad home to Texas with you, I am not so sure of this. Chad hates Texas. He thinks it's violent and − a whole many different things − gun-toting and, well I suppose that's the violent aspect, but you know what I mean."

"Oh, that's just so darned irritating."

"Pardon?"

"Irritating, Aksel."

"I didn't mean for you to repeat it. I meant pardon because I don't know which *part* is irritating you."

"Oh," she said, as another hot flush rose up her neck. She didn't know if it was Aksel himself or the strangeness of his English patois, but she found their conversation disturbingly frank. "It's irritating that he says he hates West Texas, because he doesn't, and certainly not for anything like − *that*. For goodness' sake. Can you really hate a place, anyway?"

"Yes."

"I think it's always something else you hate."

"Not always, Roberta. You can hate climate, customs, culture, the things that make a place a place, the events that happened there to scar you. Often you hide the reason. My grandmother is repulsed by Trondheim – yes, *repulsed* – and you must never mention it to her – tears and wretchedness if you do. But she does not say, 'my heart was broken by a Scottish sailor boy in Trondheim, who used my body as a plaything and then abandoned me in shame,' she says how gloomy and icy and bleak it is, how forlorn, how thoroughly miserable and ugly a city."

"But see, y'all have just proved my point – because it's not – whatever that place is that she hates – it's the Scottish boy who misused her. *Right*? And, in Chad's case, it's all about my Aunt Helen and not about Texas."

Aksel nodded in some agreement.

"Helen has always been a projection. Chad put every darn negative thing on to my aunt Helen, all his feelings about being – you know, gay, about not fitting in, all his – *otherness*. That's what I think and I'm sticking it to it, Aksel."

"Otherness," Aksel said, mulling it over, watching her intently. Then he repeated it once more, washing it around in his mouth, "*otherness*."

"He projected it right on to Helen, that's what I've come to figure out, made Helen some kind of a voodoo doll – not that she isn't worthy of being one, but that's beside the point. Face it, Aunt Helen's been stuck with every bad thought, every fear and every anger Chad felt from the age of twelve. And she knows it too."

Aksel nodded wistfully, thinking perhaps of a Norwegian mother somewhere, a mother with whom he might well have his own disagreements and upon whom he might have projected his own angers, sufficient to drive him to his life in Paris. "You are right, this is reminiscent of the Trondheim story I told you, so I see the sense in it – and, by the by, I think it is not so politically correct to speak of voodoo in this manner."

They were silent awhile and then, thinking about Aksel's earlier comment, Roberta said, "I can't say you're a type, Aksel,

103

unless I'm missing something, which I probably am, knowing me. I don't think being Norwegian is a type, is it?"

"Depends on whose doing the typing," Aksel said, smiling. "But mostly you're right. Norwegian is too vague a thing to be a type. And maybe American from the heartland is too vague as well."

Roberta unapologetically finished the last chicken finger. "Could be. Why was it so important to him, this — I'm sorry, y'all are going to have to tell me his name again, this Frenchman?"

"You know, I'm not sure I remember that part. I always think of Hippolyte Taine because I had to read him in my studies and I liked the idea of types — you know, mean policeman, nasty banker, kindly grandmother, generous whore — but I don't think I read him that carefully, even if I do quote him from time to time. Shame on me."

"Oh, goodness, don't worry. It's like me and certain parts of the bible," Roberta said. "I'll be right there in Sunday school, just teaching away and all of a sudden I'll realize what a big old crock it is that I'm trying to sell, because I never even *read* that part, at least not carefully."

"Sunday school?"

"Yes."

"I do not know of the last time I met a person who went to church," Aksel said with a whistle.

"Are y'all pulling my leg?"

"No, I am not pulling it. Sebastian and I live in a secular world and we like it. We put our faith in evolution." Then he said, with an enormous and quite sudden smile, "I think we should be friends, Roberta."

"Okay. Y'all have certainly been nice to me, that's for darned sure."

"I meant it more in the way of 'do you not you feel as if perhaps we have made a connection,' strange as it seems."

"Why 'strange as it seems?'"

Aksel looked into Roberta's eyes a moment. "Because you ask questions like that perhaps."

"Like what?'

"Like that too," Aksel said laughing and waving for the waiter. "This one is on me, since you have been lying in Tuberculosis germs. Next one is on you, so please to save up. I am not a cheap date, although Sebastian may disagree with this. You are not really trying to lose weight because of a man, are you?"

"Not entirely, but I am kind of – " Roberta realized that she was about to say 'desperate,' and then, because there really *was* some connection with Aksel, she went ahead and said it anyway, "desperate."

"For a man?"

"I've been crazy mad to have a man since I was fourteen, and he hasn't walked through the door yet. I'll die an old maid without – well without ever finding him."

"Without having a real man fuck your lights out, you mean?"

Roberta felt herself blush and, despite this friendship connection with a non-church attending homosexual foreigner (who didn't seem at all embarrassed about what he just said), she demurred. "Oh, gosh no, it isn't even about – that, I mean about sex. I just want, you know, all of those normal things, a husband, some babies – all of that."

Aksel made a face. "I don't like this word normal."

"You wouldn't lose weight if there were a – well, okay, I mean if there was a man you really liked – and you weren't already in some kind of a thing with Sebastian – and you were trying to catch him?" Roberta asked.

Aksel reflected before saying, "perhaps. Men have tended to like me as I am, though. I was never desperate. Back in Oslo, I tell you, Roberta, I had to fight them off."

Roberta laughed. "I *wish*."

"No, you don't. Trust me."

Having scraped up the last of the crumbs from her chicken fingers, Roberta said, "My God, that was delicious. Everything you eat here in Paris is delicious."

"Not everything," Aksel said. "Not as once it was. Now the kitchens of Paris are staffed by illegal Bangladeshi cooks and men from Africa."

"That's not really too politically correct, is it?"

He shrugged. "You are right, shame on me again – but there is always wiggle room when it comes to political correctness. Is that the expression?"

"What? Wiggle room? I guess so."

"Then I am wiggling the room. Anyway, I was food-poisoned last year off a *salade de campagne* I ate in the Marais. It had been sitting in the sun the doctors suspected, prepared in advance. Very bad."

"I'll bet it was delicious before it sat in the sun."

He thought about that. "Yes, a flavorsome salad before it nearly killed me."

The waiter took away the plate.

They sat in silence, watching the passersby and each other.

"What's his name, the man you're losing weight for?"

"Simon. Simon Matthews."

"*Simon*," he shrieked, "oh, but this is wonderful. Simon Matthews? This is a great friend to me. I like Simon very much. Yes, Roberta, I too would starve for Simon. He is definitely a man to starve for."

"That's for sure. Oh, Aksel, he's got a well-built hairy chest and terrific arms. He's a real, real masculine guy."

"You like them butch. Okay. That's cool, so do I. Does my friend Simon know that you have the hots for his well-built hairy chest and arms?"

The expression 'the hots' made Roberta blush again, but she said, "I reckon so and –I think he might be just a little bit interested in me. I mean he asked to take me out to dinner again and to go to Versailles with him."

"I suspect he is interested in you, Roberta, because Simon is always liking big breasts and you have got quite lovely large breasts."

"Thank you," Roberta said, looking down at the objects she had never once in her life discussed in public – and certainly not heard mentioned in a complimentary fashion.

"Come on," Aksel said. "I'll walk you home."

108

7

"I guess you must have heard about me fainting," Roberta said, looking up at Chad from where she read a book on the fold-out couch, which she had faithfully folded away that morning (as she always did). "The neighborhood must just be buzzing about the big girl taking a hard fall."

He looked at her a moment or two, assessing, "a psychologist might say you're hoping I'll refute that."

"For goodness' sake, of course you're supposed to refute it. You're Chad. I wouldn't dare try that on people back home, they'd just snicker and say something like, 'Roberta, y'all are just so funny.'"

"But I'll say – what?"

"Something like," she thought a moment, "'your self-loathing is unbecoming, Roberta.'"

He laughed at her imitation of his voice. "Which it is," he said.

"But it's not *real* self-loathing or I'd say it to everybody, wouldn't I? It's way more complicated than that."

"You're very serious this evening," he said, sitting beside her.

"I tend be serious after near-death experiences."

"Fainting?"

"Yes, sir, and falling – and waking up, or coming to I guess you'd say, all bruised up and battered on a sidewalk full of strangers – and having dream thingies about Aunt Vivian. You remember Helen's friend, the one we call Aunt Vivian?"

"Sure."

"I was having fantasies about Aunt Viv being pregnant."

"No bright lights at the end of a tunnel?"

"That would have been better than imagining Aunt Viv pregnant."

"Ghastly thought."

"Ghastly," she said in echo, her smile widening, "now *that's* a Chad word."

"Ought to have been a clue, those words I use," he said.

"But it wasn't. People just thought you were egg-headed. Most people back home *still* don't get that you can be normal looking and athletic and — you know. You've got to have the — *what*? Hand movements and voice, like that Galsworthy guy. They wouldn't guess from using a word like ghastly, not when y'all were so — " She shrugged. "I made a friend today. Aksel? He helped me after I fainted. I like him a lot." She was quiet, then, and after a long silence said softly, "are you afraid, Chad?"

"*Afraid?*"

"Because of — "

He seemed to understand that she referred to his sexuality, and perching on the edge of the sofa he asked, "AID's?"

"Oh — I didn't even think about that. No, not that, more — you know — "

"You mean, am I afraid I'll go to hell? Because I'm gay?"

"It doesn't quite sound right, when y'all say it — but I reckon that must be what I meant. Are you ever? *Afraid?*"

"Never."

"Never?"

"Never."

She thought about the vehemence of his answer, looked at him, thought some more. When she opened her mouth she wasn't entirely sure what she intended to say. What she said was, "you're brave to break free, I guess, from those kinds of fears."

"I think so."

"But in order to keep on being brave," she said, admiring bravery very much, "it would mean you'd have to stay here in Paris."

"You don't think it would be brave of me to face down mama and her posse of religious kooks?"

"Not much of a posse, just Loreen K. Albrighton — and me, I guess, though I just tote their stuff and clean-up after them. But, heck yes, that would be brave too. In a different way. Funny how Aunt Helen didn't tell me about you being gay. Do you think she's ashamed? Is that why?"

"Of course she's ashamed."

Roberta cocked her head at him. "Then why's she want you back so darn bad – that's what I'm wondering."

"Because she's dying, remember, or legless first and then dying."

"Maybe. Boy, that Helen sure is good at keeping secrets. I remember when Thornton Hamilton from one street over turned out to be related to that weirdo who cut off his wife's head and hands and dumped the rest of her body off the Caprock – remember him?"

Chad shook his head.

"Maybe you were already gone by then. It was in all the news and everything. They sent her head back in a cooler. I know about that part because Anita from clerical – at the library – she heard that somebody saw the cooler at the airport and looked in it and about died, they had to take him away to the Lubbock General Hospital psych ward and everything, after seeing a cut-off head like that in a cooler. *Anyway*, Helen found out about how Delbert was this guy's first cousin and, you know, she kept that a secret to herself for a long time."

"How long's a long time?"

"I don't know when she *first* heard about it, of course, but she didn't tell me until the night of Celeste's birthday party over to the Lakeridge Country Club. Celeste's mama bought all of that champagne," Roberta added, as if that explained the loosing of the secret.

"How do you feel about it?" Chad asked.

"I don't reckon you mean about Helen keeping secrets or Thornton being related to weirdoes."

"No."

She met his look. "I'm trying to be modern."

"What's that mean?"

"It means I've got an idea about how I *should* feel and I kind of know how I do feel and then again I know how I probably will feel – I mean, you know, when all the dust's settled."

"How's that?"

"Which one?"

"All of them, I suppose."

"Okay." She took a deep breath. "Take me out for a drink? A real drink? I mean one with alcohol in it?"

After a walk across the *Ile St. Louis*, they found themselves in the Marais, surrounded (as Roberta detected immediately) by gay men and then, ultimately, ensconced at a corner table in a place called the *Open Café*. It curved behind the sidewalk of two streets, one large and one small, and the tall windows were open. The crowd struck Roberta as almost frighteningly mixed up, rich and poor, French and not French, women with hard-looking faces sitting at tables with bruisedly cute young men with cell phones. Everyone seemed to be talking or texting on a cell phone or Blackberry and drinking – or sometimes all of them at the same time. The music was loud and, she thought, if she didn't know better she'd swear it was Madonna. The bartenders moved slowly around the interior of a circular bar, speaking sharply to the waiters, all of whom seemed to be North African. She noticed that the name of their waiter (on the ticket he gave them with their beers) was Mehdi.

"Mama really didn't say anything to you about my sexuality?" Chad asked.

"Nope. She might have been hinting – I mean, over the years she used a lot of – well, *adjectives* and all, but I didn't catch on."

"You don't really believe this whole amputation nonsense, do you, Bertie? Me needing to go back there to take care of her?"

"No."

"Did you ever?"

"Maybe."

"But maybe not?"

She looked around the bar, listening a moment to the Madonna music, and watching the young men with their tight shirts and cell phones. Then she shrugged. "You don't question what you've never been allowed to question."

"Who didn't allow you?"

"Money – circumstances – religion. Me, an orphan and poor, told how she was fat and butt ugly. That's what didn't allow me, Chad."

"No one could possibly have said you were butt ugly. No one."

"Your mama did. Said it right to my face – at Thanksgiving. Of course, at the time I blamed the *Gewurtztraminer*. They were having a sale on it out at Pinkies – you know, on the County line? Helen bought a couple of cases, and she couldn't get herself away from it, she thought it was that good."

"She's not just a liar, Bert, she's a mean liar, *Gewurtztraminer* or no *Gewurtztraminer*."

Roberta shrugged.

"I'm glad the cat's out of the bag," he said, "I'm glad you've met Imad – and I'm glad you like each other."

"I hope we do. He's awful worried, can't you tell?" Then she surprised herself by asking, "Do you love him, Chad?"

"Of course."

"As much as he loves you?"

"How could I know that?"

"You can do a guess-timate."

"Then – sure, I guess I do. I wonder if my mother knows about him? Think she'd have sent you if she knew the extent of my – what? Sinful fucking with a moslem?"

She flinched at his expression and sipped her beer. "Why do you describe it like that?"

"Like what?"

"Crude and nasty."

"How better to capture mama's feelings on the subject, Bert?"

She shrugged again, thinking of Simon and what he might provide in the "sinful fucking" department. It did have a ring to it, come to think. "I already told her you have a roommate, and she said it was a fancy word for something else, so I'm supposing she knows about him, or at least she knows something." She looked at him over her beer. "You know, I worry that if I don't get things right, Chad – whatever that means – that she'll come over here herself. In fact, it's almost like I'm just waiting for it now. You know?"

"Sure I do. It's been my fear for years – coming home one afternoon to find that overly made-up troll in my living room. I never expected to find *you* in my living room, that's for sure. You were a pleasant surprise compared to everything I've feared."

"You've been worried about Aunt Helen coming to get you?"

"Get me? As in take me back? No, no, not that. I mean, just showing up. When I hate the woman all to hell and back, just the thought of seeing her is enough to make me worry."

Listening to him, Roberta felt a lot of sympathy. Being away from Lubbock and Aunt Helen made everything seem – and feel – different. She had created a necessary life around Helen and now, because of that careful fiction, she stood to get a real home and money – and substantial possibilities for her future. All she had to do was bring Chad home. At the moment of truth, however, she found herself changing. Suddenly, she was feeling some rather angry things toward Helen, and she was enjoying her beer far too much (no *wonder* they preached against alcohol the way they did, it was so darned refreshing and – liberating).

Chad met Roberta's eyes, and seemed to read her mind. "You're fed up with her, aren't you?"

"No. I'm still afraid of her and you can't never be fed up with the things you're afraid of. They keep you on your feet. Could be I'll get to the point where *I* want to stay here in Paris too."

He looked at her a long while.

"Don't you just know that Helen's back home giving Loreen K. Abrighton lip about how I've fallen down on the job," Roberta said. "Helen's got antennae like she was built by NASA. She'll already be figuring out that I've gone over to the dark side."

"Loreen K. Albrighton." Chad laughed out loud. "Oh, hell, I remember *cette petite chienne* – she's still around?"

"*Around*? Heck, she's still Aunt Helen's best friend and callin' me names every chance she gets and – I'll just bet you – chomping at the bit to get on over here herself and see if she can't do better at what I'm failing miserably at. Last time I saw her, by the way, she told me my stripes was going the wrong way for a fat woman."

"Ah," Chad said, "still as charming as ever."

"You know how you told me you think about Great Grandma and the tornado?"

He nodded.

"It's something to remember – we got her blood, the two of us, Chad."

"Meaning."

"Meaning, she was a tough old bird – and pretty darned determined."

They sat a moment, thinking about that.

"Wouldn't you like to know what was running through her head?" Roberta asked.

"Nah," Chad said, "I prefer making it up. I mean, what if it was all an accident? What if she was only chasing after something – a cat, a blouse, some money most likely – and the thing just slammed into her. The romantic version we make up, it's bound to be better than the truth."

She nodded her agreement. "The romantic version is always better. I speak as the expert on this, Chad, having spent my life making up romantic versions of things."

"Including me?"

"Particularly including you."

"And now I've ruined all the stories."

She closed her eyes a moment, the beer jostling her mind. "Oh no," she said, "not at all, and I may be damning myself all the way to hell for saying this, but I just can't think of anything more romantic than the life you and Imad have here in Paris. Now isn't that just the funniest thing?"

"Thank you for that."

"How come?" She asked with real confusion, wondering he had tears in his eyes. "You're the one who found him."

At precisely four in the morning on the digital clock by her bed, Roberta was awakened by the insistent trill of the telephone. Leaping from bed she remembered that she had forgotten to phone Helen as promised. She snatched up the phone, which was fortuitously poised on the edge of Chad's desk.

"Oh, my word, Aunt Helen, I'm so sorry — I mean, you can't *know* how sorry I am — but I forgot."

"You *forgot*?"

"Yes, ma'am."

"How in the blue jumping jeepers could you forget to call when that's the whole darned *point* of this ridiculous escapade?"

"I'm so, so sorry."

"I have half a mind to — well, I don't know what I have half a mind to do. Call up the embassy and say something about you to whoever's over there. The marine guard or somebody like that."

"Say what about me?"

"Something that'd get you into a whole heap of trouble, missy. These are dangerous times. Maybe you're planning to put a bomb in those Wal-Mart shoes of yours, how would I know? Clearly you can't be trusted."

"*What?*"

"Of course, I know you're not planning to bomb anything, Roberta, don't be an idiot – but the marine guard doesn't know that, you're just another stupid terrorist girl to him. So don't mess with me. Because what I do know for damned sure is that you're irresponsible, and for that – for that, well, I don't know, maybe I *should* report you – maybe it's my patriotic duty."

"To report to me to a marine guard?"

"You think I won't do it?"

"I reckon you would, Helen. So I shouldn't mess with you. Right. I get it. Threat taken."

There was a long, crackling silence on the line – then, "are you sassing me now on top of it?"

"It's four in the morning. You woke me up. I'm not sassing, I'm exhausted."

"Do you think I give a fig what the heck time it is? When I've been sitting here twiddling my thumbs just waiting for a phone call from some fat old tourist over there to Paris who *forgot* about me? A fat tourist on my payroll, I might add."

"I didn't forget about *you*, Aunt Helen. I just forgot to call. That's way different. I could never forget about you. And I've lost a lot of weight already. I'm not fat, so you can stop saying that please."

"Oh, good grief, I'm not paying good money to talk about your weight."

Imad had appeared in the doorway wearing pajama bottoms, his hair rumpled, his eyes concerned. Roberta gave him a look of despair. He nodded his commiseration.

"You've got a whole lot of explaining to do, missy, I'll tell you that. And you'd better have something good to tell me or I've going to be even madder than I am already."

There was silence on the phone. Imad went into the kitchen, where Roberta heard him drawing a glass of water.

"*Well*," Helen demanded.

Imad came back into the room and handed Roberta the water. She noticed as if for the first time how beautiful his skin was, like burnished copper.

Sipping the water, and allowing Imad to hold her hand, Roberta said, "I've made myself known to him, Helen – I mean, he knows why I'm here and he knows all about how you're sick and how they're fixin' to cut off your legs. I've put it all out there on the table."

"And?"

"And now –" but Roberta couldn't think what to say about the "and now," so the line merely crackled with her indecision.

"Now *what*, you numbskull?"

"And now we're waiting," Roberta said softly.

"Who's we? You and me? You and Chad?"

"All of us, I guess," Roberta said.

"And so now we're all waiting for what exactly?"

"To see what happens," Roberta said, with complete honesty.

"Have you up and lost your marbles? What in the name of sweet baby Jesus do you mean we're waiting to see what happens? I'm not paying you to wait. I'm paying you to work it – to work it hard, to work it every minute you're over there prancing around on the *Champs Elysees*. Am I understood?"

"It's beautiful, the Champs Elysees, it's like – like a magical place. And Chad and I have really connected, Aunt Helen. That's something. That's something real important, I think."

There was a long and suspicious silence, followed by, "I don't like the sound of this one iota, no not one *iota*, Roberta Martin." Another long silence. "And I've got me some thinking to do. *Now*. You suppose we can agree on a phone call and this time you won't forget?"

"I can try," Roberta said.

"You better do more than try or you'll be the sorriest fat woman in Lubbock County, and there's a whole heck of a lot of 'em competin' for that title. Do I make myself clear?"

"When do you want me to call?"

"Tomorrow – no, night after tomorrow. Before you go to bed. You call me – and you tell me that Chad's either coming home or seriously thinking about coming home. Anything less than that and I'm telling you you'll be on the terrorist watch list sooner than you can say Weight Watchers, and I'll see that they revoke everything from your membership in the Ranching Heritage Center to the library reading circle."

Roberta sighed, holding Imad's hand a bit tighter.

"What was that?"

"What was what?"

"That noise. And I do indeed swear that you are sassing me, young woman."

"I'm not sassing you. And y'all heard me sigh, Aunt Helen, that's what you heard."

"*Uh huh.* You'll be sighing a lot more than that if you screw this up, missy. So when are you calling?"

"Night after tomorrow," Roberta said, "before I go to bed."

"Darn tootin'."

"Good bye, Aunt Helen."

"I've half a mind to hop on the next plane and get over there myself and − you still there, Roberta? Roberta? Say something gosh darn it, if you're there. Now, you listen here −"

But before Helen could finish her sentence, Roberta put the phone down. After all, she'd said goodbye. She could honestly claim to have thought the conversation was over. But her hand still rested on the receiver, and despite her resolve in ending the conversation her eyes filled with tears.

Gently, Imad leaned over and kissed her cheek.

"Are you all right?" he asked.

"Oh yes," she said, "righter than I was when I was lying on the ground looking up at Aksel, at any rate."

"I'll go on back to bed, then," he said.

"Okay." Then, "Imad, I think she's coming over here."

"Yes?"

"Yes."

"Well, as Simon says, won't that just put the cat amongst the pigeons?"

Roberta thought about that expression and liked it. She closed her eyes behind her tears. "Won't it just."

Roberta had no sooner fallen back asleep when she was roused by arguing voices. She sat upright, holding her covers to her chest protectively. Then she slid slowly back down to her prone position, staring at the ceiling and listening sadly but without fear.

"Come to bed," Imad said, "I can't talk to your back."

"Then don't talk to my back. Just shut up."

"Chad, look – think about it. If she were going to come over here, wouldn't she have done it before now? She has the address. Roberta got here easily enough. If your mother wanted to come and confront you, she would have done it by now."

"No, she wouldn't have. And coming now punishes Roberta, don't you see? My mother lives for punishment. Her God is a mighty God, a vengeful God, and she likes to imitate him. She likes to dole out punishment, and Roberta's in her line of fire – Roberta's always been in her line of fire. I *hate* that woman, Imad."

"Chad," Imad said, "Don't."

"It's who I am. I'm a mother-hating atheist. Know that or know goddamn *nothing* about me."

"Please," Imad said, but Roberta couldn't tell whether he meant please stop, or please come back to bed.

"She'll show up here all right. And then – "

A long silence.

"And then what?" Imad asked.

"Never mind. Just fucking go back to sleep, okay?"

Another silence.

"And then what, Chad?"

"If you don't shut up, Imad, I'm going to fucking put some clothes on and walk right out the front door – I'll fucking go wait for her at Roissy – she'll be on American Airlines, she's as goddamned predictable as West Texan dust storms. She wouldn't want to miss out on her Frequent Flyer miles, even when she's on *une mission de guerre*."

Another silence extended farther and then farther still, beyond the silences which had preceded it, beyond the silence of the night which had been disturbed by Helen's phone call.

Then, more quietly, Roberta heard a final comment before the apartment fell completely quiet: "Don't touch me, Imad – just leave me alone. Don't fucking touch me."

"I have to stay behind," Chad told them.

"Why's that?" Imad asked, from where he, Roberta and Simon stood by the front door.

"Bernard."

"*Pardon?*"

"Bernard called." Chad looked at Roberta, "Assistant Head of School. He wants me to meet – you know – those people from Ohio."

"Which people from Ohio?" Simon wondered.

"The ones with – the girl."

"Ah," Imad said, "the ones with the girl. Of course."

"When did he call?" Roberta asked.

"This morning."

"Okay," she said, realizing – as they all did – that there had been no phone call that morning.

"So enjoy yourselves," Chad told them.

Imad crossed the room and kissed Chad's cheek. "Check in by the front courtyard at noon, if you're able to catch us up. We'll have lunch together."

"Don't wait for me."

"We won't."

"Bye, all."

Imad joined the others at the door and they left. Chad heard their feet cascading down the stairwell, heard the front door in the lobby open and then slam shut. He stood motionless in the middle of the room, listening. He couldn't go into the den, his proper refuge, because now it was Roberta's bedroom. Yet his desire to be alone, a weary, bone–deep, fearsome need, demanded attention. He put a cap on his head and plunged out of the apartment, down the stairs, out to the street.

She spotted Simon as he came toward her across the gravel. Half a dozen others would by now have spotted him as well, she figured, such a good–looking man, over six feet tall, virile, with his five o–clock shadow and T–shirt form fitting over his curly–haired pecs. Dear God, she thought, was this man really spending the day with *her*?

"Hey," Simon said.

"Hey back."

He juggernauted toward her, handing her one of the two bottles of water he carried, slamming his body down on the rim of the fountain like a steel girder. "All I could find."

"Thanks."

"And Imad's staying in the *Orangerie*; he's decided to do some sketching."

"I thought he might. He kept talking about it on the train."

They were quiet, drinking their water. Then Simon shrugged. "Penny for your thoughts."

"Is that all they're worth?"

"Can't judge their worth, can I? But you were definitely thinking about something."

"I was, sure enough. You know, it's so strange, Simon, finding out the way I have – you know – about Chad and Imad and everything. And what's really, really bizarre is that the two of them seem – and I can't believe I'm saying this – but they seem downright –" she paused, hesitated. "Normal, I guess you'd say."

"Of course they're normal. Who says they aren't?"

"Plenty of people, from the Pope to the preacher at our church, who's managed to get himself and a lot of others worked up over this whole gay marriage thing, to – oh, heavens, plenty of people. By the way, this Bernard guy never called, did he?"

"Of course not," he said, smiling.

She looked puzzled, querying his smile.

"'Bernard guy,' something too American in that – and if you knew Bernard. He is a guy, but only just. An more effeminate cousin of Jaba the Hut."

"That nasty old thing from Star Wars?"

"Bernard is perhaps not *quite* that handsome, but yes – that's the one."

"So why didn't Chad just say he needed to be alone?"

"Because that's not how people do it. They don't walk around saying, 'I'm disturbed, leave me alone.'"

She peered across the fountain into the woodland surrounding Versailles. "Don't they? It seems like that's precisely what I do." She sighed. "How the heck is this all going to turn out, Simon? *Huh?*"

He put his legs out into the sun and held his face up. Then, waving a hand as if painting in the vista of palace, he said, "I have no idea. But Chad, now, he has to figure out whether he's true to his beliefs, whether or not he did the right thing, leaving West Texas all those years ago, coming here, living with Imad. It's a big challenge to the status quo, your arrival. It's not really a question of going back or staying here – it's just a significant moment in Chad's life. It will tell him whether he was right or whether he was wrong."

"What will?"

"This." Simon shrugged. "Everything. When it's all done he'll know. When it's turned out in whatever way it's going to turn out – then, he'll have his answer."

"Y'all sound like some tarot card reader at the County Fair."

He laughed loudly at that.

"But I think you might be saying that he won't be coming back to Lubbock. Is that part of what you're saying?" she asked.

"Look, Roberta. Who knows? Chad can resolve his crisis in whatever way he wants. Maybe that means returning to the *llano estacado* – maybe not – probably not."

She gaped at him, struck by his unexpected knowledge of West Texas, even using the Spanish term for the staked plains.

He smiled at her response. "I had to learn a little about this place you come from, didn't I?"

"Did you?"

"I think so, yes."

She thought about that, admiring his well-formed, suntanned, hirsute legs. "You're so – nice."

"Nice?" He seemed startled, as if he had been expecting a comment on his legs. "No, I'm not nice," he said, with a tone suggesting he'd been insulted. "No, I prefer to think I'm whimsical, sometimes even shallow in my whimsy."

"Whimsy," she repeated, wanting to be sure she actually knew what whimsical meant. She thought she did. "That sure is a pretty word. It makes me think of an English children's story. I guess it's the kind of word a teacher would use, isn't it? Do you like being a teacher, Simon?"

"I could have liked it, given a different set of circumstances – yes, maybe then. But, to tell you honestly, Roberta, I've not found in teaching what I'd hoped to find."

"What was that?"

"I wanted to bring light to the darkness, patch up the mindless savagery of our modern world. It didn't work out that way; that's not at all what teaching's about."

"What's it about, then?"

"Making sure the world stays the same. Education is the single biggest force for conformity we have, that's what I've discovered. Of course, maybe if I were more *whimsical* in the classroom — more innovative and daring. But I'm not. Well, okay, maybe sometimes I'm whimsical, but I'm never daring. I'm just mediocre."

"I don't think you could be mediocre at anything, Simon."

He gave her a smile for that and shrugged again.

"Will you go back to Australia?"

"When?"

"Some day."

"Go back and start where I left off, you mean?"

"That depends on where you left off," she said, remembering his story about the woman and her possibly wanton ways. "Don't you miss it?"

"No."

"Not even a little bit? It's your birthplace."

"Are you practicing on me?"

"Say what?"

"For coaxing Chad back to Lubbock, Texas?"

"Oh," she said with honest surprise, "no, I wasn't. I was only thinking about you, Simon — only you."

He seemed pleased. "I miss it the occasional littlest bit maybe."

"Where in Australia are you from?"

"Melbourne, born and bred, mum and dad, grandparents too. Real Victorians we are." Then, seeing her look, "the state. Melbourne, Victoria."

"Oh. I didn't know that was a state. I didn't even know Australia had states. You mean like the United States? Simon, do you have a — are you seeing someone?"

"Aha. I knew you were giving my legs the once over. I was waiting for a compliment on my calf muscles. Are you telling me you fancy me?"

She felt her color come up and she stood and fumbled for her guidebook, monstrously embarrassed. They looked at one another. "I want to see that Trianon place," she said.

He pointed off over the trees.

"Isn't that where Napoleon lived?" she pursued, as if really interested. "After he divorced Josephine?"

"Grand Trianon." He stood up as well.

"I don't get why he had to divorce her, just because she didn't have any children, when he loved her and all —and she'd stood by him through everything. It just seems downright mean to me."

"Look, Roberta, there's nothing wrong in fancying me. I rather liked it when you were ogling my legs. Yeah?"

"I'm sure I'm not the first to *fancy* you."

"I wouldn't be much of a catch if you were now, would I?"

She looked into his face and smiled despite herself.

He took her hand, squeezed it. "You can fancy me without being embarrassed about it."

She felt suddenly breathless, as if she might faint again. "Okay."

"And about your question. Would I have asked you out if I already had a girlfriend?"

"I hope not, but I don't know what signs to look out for or anything. I'm out of practice, which probably makes me sound desperate, which I'm really not. It's just that I haven't dated much recently, though I can't say I've minded – I get by pretty much okay on my own."

"So people always say."

"In my case it's true."

"So everyone also says. Not that I don't understand about enjoying your own company. I like my own company well enough at times too, but not all the time."

"I didn't mean *all* the time," she said.

Dropping her hand and looking at her earnestly, he said, "I like you Roberta. Got it? In the way a man likes a woman. That's how I like you."

She smiled, fixed in his passionate gaze, his eyes glittering with a passion she had never had directed at her before. Something quivered in her stomach. Turning away, she began to trace a route in her guidebook. Having lived her life vicariously, through the quixotic escapades of more exciting others, she had no reference for adventure of her own. In sending her to Paris, Aunt Helen had inadvertently given her the best gifts anyone had ever given her: romance, adventure, in fact her own life. Feeling in possession of a genuine life for the first time – not merely the reflected life of one of the girls from upstairs in fine collections or the alluring sales lady with hot pink fingernails from Dallas who came to talk to them once about the advantages of a new photocopying machine and flirted with every man in the library – dizzily disoriented Roberta. She had never been (had never anticipated being) in this place, at this time, with this man. *Never.*

"Roberta?"

"Okay, then," she said.

"Right." He nodded. "The Trianon?"

And they started walking along a wide, long path through woodland, in the direction of the Grand Trianon.

8

It wasn't the first time Chad had been unfaithful to Imad, but it might well have been — it was that gratifying. Blond Etienne had drawn Chad toward him in the *Etoile Manquante Café*, eyes meeting, smiles linking, and finally a hand on a shoulder. Not that Chad had resisted, not that he would have gone to the Marais if he were intending resistance. Etienne lay now on his back, Chad straddling him, his hands caressing Etienne's smooth chest. The window, wide open in his tiny room, let in the sounds of traffic as it snarled along Boulevard Beaumarchais toward *Place de la Republique*. Antidote to traffic, the young man's blond curls fluffed over the pillow, his long hand reaching up now and then amorously to grasp the hair on Chad's chest. Chad's own intense erection amazed and certainly pleased him, a denial of that looming fortieth birthday. His beautiful hard-on throbbed like a twenty year old, as eager as ever it had been.

Chad felt as if he might come just putting on the condom, Etienne's hand as he stroked lubricant on Chad in some manner a fulfillment of — of what? Of *something*. Etienne's legs squirreled up around Chad's shoulders quickly, knowledgeably, and Chad found his mark. Each thrust was somehow, again, like the first time fucking, better than the first time, more extreme, more cogent, Etienne's squirming, the patina of sweat over his pale face, his increasingly limpid curls, then Chad's own gasps and Etienne's cries. Chad came in a fervid ecstatic rush, loud grunting, ramming Etienne on to him as if to impale him, twisting him like a rag doll.

"*Je t'aime*," Etienne said as he too came, shooting across his smooth chest with youthful energy.

How could you not, Chad thought, thrusting once more, deeply, so deeply?

Etienne's hand grasped Chad's sweaty chest hair.

How could you not?

From the Peristyle linking courtyard and gardens, Roberta and Simon proceeded into the ascetic rooms of the Grand Trianon, through the *Salon des Glaces*, with its silk hangings done to Marie Antoinette's specifications. In Napoleon's bedroom, Simon provided Roberta with historical background on Napoleon, Louis-Philippe, their families and, finally, Charles de Gaulle, who'd apparently had a soft spot for the Trianon and ordered fresh renovations in the 60's. They went into the reception rooms and the *Salon de Musique*. Crossing through the *Salon de Famille*, Simon showed her the tables in which numbered drawers once held the embroidery of the daughters of Louis-Philippe, the citizen King. In the Malachite Salon they marveled at what had once been the bedroom of the Duchess of Burgundy, filled with the malachite *objets d'art* given to Napoleon by Tsar Alexander I at Tilsit.

Back again in the Peristyle, they walked hand-in-hand, shoulders brushing, down the stairs into the clear, clean light of the upper gardens. There, on the terrace of the *Jardins Bas*, in full few of numerous tourists, Simon pulled Roberta to him and kissed her.

She clung to his hard chest with a shocking immediacy, clung like epoxy or Velcro.

"Nice, that," he said.

"Yes," she said, her head tilted back, looking up into his eyes, tenderly jolted in some female place she couldn't even locate.

He released her.

She stared at him.

Then, flushed with passion, she looked away. From where they stood, at the top of the horseshoe staircase, she could see the green-hued lower basin and the vast span of the *Petit Canal*, the flower beds behind them, the woodland which embraced the canal. Over Simon's shoulder she observed the chateau and the Peristyle and the people sitting on the stairs of the *Trianon-sous-Bois*. A mother pushing a baby in a stroller crossed slowly through the flowerbeds toward Mansart's *Buffet d'Eau*, where Neptune had been cavorting with Amphitrite since 1703.

"Really nice," Simon said, gesturing back toward the Chateau, toward the parkland of Versailles. "Now. How about an ice cream?"

"Okay," she said, softly, one hand against the heat of her face.

"Okay," he echoed, leading her off by the hand.

"I've been getting my fortnightly coiffure," Galsworthy said to Chad, from the aperture of Mod's Hair, the salon across from *Open Café* and *Agora Presse*, "what's your excuse?"

"I have no excuse."

"That you care to share."

"That I've had time to think up."

"Indulge yourself then," Galsworthy said, "and buy me a coffee and *tart aux pommes*."

Chad hesitated. He needed a shower; he needed solitude. He did not need Galsworthy.

"Or *tart aux poires*, it's scrumptious too. Henri has the touch." He pointed down the street toward *Les marroniers café*. "In more ways than one, or so I have heard. You should see his biceps. All that pounding of dough and kneading of flesh – or is it the other way around?"

"That place has the worst service in the western world."

"It certainly does *not*, that honor belongs to *El bebé del diablo* in Chueca, in Madrid. But all gay places have poor service," Galsworthy said, "because attitude makes people feel hip. If you don't want attitude, go to Starbucks with the straights."

"All right," Chad said, "I'll treat you to something."

Galsworthy took his arm and walked him down *Rue des archives*, to a table beneath the chestnut trees. "I left the boys at home," he said, tossing his head so that his newly highlighted tresses capered on his forehead, "last month they chewed through an electrical cord and nearly sent poor Hugo back to Lisbon the hard way. I'll pick them up some liver sausage in the corner shop by way of apology."

"What do you do with them during the school year?"

"They understand seasons, Chad. They know that when it's winter, mama's out working the salt mines. It's uncanny how they know, but they do." Galsworthy held a hand up until a waiter came over. "*Café crème*, and one of your two tarts, I don't care which," then *sotto voce* to Chad, "as if there were only two tarts here, *please*," and then more loudly, "Chad?"

"Cappuccino."

The waiter left.

"What's his name?" Galsworthy asked.

"By what's his name I assume you're referring to Aksel's boyfriend?"

"Don't be coy. I mean your tryst," Galsworthy said.

"What makes you think I've had a tryst?"

"Darling. I'm like the boys with their seasonal sense. I can tell when someone's been battling the sheets."

Chad looked out into the street, at the couples passing by, the many tourists with their guides.

"Ignoring me only makes me more suspicious," Galsworthy said.

"What is Aksel's boyfriend's name anyway? My God, we all just keep calling him what's-his-name. How rude is that?"

"Sebastian is his name."

"Sebastian doesn't sound Norwegian," Chad said.

"I wouldn't know. I'm pleased to say I'm unfamiliar with the vicissitudes of Norwegian culture. Personally, I prefer what's-his-name, it has more panache."

"My mother's about to come to Paris – after all these decades of distance. *Poof*. Like the wicked witch on her broomstick, painting my name in the sky over Paris – surrender, Chad. Roberta was the ambassador who failed to negotiate my return. So, knowing my mother was about to make her move – well, I don't know, maybe feeling that 'I'm about to be forty' thing as well – I crashed today at breakfast."

"*Ah*. You crashed today at breakfast – now isn't that a quaint expression. But Chadwick, you hate West Texas. So why would the witch's arrival worry you? How could you even entertain the idea of going back there? You should be rejoicing at your life, despite your advanced age, and the chance to rub your mother's green and warted snout in it. It's a chance to shock her to the slimy green marrow in her bones. You should be partying. Cartwheels, booze-ups and pretty, pretty boys. Well, I suspect you've being doing the latter – or at any rate at least one pretty boy."

"I don't hate West Texas."

"Why did you tell me you did, then?"

"When did I tell you that?" Chad wondered.

Galsworthy waved a hand. "One of those sepulchral school parties, penny-pinching champagne and shallow toasts. However, I do remember you telling me, quite clearly, and Imad has certainly supported the view in our discussions on the subject."

"You and Imad talk about my feelings for West Texas?"

"The subject has come up."

Chad thought about that, how it indicated something – though he couldn't figure out what – about Imad.

"In fact," Galsworthy said, "your living in this perpetual Parisian exile supports the view that you are a manly man with excellent decision-making skills."

"Is that what it supports?"

"But yes. Of course, it's crunch time. Roberta the cousin wants you to go back to the cotton and petrochemical fumes and now mama's coming over to make it an even better TV docu-drama. How *exciting*. By the way, do you and Imad have one of those broad-minded open relationships where you scamper home and tell each other about your latest trick?"

"Hardly," Chad said.

"In other words I'd better keep my tongue and my lips firmly locked around my pearly whites?"

"Thanks."

"Honey, if you had an inkling of the number of secrets I keep. And, besides, you haven't given me much of a secret to keep."

Chad made a time-out sign with his hands, and brought his no-nonsense teacher's voice to bear. "Whoa."

"*Whoa*? Which I do resemble, darling, the horse or the carriage?"

"Whoa as in you need to find a new role to play, Galsworthy. You're cutting it a bit close here."

"Excuse me if I'm particularly dense today, but – *what*?"

"This sharp-tongued old queen thing is getting tiresome."

"Ah, I understand now. The petrochemical fumes remark struck a nerve – or, no, it was the reminder of your little tryst *aujourd'hui, n'est-ce pas?*" Galsworthy accepted his coffee and tart from the waiter, who'd silently appeared at their table. Then he said, "In terms of roles, I'm working up a hardened criminal *schtick*, you know, shaved head and bulging muscles, but it's a good two years from any unveiling since I haven't even located a personal trainer yet – I want one of those *scrumptious* tall Germans, though I'd settle for a Dane, even if they are rather unpopular just now, poor Viking dears – so I'm afraid we're stuck with the Bette Davis tired old queen thing for a while longer. Of course, you could get together a contribution and send me to Bead Clutchers Anonymous. That might help."

Chad rolled his eyes.

"So, back to our story. Filled with an inarticulate emotion about your nearly-forty life and fear of your mother the witch, you ran off to the Marais for a wander around the over-priced tourist stores and a little therapeutic bonking of boys."

"I don't know if bonking can be called therapeutic," Chad said.

"Don't be silly. That's just about all it is, especially for us queers — we're not procreating, we're *re*creating — we're unloading our pressures. We're preventing prostate cancer by getting those toxins out. We're relaxing. And Insurance companies pay for impotency pills. I rest my case."

Chad sipped his cappuccino. "If I said I hate West Texas, I was wrong." Then, he looked toward a table where several couples laughed and said, with soft pain, "I hate my mother. I mean I really and truly detest the woman."

"And you think *I* sound like Bette Davis?"

Chad sighed, consuming the remainder of his cappuccino, "I said sharp-tongued old queen."

"Perhaps more Joan Crawford then? You can only hold things at bay for so long," Galsworthy said, "sooner or later the tide of battle turns. Nothing stays the same, darling, nothing. It all changes. This hatred you've been bottling up, it was bound to fizz out of the bottle. Did you get his number?"

"Who?"

"The secret I'm keeping."

Chad shrugged.

"Are you seeing him again?"

Chad shrugged.

"This isn't a convincing no, lovey, is it?"

"Bitterness of the kind I have for my mother," Chad searched for words, dipped a finger once more into Galsworthy's tart, "it isn't — right.'

"*Right*? Is that what this is about? Our little bible-thumper Christian girl has got you all tied up in knots about what's right and what's wrong? Now, I admit, you've just taken me by surprise. Which is not something that happens to me much anymore, jaded old thing that I am. Sorry. Sharp-tongued. I keep interpreting, don't I?"

Chad looked at him.

"Well, for the love of whatever," Galsworthy said, "just how does one define right? For God's sake — if she's still around, the meddling old bat – we live in a world where thousands of Bengalis die year after fucking year in cyclones. That isn't *right*, is it? No, I hate the word right. If that many people died every year in Iowa, they'd fucking drain the Mississippi and erect cloud barriers, wouldn't they?"

"Actually, they might not for Iowa, the Hurricane Katrina fiasco proves that – although they'd probably be able to subsidize a few more farmers."

"Oh. Nice *riposte*," Galsworthy said.

"Thanks."

"And I suppose it would depend on the administration, wouldn't it? One of them likes corn and dust and guns one of them prefers the westcoast and busty starlets, but I get it all confused. So why is the bitterness you feel not right?" Galsworthy asked.

Chad stretched, held his hand up for the waiter, "Because ultimately it's all about me, which is what's happened here. It's not even about my mother anymore, I can hardly remember what she looks like, certainly I've no idea what she looks like right now. It's my thing."

Galsworthy twisted a ring off his finger and handed it to Chad.

"What's this?" Chad asked.

"Look at it."

Chad examined the ring, saw it was from a convent school in Quebec.

"I bought it at an antique store in Montreal. I loved it. I thought, 'that's the life I want, it's not fair, I want to be a fetching young *Quebecoise* at a convent school in the leafy countryside. Did you see *Lilies*? The film?"

"No."

"No matter. Anyway, I bought it; I wear it. It's the me who would have been, if things were fair. I understand bitterness. But, *quelle surprise*, I disagree with you. I *do* think bitterness is right."

Chad gave him the ring back.

Galsworthy wriggled it back on his finger. "I never knew my father."

"Not at all?"

"Not at all." He stopped playing with the ring and placed both of his hands flat on the table. His voice, when he spoke, was suddenly, unmistakably middle-American, a boy who'd gone to a big public high school and fellated horny basketball players under bleachers but pretended to be straight when he went to the prom with a girl named Darcie who wore braces and studied AP chemistry, a real, an historical person, someone who existed long before the invention of this other person named Galsworthy. "No. I was a date rape baby, I think he was some stud muffin sports dude from out of town, met my mom at a basketball game, charmed her and screwed her in his Camaro. Did they have Camaro's way back then? Oh, of course they did. It's now they don't have them. Or do they? Anyway, *voila*. Here I am. Not many abortions to be had back then in rural Kansas, it wasn't even an option. I have absolutely no idea who he was."

"Your mom must have married someone — at some point. Don't you have a step-father?"

"Nope. She never married. Just grew fat and mean, like my aunties, they were meaner than hell too though they had husbands. Quite banal, really, how mama blamed me for most of it, our poverty, our status. Such a *cliché*. So, when I graduated from high school I took my little old scholarship to Rice University and I never looked back. Sent her cards at Christmas for awhile, until even that seemed phony; then I called her now and then at holidays, but finally I stopped doing even that much. She's probably dead or in a home by now. But unlike you, Chad, I have never felt bad about my bitterness. Never. Not once. *Never*."

"Do you hate her?" Chad asked.

"Of course not," Galsworthy said, "that's my point. I'm trying to help you. What a waste of energy it would be. I reserve hate for people like the man who cuts the boys' toenails — such a clumsy lout, poor Alcazar is forever shrieking in pain — or the school administration, now *them* I hate. No, I loathe how I grew up and abhor how mean mama was to me – you've no idea, no idea at all how mean Kansas trailer trash can be until you've been beaten raw by a Harlequin romance novel and then by a wooden spoon because your bare backside tore off the top of the aforementioned Harlequin romance novel while you were *being beaten with it* – but I've never felt anything even vaguely like hate for her."

"This woman can't have named you Galsworthy."

"Oh, you shrewd detective you. No, this woman christened me Delbert. I went through high school as *Del*, if you can believe it."

"I guess Galsworthy does have it over Delbert."

"Girlfriend, just about any name you'd find scrawled on a toilet stall has it over Delbert, unless it's Torvald Aksel. Delbert is musical compared to Torvald Aksel."

Galsworthy was back; Middle America was gone.

Chad laughed, despite himself.

An appealing older couple passed by on the pavement, tourists clearly, well-attuned to one another, that beautifully-groomed, successful male American look about them, designer label-wearing denizens of West Hollywood or Hillcrest or Chelsea or the Castro. Chad watched their familiar banter as they ambled through the Marais, nudges, pointings, noticings. They wore their short gray hair well, still sporting admirable pecs, nice legs, clean dental work and designer eye wear. No wonder terrorists and Baptists had them in their sight. They looked entirely too good for sinners and extremists to be pleased.

"Oh, to grow old gracefully," Chad said.

"Oh, to grow old kicking and screaming," Galsworthy said, "whatever is the matter with you? You must fear the great beyond, my dear, and resist, resist. Of course, mommy's big old urgent plea that you come home and go to Sunday services can't be helping. That's downright existential – I mean, there's a sure-fire reminder of death if you ever you needed one. But it's all to be expected – everyone ends up where you are. True, we want our sufferings to be deep and personal and meaningful. But they aren't. They're usually simple – and cheap. They even have a name for what you're going through."

"Breathe the words mid-life crisis and I'll smack you."

"Oh, you *manly* piece of mischief, you. Promises, promises," Galsworthy sighed, "I'm all through with promises, promises – " He closed his eyes a moment, eyelashes fluttering, then opened them, looked into Chad's face, "I can't remember the last time a real man smacked me. Must have been Paolo, back in '86. Good lord. Was it that long ago? Anyway, call it what you will. It's predictable."

Chad nodded. It was predictable, wasn't it? He thought about beautiful Etienne and the quality of their coupling. Was that also predictable? He'd felt more alive in the middle of sex with Etienne than he had in months, if not years. That was a denial of what Imad described as Chad's hare in headlights reaction to being forty. He circled around a watercolor memory of the afternoon, and yet in that circling there was little guilt, little decision-making about the future, about whether he did or did not tell Imad, whether he did or did not see Etienne again. He savored the watercolor, catching it from angles, but wondering now if it had only been painted by numbers.

"By the way, I'm not noteworthy in choosing to play a role," Galsworthy said, "in fact, we all play them."

"You're not one-dimensional, yes, I remember you telling Roberta that on the staircase."

"Sweetums, I imagine a few minutes ago, with whomever he is, you were playing quite a role yourself – a very dimensional role, I'm sure."

"Etienne," Chad said, surprised both by saying the name out loud and by saying it to Galsworthy, whom he did not think adept at keeping secrets, despite his protestations. And yet there was a thrill to this recklessness, a continuing adrenal rush, like the brilliant sex, pushing any need for resolution of his mother and exile and Roberta farther into the background.

"French?" Galsworthy asked.

"Yes."

"*Quite* a role, then. Those French boys are so demanding in bed."

"There's not so much balance with you, you know? That's all I meant, Galsworthy. Most of us get assigned our roles, sure there's some choice involved, but not as much as you've – well, taken on."

"I shan't sit here and argue, poppet, it's unseemly. But what if this is who I am, what if it's not a role at all?"

Chad said nothing.

"If this *is* a role," Galsworthy said, "take note: I've been successful in my life. I've done well. You've seen how I live."

"By that standard, I'm every bit as successful as you are."

"I never suggested you weren't, darling – and I haven't yet provided my standard," Galsworthy said.

"Haven't you?" Chad challenged.

Galsworthy – Delbert – looked at him.

Chad looked back.

"Good luck," Galsworthy said, "and you know what I mean."

"Thanks," Chad said, "and you know what I mean."

Chad awoke to a thunderclap and flash of lightning.

"It lives," Imad said, from where he stood at the *porte-fenetre,* looking out on the rain.

"I didn't actually intend to sleep." Chad indicated the book he'd been reading and which had tumbled to the floor. "Are we having a thunderstorm?"

"Your other guess would be – ?"

Imad wore his Winnie the Pooh apron flocked with flour; he'd obviously been working in the kitchen when he came out to look at the storm. His domestic frumpiness troubled Chad.

"Oh God," Chad said, as he stood up, rubbing his eyes, "Roberta?"

"I left her — quite literally — in Simon's hands at Versailles."

"They'll be caught out in the rain."

"Won't be the only ones today," Imad said.

"No. I guess not. I didn't hear you come in."

"You were snoring away."

Chad walked over, stood beside him at the *porte-fenetre*. "Successful outing?"

"I did some sketching in the *orangerie*, the *palmiers* are stunning."

"They're outside this year?"

"Yes, some of them," Imad said, "a couple of lovely ones still inside with the citrus."

"So a good day."

"Yes. A lot to think about just now. The sketching helps."

Chad nodded.

"And you?" Imad asked. "How've you been? You benefited from your time — "

Chad shrugged, committing nothing to words and wondering why Imad had left his own sentence unfinished.

Imad took Chad's hand, squeezed it, then touched his apron. "Apple pie," he said, "crust from scratch."

"Yummy."

"So you're all right, Chad?"

"All right?"

Imad merely looked at him, eyes glistening behind his glasses. A dab of flour hung between his eyebrows, where he'd adjusted the frames while making his crust.

"Of course."

Imad kissed Chad's cheek and together they watched the progress of the storm.

Sheets of water splashed over the faces of the apartments across the street. Another lightning flash froze shadows in their places; thunder rattled the windowpanes.

Rivulets flowed down *Rue des Bernardins*. Chad opened the *porte fenetre*, tasted the rain, and held a hand out into the downpour. Then he stepped out on to the balcony and stood with his face tilted up, his eyes closed. When he opened them, drenched, clothes soaked through to his underpants, he saw that Imad had returned to the kitchen.

The living room was abandoned.

9

They sprinted up *rue des Bernardins* through the rain, laughing past the boxes someone had pushed under the awning of the fruit shop, then into Imad and Chad's building. The door slammed loudly behind them; puddles of water collected around their feet.

"You can run, you can," he said.

"For a girl?" she asked and – significantly – she made no joking reference to her weight, no sarcastic or self-deprecating quip. She had never felt more attractive.

"For anyone," he said.

"The secret of sensible shoes."

"Is that what it is, then?"

"That and good calves," she said, "These babies will take me running *away* from any tornado, I can tell you that. I'll tell you some day how I ran clear through The South Plains Mall – without even slipping once, and they polish that thing like a deathtrap – just so's I could get back to my car before that fool in his little golf cart found out I'd parked in one of them handicapped spots. There wasn't any place else," she said, realizing what she'd just confessed to, "and generally speaking no one really checks, except that day – well, lo and behold, there he was, golf carting around like the parking lot emperor. I'm here to tell you – I beat him and then some."

Simon smiled, his smile grew, and he laughed.

"What's so funny?" she asked.

He looked at her a long while, his hand gently caressing the side of her face. "You just don't fit the mold, do you?"

"What mold?"

"*The* mold."

"There isn't a mold, silly, even in West Texas – and we were pretty near the last to throw it out. You're old-fashioned, you are, Mr. Matthews."

"You mean I'm chauvinistic."

"Simon," she laughed, "I don't even think anybody in *Lubbock* still says Chauvinistic."

"You're saying that even my lingo is passé?"

"Lingo? *Sigh*," she said.

"I'm not an up-to-date sort of lad, am I?"

"No, you are not. I will say, however, that old fashioned an accessory as they are, I rather like the way you wear your T shirts."

"Fill them out all right, do I?"

"Why don't you come up?" she said. "It's okay."

"I don't think so. Given the day. Chad's — feelings — all of that. No, no, I'll say good-bye here."

But they remained together in the lobby, her arms around his neck, and his arms around her waist. Not once in her life had Roberta really stood like this with a man, although in too many erotic imaginings to count she had done just this with a man just like Simon. Nothing in the reality of her life's expectations, however, had come close. She leaned her face into Simon, inhaled his wet smell of soap and shampoo, felt him against her, hard, male, enigmatic, and boyishly aware of himself.

He kissed her.

Outside a car splashed down the street.

"I have to call my Aunt Helen this afternoon," she said, "I've put it off. I haven't been able to do it like I promised, which is just terrible really. *Terrible*. But I'll try to buck myself up and give it a try today."

"Why've you not been able to phone?"

"I don't know." She shook her head. "Something about the way I feel at the moment and — well and some kind of loyalty I feel now toward Chad. I've got to call her, Simon, or Lord have mercy the woman really *will* show up here. But calling her doesn't mean I'm going to say what's on my mind, that's for darned sure."

"Probably for the best," he said.

"Yup." Then, "Such a wonderful day," she said, her breath hot against his skin.

144

"It bloody rained all afternoon."

"That only made it better."

He laughed and kissed her again.

"So when do you show me your other side?" she asked.

"Which side would that be?"

"The side which isn't this Cosmopolitan-ideal-man-quiz come to life."

"I'm a Cosmo boy now?" he asked.

"Well – y'all have that significant catch thing going."

"What if this is my only side?" he said.

"Everybody has a dark side," she said, remembering their conversation about depression, and the too-many conversations she and Helen had conducted on this subject. Helen was a firm believer in people's dark sides, which she always said were apt to "get you" when you least expected it, like the time Dorothy Sinclair "turned on her like a rabid little prairie dog at the Lakeridge Country Club." Dorothy Sinclair was forever after that the example both of peoples' dark sides – and of what happened when you let your guard down.

"What if this is my dark side and the other is even better looking in his T shirts?"

"It would be *impossible* to look better in a T shirt," she said, leaving her hand open-palmed in the center of his chest.

"And do you need to know that now? My bad side?"

She thought. "I guess not."

"We've plenty of time to find the warts," he said, then, kissing her lightly again on the lips, "and the parts that don't have warts too."

She flushed warmly, smiled into his face.

"You really didn't mind the rain?" he asked.

She thought about his question, about what he was really asking. It was one of those momentous things, a moment that led ultimately toward bed and relationship, or toward – well, toward nothing at all. She'd never been much good with important moments. But this time, she peered up into Simon's face and recognized the moment in his eyes, quizzical now and insecure.

"*Hey*?" he asked.

Snuggling tighter against him, feeling the hair of his chest through his wet T shirt, she said, "I didn't mind the rain, Simon, I didn't mind anything."

"Ah, right, then."

"Yes."

"I'll give you a ring," he said.

"*What*?" she said, dismayed by the sudden commitment – though she was not exactly displeased by this turn of events.

"I meant, I'll Phone you."

"Oh," she said, a hint of disappointment in her voice, and she remembered hearing this use of 'ring' in one of the Austin Powers movies, "I should hope so, you scamp."

He pulled away, stepped to the door, turned.

"My dark side is my fear, Roberta."

"Fear?"

"Yes."

"I meant, fear of – ?"

146

"Things real and imaginary, most particularly the imaginary. When I –when I fear things, I retreat."

"To where?"

"Inside," he said, "into my head. It's not always a good place, my head. There are a few cobwebs there sometimes."

"It's okay. The cobwebs. I've got a few myself, you know. And a bat or two in my belfry, I do believe."

"It's about the best way I know to tell it to you," he said.

"Thanks, then. But it's okay," she said again, so softly her words were barely audible, "really okay." And somehow she knew it was.

Simon lay so immobile in his bath water that he could hear the drip from the tap in the sink, fragments of dialogue from the downstairs apartment. Candlelight sparkled in the mirror, flickers refracted in the window. Puffing a ripple across the water, he watched it touch against his toes. Then, head back against the porcelain, he closed his eyes, breathing the aromas of the scents he'd put in the water, lavender and rosemary, insinuation of eucalyptus. Someone knocked roughly on his door. He sat bolt upright, water sloshing. Whoever it was knocked again. Grabbing his towel, swiping at his hair and legs, wrapping the terry cloth around his waist, he crossed the living room and opened the front door.

"I've pulled you out of the shower," Imad said.

"Bathtub, actually," Simon told him. "How'd you get in?"

"Street door's propped open."

"Fucking *gardien*." Then, briefly putting his head out the door, "The great gormless git. I've fucking told him a thousand times. We'll get those bleeding homeless blokes with head lice in the stairwells again." Simon pulled the door wide. "Come in, come in."

Imad stepped through to the long living room. He loved Simon's apartment, the furnishings suitably Spartan: a couch, a bookcase, a computer desk and word processor, an unplugged torchiere, Simon's backpack sprawling on the door side of the couch, a beamed ceiling leading toward a fin-de-siecle *porte-fenetre* and a balcony overlooking the Cluny Museum. The darkened room caught a glimmer of the candles in the bathroom, and even here, the clean smells of herbs.

Simon stood with his towel around his waist, staring at Imad. "You just here to admire my place again?"

"I need to talk," Imad said.

"No problem."

Imad crossed to the settee and plopped down amongst the cushions. A vanilla smell wafted up from them. Simon settled down on the overstuffed arm, still in his towel.

"You know you've got a smashing flat. I love it here. I'm always envious."

"So you've said. But yours is more refined — better decorated, and I pay through the teeth for this view of the Cluny."

"It's worth it," Imad said. Then, after a clumsy moment's silence, "Do you need to dry off — throw something on perhaps?"

"I'm all right as I am thanks. What is it? What's brought you here like this?"

"I don't know where to start."

"At the beginning if there is one, anywhere if there isn't."

"Okay. I have a bad feeling," Imad said.

"How's that, then?"

"It's hellishly complicated, so I guess it's a start anywhere thing — what's the smell, by the way? It's lovely."

"Aromatherapy," Simon said. "Lavender, rosemary, some other bits and pieces."

Imad nodded, sinking into the soft vanilla couch. "I've this feeling of — how do I call it? *Prémonitoire*. Foreboding. Simon, I think Chad's seeing someone else."

"*Hey?*"

"He was sleeping on the divan when I came in; I left him to it, as one does, tiptoed around. But when he woke up and he stood beside me, well, honestly there was the smell of sex on him — as if he'd been *having* sex, I should clarify."

"If Chad fools around, you haven't told me."

"He has done from time to time, Simon."

"But you've nothing solid to go on today? Just a smell?"

Imad shrugged. "It's more than just wondering if he's stepping out on me — I mean, he's about to turn forty, so he's bound to behave strangely. But it's started me wondering how much he might be questioning everything — us — you know? On the other hand, I'll be absurdly angry if there *is* someone else"

"Why absurdly?"

"Because — what good does making a fuss do? You always end up looking unsophis-ticated and getting gossiped about at parties. It *is* absurd."

"I wouldn't stay with someone who slept with another bloke," Simon said. "No way. I'd chuck her out the moment I found out about it. End of story, unsophisticated or not, they can fucking gossip about me all they want, which they do anyway, as you well know. Yes, indeed. Nylons and blow dryer out on the pavement," he gestured, "bang, right out the window on top of some fucking tourist queuing up for the Cluny."

"I wonder if perhaps fidelity isn't different for us."

"Us?"

"Gays."

Simon thought about that. "Don't see why it should be."

"Anyway, it's not just the possibility that he's doing some other guy." They looked at one another. "I don't know what it is. Simon? What is it? Why *am* I here?"

"I don't know."

"Nor I," Imad said.

They sat quietly a while, Imad in the cushions, Simon on the arm. Imad gazed through the darkness of the high-ceilinged living room, toward the candles.

"Did all of this start with Roberta's visit?" Simon asked.

"All of what?"

"That's what I'm trying to find out," Simon said.

Imad stood up, went to lean against the fireplace mantle. He sighed loudly. Nowhere in Imad's story of his life had this scene been envisaged. He felt scriptless; as if he knew where he was and what he was doing, but could grasp neither its context nor its progression. Closing his eyes, he felt an ache, not a headache exactly, but something similar. When he opened his eyes again the pain increased.

"It's a super fireplace, isn't it?" Simon said.

"Yes."

"These buildings have a more modern design," Simon told him, "they don't diminish in quality as you go up the floors. I wouldn't want anything older than this — or more recent either. This is just the right age. Hausmannesque, so to speak. Before the Second Empire, before Hausmann I should say, the top of the building was the least desirable, cramped, the place where they put the maids and paupers like *Père Goriot*."

"The invention of the elevator?" Imad asked.

"In part. Hausmann turned everything in Paris on its head – psychologically speaking. The effect of that one man on this city, it's bleeding amazing. I've got some tins of lager in the fridge," Simon said.

"I'd like one, Simon, thanks."

Simon went into the kitchen, opened two beers, and brought them back.

"Thanks." Imad drank fiercely. "Simon, I felt liberated in Barcelona, on the school trip. Did I tell you that?"

"No. How did you feel liberated?"

"I felt free."

They were quiet a while.

"Really free," Imad said.

"Just how free is that?" Simon asked.

"I didn't do anything, if that's what you're implying."

"Tempted to?"

"No. No, it wasn't that at all – it was just a feeling."

They looked at one another. What Imad wanted to say was that he might be a little glad that Chad endangered their relationship with his philandering; he wanted to say that it fit with his discovery of freedom in Barcelona, that it – confirmed something. But, of course, he did not. He could say nothing like that. He merely looked at Simon, softly said, "nice beer," and then turned to look at the books strewn across the bookcase next to him.

Simon drank from his own beer, lifted a corner of towel, and dried the inside of an ear. They looked at one another, one of those unraveling looks, a shifting of weight, a parting of curtains.

"It's dark in here," Imad said.

"How I like it, Imad."

"Can't be wise – can it?"

"How can light in my apartment be wise or unwise, mate?"

"For your mood?"

"Ah. Right. My moods. On the contrary, Imad, bright lights – they make me sad. Bright lights are bad for my mood, so you can pass that on. The rumor mill should know it."

"Lights make you sad?"

"Yes. Bright ones do."

"I've never heard anyone say lights make him sad."

"They do me," Simon said. "I prefer candles."

For a long while they looked at one another, assessing, thinking, then Simon walked over to Imad, and with an arm over his shoulder, brought him to the window. "You can see *Sacré Coeur*. Just."

"Can you?"

"Just there," he said, pointing.

Imad's head leaned against Simon's upper arm. Simon's grip tightened around Imad's shoulder. It wasn't calculated, wasn't planned, the way Imad's hand moved up against Simon's chest, feeling the strength there, the tactile energy of his chest hair, the powerful – *something*, which defined him. And it was in every way natural that Simon tilt Imad's head up and kiss him with a surprisingly intense passion, drawing Imad's arms around his neck and pulling him close in an intimate, protective embrace, kissing him all the while. They stayed together for a long time, too long for the thing to be dismissed as inconsequential.

But it was also the natural conclusion that when Imad's hand dropped down to cradle Simon's erection that Simon should say huskily, "no, that's too far, isn't it?"

"Is it, Simon?"

"Yes."

After another long kiss, Simon released Imad, turned around and walked back to sit on the couch.

Nearly dizzy, Imad felt himself suffused with – something unknown to him, as if he'd never been kissed before. More than that, it was as if he'd never before felt spontaneously regarded and – perhaps, even this – *loved*. Never had the idea of kissing Simon or of being kissed by Simon crossed his mind.

151

Another of the present unscripted moments, another of the chaotic jumble of unforeseen happenings, a thing unheralded, a thing so abruptly dazzling that it left him shaken.

He looked at Simon and Simon looked back.

"I haven't had enough poetry in my life," Imad said, though that wasn't wanted he had planned to say. "I haven't had enough lyricism." He gestured, toward Simon's chest, the flesh and blood of him, muscle and skin and hair and sex, "I think there's this part of all of us – well, honestly, I can't express it, and to express it – I mean, if I were to express it," he sighed and flushed. "Thank you, Simon."

"Stay awake, Imad, and be alive," Simon said.

Imad observed him, startled inexplicably, startled beyond the fact that Simon had taken him in his arms and kissed him. It was a manner of startled for which he lacked vocabulary, a memorable life-altering startled, nearly religious in its fervor. Miraculous, even. He looked then at Simon and realized that he was only just figuring him out. He admired the way Simon calmly returned to the couch, and sat with only his towel around him, a masculine centering force. He'd so often been dismissive of Simon, been led into the malicious school humor about Simon's troubled moods. Seeing him there, like that, honest, open, strong, too very real, Imad felt that he'd been wrong for a long time.

"A strange thought has just come to me, Simon – that I've been missing the really salient features of your personality all these years."

"Can't have done or you wouldn't be here right now, unburdening yourself and knowing you'd find solace."

Imad thought about that, felt an intense rush of blood to his face, embarrassment and perhaps even a return of the passion he'd experienced in Simon's embrace. "Yes, you're right, of course."

"Then again, you do have a point. And, then again, you haven't unburdened yourself much, and then again there wasn't after all much solace that my arms and my kiss could offer."

152

"Oh, I don't know about that," Imad said, knowing that they would never speak of these things again, "I rather suspect I'll remember your kiss for the rest of my life."

"So, mate, there you are." Simon raised his beer bottle and winked. "To the kisses we remember for the rest of our lives."

Roberta finished writing her postcards, stacked them neatly on the corner of Chad's desk, and went to the window. It seemed odd now to write postcards. Shouldn't she just log-on to *Yahoo!* and send an email greeting? She had considered that, but she didn't like Helen's habit of forwarding emails to her friends along with interpretations, like, 'read this letter from Louise, Roberta, and see if you don't agree that she's gone and lost her marbles again.' So Roberta clung to the postcard tradition, silly as it probably was. Helen would have a harder time mocking her with postcards. However, far more pressing a concern than writing postcards was that the fact that she had lost touch with her mission. She could not see herself even trying to change Chad's life now, and not merely because of falling in love with Simon. It was nearly dark outside. She stood for a long while at the *porte-fenetre*, looking northeast over the shadowy Paris rooftops, watching young people gossip on the pavement below. The clouds were gone; it felt hotter.

So far neither meal nor suggestions for dining out had materialized. She'd heard Imad leave long ago, the lingering smells of the apple pies he'd baked doing nothing to slake her hunger, but Chad had remained silent. He hadn't sought her out, hadn't moved, and hadn't spoken on the phone. Hungry, she went now in search of him. She found him on his back on the bed, one arm forming a shield over his face. For longer than she'd stared at Paris, she stared at her cousin, who was either asleep or choosing not to acknowledge her, rigid as a corpse in

153

the warm light of the bedroom. Turning finally, she got money and her passport, tucked them into her front pocket, made sure she had the key, and plunged down the stairs, out to the street.

"Are you on your own?" Aksel asked her, from the balcony above her head.

"Oh, Aksel. It's you," she said, looking up. "Yes. Imad has gone out and Chad is – well, I think he's asleep."

"May I come? Sebastian is bowling tonight with his group out in Meudon. He won't be home until quite late and sometimes he must stay over with a friend."

"Of course," she said.

"I will be only a jiffy."

Aksel disappeared into the building and she waited, with this continuing, perhaps even rising sense of elation, as if something in her life had reached a summit.

The door opened, Aksel emerged on the street.

"Any suggestions?" she asked him.

"There's a Savoyard place on *Rue de Montagne* – do you know Savoy?"

"No."

"It's an area of France, near Switzerland and Italy. The Memise? They are an extension of the Alps. They eat game birds and fondue, things of that sort. There," he pointed, "just before the Pantheon."

"Oh," she said, wondering what the 'things of that sort' included which she could herself eat, "okay, then."

They went up the hill from the apartment, speechlessly fighting their way across the main street, then walking amid an astonishing crowd of tourists past a string of restaurants – Vietnamese, Italian, Chinese, generic French – until they came to the place Aksel had mentioned. Unlike the other places they'd passed, it wasn't busy. Perhaps she wasn't the only one who found the idea of fondue and game birds less than tantalizing on such a hot evening. They were shown to a table in the window, with a view of the cobbled street, the Pantheon and the knurly panorama of the Latin Quarter.

She looked up at him over her menu. "Do y'all have any recommendations other than greasy birds and cheese?"

"Even though it's a bird, I can recommend the chicken," Aksel said, "crisp and savory, with *frites* — *pommes frites* – French fries? Or do you call them something else now? I believe they were renamed."

"Oh, good grief, that was just some hare-brained gimmick by some idiot. Like we were ever going to go down to Burger King and say, "I'd like to have me a large order of freedom fries, please.' Isn't that just the *stupidest* thing you ever heard?"

"No," he said, "it is not the stupidest, actually."

"*Hmmm*," she demurred, thinking that her days of French fries should probably be over. If her dream of being naked in front of Simon were to come true — and she knew, somehow, that it would — she needed to be the sveltest version of herself that had ever existed. Fries wouldn't help peel away those pounds.

"Everything is good, however. Even Galsworthy eats here."

"The true test?"

"For our group."

"He's that picky?"

"So he says."

"I guess he would, wouldn't he?"

"Yes."

They both laughed.

She glanced over the menu on her own then, marveling at the names and the artwork and the flourishes in the way prices were noted. The menu itself was delicious. It was kind of like the new menus at the Lubbock Club, only a little less pretentious. Helen never tired of denouncing the Lubbock Club for being pretentious, though it didn't stop her eating there every other Saturday with "the girls," and telling Roberta afterward what everybody ate, including Loreen K. Albrighton who, invariably, "ate herself sick, the little piglet." Finally, Roberta settled upon onion soup, which was improbably wrong for the heat but seemed to have a mouth-watering description and didn't seem like it could be too fattening, and a lamb dish of some kind. She didn't know if lamb was fatty or not, though when she thought of curly-headed lambs in meadows she thought maybe they weren't. The lamb dish had an enticing drawing of a stone cottage beside it.

They ordered a large bottle of water to share and a cheap pitcher of wine, which Aksel said was good.

"You are enjoying Paris?" Aksel asked.

"Oh, my yes. Here I am drinking wine like there's no tomorrow and — everything. I'm a real happy girl right now, Aksel."

"To friends back in Oslo, I always describe Paris as seductive. Which it is. And you have been seduced, Roberta?" Aksel asked.

She looked up at him, thinking as she answered of Simon, to whom Aksel had obviously referred, and though she meant to say something coy and West Texan like 'sadly, no, sweetie,' she instead said quite bluntly, "Sure have, though I'm still waiting for the big moment — like all the others, I suppose." Then after a moment of quiet she asked, "Are there many others, Aksel?"

"Waiting for the big moment of being fucked by Simon? No, not that many." Aksel shrugged. "True, he turns heads; true, he arouses passions. But there is no line formed."

"He's not the kind of guy I ever did think of myself — you know — being with."

"Fucking you mean?"

"Oh no, much more than that — though that too, for sure. I mean, all that competition for one thing. Competition for a man is not my cup of tea, which I pretty much think you could guess. I could never win in a competition."

"It's not real competition," Aksel advised her, "only competition for something physical. Simon is very physical to people, and sometimes he is *only* physical to them. People like Simon, they come to hate this, I think, this knowing that they can use their physicalness to get many things. They know they

156

are objects, so they like most the people who see beyond the physical. The real competition is competition for Simon's heart, and that is a different thing than competition to undo his clothings and leap on his hairy body. I think you are seeing Simon not as a sexual adventure, Roberta, but as – ."

"But I *am* thinking of him sexually," she said.

"But not only that way."

"Okay. Not only that way," she agreed. "But – well, face it; can you *imagine* the kids he'd make?"

Aksel made a warning movement with his hand. "Genetics is a tricky business, Roberta. I could tell you stories. My cousin Arnulf, very beautiful parents – my aunt Sigrid is beautiful and my uncle Karl could stop the traffic – but Arnulf, he resembles a lizard, with little teeth and big eyes – a tragic failure of genetics."

"Whatever. I mean, I'm sorry about your lizard cousin, but to answer your question, I have most certainly not been seduced yet. I think I'll know when I have."

They both laughed again.

The waiter appeared; she took her soup and Aksel his salad. To her dismay the soup was covered in a two-inch think layer of cheese, some of which had bubbled over and was now oozing down the sides. This was not at all what she expected, although it smelled delectable. "Here we are talking about me and Simon, which is just too weird for America, and all the time we both know I came here to fetch Chad back to Lubbock. So how come I've gone and – " but she didn't say what she'd gone and done. Perhaps she didn't know.

"Maybe the reason you came was all along a pretext."

"It wasn't a pretext, Aksel. My Aunt Helen really is sick with diabetes." Conversation paused as Roberta pushed through the cheese and savored the soup. Then she looked at Aksel and said, "okay, so she's not all that sick. Not yet at any rate. Oh, what the heck – for all I know it *is* a pretext. And maybe I was a big old pretext too, maybe I said yes so's I could escape, just like Chad did." She thought about that, nodded. "But maybe I also said yes because I do want Chad to come

157

home – that's for sure no pretext. Of course, I never wanted to be the ruination of his happy home. But I never really thought about him having a home in the way he does. I honestly don't know what I thought about that part."

"A *happy* home?" he said, shaking his head. "Roberta, I do not know if it is a happy home."

10

Aksel's remark called to mind the argument Roberta heard after Helen telephoned. She also remembered how Imad had stumbled over calling Chad happy, that day in Luxembourg Gardens. Perhaps it wasn't a happy home.

"Of course," Aksel said, munching on his salad as he talked, "we spoke of this before, I know, but Chad can't go from Paris to a place like Texas – a place where even your vice-president went shooting at people for his pleasure. And that caricature of a man you twice elected as your President came from Texas."

"W? He's okay really; he's a nice guy, Aksel."

"*Nice*? Not so nice to the Iraqi women and children in Fallujah. Apparently they were in this nice man's way, so he blew them to pieces. In Norway, we have other words for this than nice, Roberta."

She shrugged, having already been in Paris long enough to grasp peoples' opinions regarding that particular American president. At the moment, she cared more about her soup, with its crust of cheese and filaments of onion. "Yes, we talked about this before, Aksel – and Chad being here and wanting to stay here – it's not about hating Texas. It's like your grandma and whatever the heck that city is you told me about, that *Trond* place. It's about what he projected on to Aunt Helen. Who was and I won't dispute it anymore, a mean-hearted shrew of a woman who terrorized Chad and made his life miserable. I was there, by golly. I saw and heard it." For a moment Roberta looked stunned. She wiped her lips on her napkin, closed her eyes, and then opened them with watery befuddlement. "Did I just say all that?"

Aksel also looked around the room, then back at her. "Yes, it was you."

"Okay, then, fair enough. True is true. But to accept his West Texas past, in any shape or form would mean accepting himself – and he's not going to do that, not as far as I can see."

"Have you talked about this with him?"

"How do you talk about something like that?" she asked.

"Bring it up, perhaps?" Aksel finished his salad, drank some water. "See what he says?"

"He's superior to me intellectually; he'd make mince-meat of my arguments. He'd ignore me."

"You could try."

"I could try," she agreed, devouring the last glob of cheese in the bottom of her bowl.

"Is there room for a third?"

"*Chad.*" Roberta had not seen him come up the street and his presence seemed conjured up by their discussion. Had he heard anything? She felt another flush rise up to her cheeks.

Chad sat beside Aksel. "I heard you two talking through the *porte-fenetre* in the bedroom. This is where Aksel always brings the unsuspecting."

"The unsuspecting what?" Roberta wondered.

"Diner. Tourist. Initiate into the mysteries of fondue."

"I didn't know if you were sleeping or not. I thought I shouldn't bother you. I'm sorry if I got it wrong."

"You didn't — and I almost didn't come. In the end, I thought I'd better eat something. Fretting makes you hungry." He signaled to the waiter, ordered chicken and *frites*, same as Aksel. "I've probably interrupted deep discussions."

"Indeed you have," she said, remembering something she had heard once about hiding more behind the truth than you can ever hide behind a lie — or something like that. "Is Imad home yet?"

"No."

"Is there a problem?" Roberta asked.

"What sort of problem are you imagining, Roberta?"

She met his look. "I heard y'all arguing this morning, so that's what I'm imagining, Chad."

"That's what comes from having a spare pair of ears in the house, I suppose."

Her flush, which had started to fade, flared back up again, and she looked away from him, out the window.

Aksel shifted nervously in his chair.

Chad poured himself some water, held it up, examined it a moment, and then sipped from it. "You've done your hair differently."

A long moment of indecision fell over the table, then – looking at Chad's reflection in the window – Roberta said, "I pulled it back in a clip. That's all."

"It looks nice," he said. "Young. Makes your face look even prettier."

"Thanks."

"Look. You heard what you heard, Roberta. The fact of the matter is that I'm not dealing well with the idea that my mother is most likely on the verge of appearing here, or rather I'm not dealing well with myself as a consequence of the idea and, well, goddamn it, I'm not dealing will with everything else, from my birthday to you being here to – *everything*."

"Okay," she said softly.

He looked at her a moment or two, took her hand, and brought it to his lips.

"*Chad*?"

He put her hand down on the table. "I love you, Roberta."

Shocked, she said, "I love you too, Chad."

"That's good, then."

"Yes," she agreed, "It is."

Imad walked slowly home from Simon's flat, along the length of *rue des Ecoles*. He stopped on the corner of the *rue St. Jacques* to read a poster about a concert at the church of *St. Julien le Pauvre*, admiring the printing and the colors – burgundy and white – more than the idea of the music. In the Mariette park a group of girls in uniform sprawled over the grass, smoking, chattering, and he watched them a long while, ogling their animation, their youth. He waved to an acquaintance, dining across the street on *Jean de Beauvais*. The humid warmth added a quality to the evening, a summer richness that he liked, men in shorts and tank tops, young backpacking tourists, unshaved and sweaty. At *rue de la Montagne* he went into their wine shop, spoke briefly with Laurent, the owner, who asked after Chad and their summer plans and Roberta's visit, and then he browsed through the racks until he'd selected a good white and a serviceable red. When he'd paid for them, he crossed the street and went down *Bernardins* to their building.

The phone was ringing as he came in and he snatched up the receiver, clanking his wine bottles on the sofa.

"Hello."

A crackling phone semi-silence.

Then, "Chad?" the voice asked, in a French accent.

"No, this is Imad."

"Oh. I see. Is Chad at home?"

"No, he's not. Could I take a message?"

A pause.

"Perhaps you would be so kind as to inform him that Etienne phoned?"

Another pause as Imad reflected on what it meant that Chad had given out his home phone number. Reckless? Intentional? What?

"Of course, Etienne. *Je l'informerai.*"

Chad and Roberta sat in the shadow of Notre Dame, in the park honoring the Jewish deportees of World War II. Behind them a conga-line of tourist buses dozed beneath chestnut trees. On both sides the river lapped, the lights of the left bank and the *Ile St. Louis* starting to sparkle as the sun sank and night rose. Roberta looked across the deck of the lighted *Pont de la*

Tournelle, visible above the engraved words of the *Crypte Memorial*.

"I keep thinking about how I'm in Paris, I mean, I'm really in Paris," she said. "Though Simon says he just thinks of Paris now as another big city. It's lost its mystique for him."

"Familiarity breeds contempt?" Chad said.

"Perhaps it's not that strong. I don't think he's contemptuous or anything."

"I've been thinking about great grandmother again just now."

"Bertha Belle? What a name. If she thought that tornado was Jesus come to take her home it was probably because some evangelist in a tent said something about God and tornadoes and got her to thinking. From what I hear, she was big on revival meetings. I think she even let them pitch a tent once out in her field."

"It's just so extreme, Roberta. I think about it all the time. Bertha Belle and the tornado." Then, as if this were logically connected to the subject of Bertha and the tornado, he asked, "So how is my mom, really? All of this diabetes crap aside."

"Oh, I think she really does have diabetes, Chad – though I don't know for sure, of course. Leastwise, I don't know enough yet to call her down as a liar."

"In general, then. How's she doing – in general?"

"About the same, I guess," Roberta said, "in general."

"Remember all those Christmas celebrations?"

"I still put up with them, don't forget."

"Christmas was always an engineering feat for mom, stackable Christmas presents and decorations in numbered boxes brought down from the attic. We always had a tree decorated by a man who came out to the house and did it up according to mama's specifications."

"He still does it," Roberta said, "rocking horses, drummer boys, toy soldiers, and an angel blowing her trumpet at the branches and lights and ornaments below."

"They were always Christmas trees to remember."

163

"Yup. That's Aunt Helen, she survives and she thrives — she lays down the law and she sets out the rules. She's been taking good care of Aunt Carol, by the way. You know she has arthritis and macular degeneration, she's too crippled up and demented to leave her lopsided trailer ver there to Plainview, which she shares with that maniac poodle named Miss Laverne what bit my thumb so bad I had to go to Lubbock General that time — I guess that's just about the best answer to how aunt Helen's doing."

"What's the word for those feelings that arise at times like this?" he asked.

"A time like what?"

"A time so far from the anamnesis of Christmas celebrations that I'm grieving for all my powerlessness to fuse the past and the present and the future into a congruous life?"

"I think I get the gist of that, Chad — but I for sure don't have any word for it."

He looked away, at the river or the trees or something he could neither recognize nor acknowledge. There was something he wished for but could not name.

Roberta stared at the bridge, then with soft deliberation said, "You need to know that it wasn't just Aunt Helen you abandoned, it was me too — and it hurt a lot. Because I loved you — because — "

"Because now I live far away?"

"No. You live a phone call or an email away," she said, "that's how far you live."

He looked at her, this new Roberta who spoke so bluntly. They appraised each other quietly and a murky reticence slithered between them. "Things must have been hard on you," he said at last, wishing now that he had never made the crack about another set of ears in the house. That was mean — that was like his mother. It was the sort of thing Roberta had spent her life hearing from people.

"The orphan girl and her tale of woe," she said.

"I'm so sorry."

"I don't know that you are really." She looked at him. "I don't know that anyone but me ever has been sorry. I don't think most people really give a hoot."

Chad thought about that. "But I am sorry. I was running away from a lot – a *lot*, Roberta."

"I know that. Now that I'm here, okay, I understand better how you must have been running hard and fast for a long, long time."

"You really didn't know about me before you came? About me being gay?"

"Nope. Nada. Nothing."

"Not even when I wrote letters home to you from college," he said, "and I was dropping hints all over the place, names of the guys I was seeing and – well, *geez*, I remember I told you once how I'd been hanging around watching the wrestling team one afternoon – I even described one guy, he had blue eyes and black hair and a body like a centerfold. I've no idea what possessed me to write that, and I was embarrassed for days after I sent you that letter. What psychologists call the confessional urge, I guess. Anyway, I can't believe you didn't pick up on it."

"I worshipped you, Chad; I just thought you were teasing me with stories about cute wrestler men. I was always a little partial to wrestlers. But I really didn't pick up on anything – it just wasn't – what? In my mind at all. I mean, I knew gay people existed, but I –"

"Would you have worshipped me if you knew I was gay?"

"I don't know," she said. "Maybe not back then." She sighed, fell silent. "I don't know. Sorry. I wish I could just say yes."

"*Will* she show up now in Paris?"

"I think you were right on the money when you said to Imad this morning that she'll come over here to punish me. That's it exactly. It's now about how she's 'got to teach that dim-witted flabby Roberta a lesson' – and because it's about me, it's all the easier for her to hop on a plane and come over here with both barrels blazing."

"I'm not the least bit ready for her – not the least little bit. But you should know something, Roberta. You should know that I'm glad *you* came. I'm really glad you're here. Honestly."

She shrugged.

"Not to change the subject, but you and Simon are getting quite cozy, aren't you?"

"*Cozy?*" She snorted as if he'd hurt her feelings. "I don't know what y'all mean by saying cozy. Simon is a great guy."

"Just be careful."

"Why should I be careful?"

"Simon's a little – you know."

"Excuse me very much, Chad, but Simon is not the tiniest bit '*you know.*'"

He observed her, thinking about this loyal resistance to his words.

She looked back at him, unblinking.

"He's a handsome man, Roberta."

"Some people are," she said, "that's the way it works. Y'all should be more accepting of people, you know that – more *open*. In fact, if you wanted to save this whole thing you'd pick up the phone and call Lubbock tonight and stop things before they escalated. Tomorrow's your fortieth birthday, seems like a good time to do it, to – " but she halted in midstream, blinked, and stayed silent.

"To what? What would I say after all this time?"

She considered a moment before she spoke, as if she might just stay silent. "You'd say, hello, mom – how are y'all doing, besides dying of diabetes and all – Roberta's lost some weight and, oh yeah, by the way, I'm not coming home so stop trying, damn you."

He smiled. "I couldn't do it, I couldn't possibly call her." He stood up and walked to the railing, where he stood with his back to Roberta, waiting in his quiet quarantine until she came to stand beside him.

"Chad?"

His lip trembled. She saw him bite it, hold it clenched in his teeth, saw him struggle for control.

"*Chad*?"

"Please, don't," he said, turning away from her.

"Don't – what?"

They stood there, side-by-side, silent.

"You know how to get home?" he asked.

"Yes," she said.

He looked at her as if he wanted to say something. But he didn't, he remained mute and pained. Then he wheeled around, strode across the path, walked up to the *Pont St. Louis* and disappeared into the crowds. She stared after him, an ambivalent mixture of horror and rapture, elation battling with apprehension. He was gone. Turning back to the river, leaning against the stone parapet, she thought, 'I'm in Paris and I'm in love.'

167

Chad awoke with Etienne's head cradled on his chest and Etienne's legs on top of his own. The flat suffocated. Sweat tingled over his face and neck and ran wherever Etienne's skin touched him. His chest itched. He turned on his side, restive, staring open-eyed into the darkness of Etienne's bedroom, not the darkness of death, but the black and white darkness of cats and dogs, objects seen but not understood, things recognized but unnamed. He realized in that moment that another Chad, the phantasmal Chad who might have been, stood forever forsaken at the end of this long road not taken. This Chad in bed with Etienne, this Chad who had taken the alternate road of evasion and renunciation, sometimes glimpsed the other Chad, and was sometimes aware of that other man, the might have been person. This was one of those times.

How did it happen that he ended up here and not there? He might have been – *what*? What might he have been?

When people said that, when they said, "I might have been," did they mean a different profession, or a state of mind, or perhaps a pathway of different emotions? What? For himself, he might have made sense of his life; he might have been centered. But he had not, and he was not. He found himself turning forty without having resolved those many motivating irritations and unhappinesses. But how did that happen? After all, how could he not have reconciled his wild dreamy remembrances to the life that he actually lived? There had been a time, of course, when the fork in the road was right there in front of him; touchable, beheld, and available for him to turn down.

He and Imad, in the bliss of their first swollen-lipped partnering, had ventured south to Italy for an August vacation in Tuscany. Artist friends of Imad's lent them a shabby but beautifully situated farmhouse, with a bedroom view of the valley and distant Church tower. It was as sensual as a Mortimer novel, the people, the food, the wines, but beyond all the garden, with flowers in feral profusion. Chad's response to those flowers had been surprising. He'd never cared for gardening, never been one to marvel at prize roses or well-tended rhododendrons. In Tuscany that changed. There, he fell in love with aromatic hillsides of yellow and white flowers, with blue, red, and pink vines crawling over stonework, flowery perfumes dropping down from the pergola roof.

A peevish woman named Teresa cared for the garden, and she reminded Chad of his mother. She even had the same way of walking. Just like Chad's mother, animals loved her; people feared her, animals loved her. As Teresa climbed the hillsides, looking at her plants, dead-heading flowers, assaulting weeds, training vines, a crowd of cats and dogs accompanied her, wrapping around her legs, perching above her head, sleeping beside her. Amazing synchronicity, Chad thought, the universe producing two similar women: Teresa in Tuscany and Helen in West Texas. The real difference lay with the sons. Paolo, the Italian son, cared for his mother. This curly-haired young man, exactly Chad's age, endured all of Teresa's cruelties with a genial shrug and a wink in Chad and Imad's direction. Sitting in the garden one Saturday afternoon, Chad watched the patient interaction between young and old. For a man who had turned his back on his mother, this different story perplexed and mystified him.

He and Imad talked about Teresa and Paolo, standing on the balcony, staring into a Tuscan twilight. Later, on the afternoon before they left Italy, Chad decided he should break the ice and he wrote a letter to his mother. He carried that letter home with him to Paris. But in their colder Northern environment it became just another letter never sent. Although it had been left to rot in a desk drawer, however, it had not been forgotten. It contained still the story of what Chad and his mother might have been, had the ice been broken. Could that one letter have changed the course of history? Could that letter have stopped him running naked into his own tornado? That letter, Chad realized, was part of his road never taken. After that, he had traveled too far down the alternate road ever to go back or find the fork again. Gently, he pushed Etienne away and stood up.

Etienne continued to sleep in untroubled oblivion, unaware of Chad's departure. Sweat glistened on his chest and forehead, and where his arm had been thrown up behind the pillow, in the matted hair of his armpit. A gift of beauty for the morning Chad crossed the border to forty, this young Frenchman naked in the bed in which the two of them had recently made love. Pulling on his boxer shorts, Chad went to the *porte-fenetre*. It had no view, except the back of another stone building. Somewhere in the western suburbs lightning flashed. Not long now until dawn, in fact a hint of rose had started tracing itself into the sky. Chad stepped back into the apartment.

He dressed quickly and left, muffling his footpads on the stairs of the sleeping building, carefully opening the door to the street and letting it shut gently. Once he was outside he felt he could breathe again. He paused at the corner and, looking right through the columns of the *Pavilion de la Reine*, saw amongst its trees Louis XIII's statue in the *Place des Vosge*s. He headed that way, down *rue de Bearn*, and when he arrived in the *Place des Vosges* he sat and looked toward Victor Hugo's house, waiting for the sun to come up. He smelled his own sweat and the sex he and Etienne had enjoyed, the miasma of passion from their hours of sweaty coitus. They'd done things last night he'd never asked of Imad. Half-naked love making in the kitchen, taking Etienne standing up, Etienne's legs caressing Chad's neck and head, his body supported by Chad's arms, their passion banging everything off the tall dresser on to the floor, photographs, keys, wallets, an ashtray, both he and Etienne finally coming with weak-breathed shrieks. Real sex. But then, expended, he'd dreamt of death.

He had dreamt of his mother dead.

He stood up and walked, not back toward Etienne's flat, but down the narrow *Rue de Brague* and onward across *Rue Saint Antoine*, in the general direction of the Seine. Pausing on *Rue Beautrellis* to get his bearings (they were warrens, these streets), he inhaled the sharp aroma of someone's cigarette, which presumably came from one of the buildings lining both sides of the street. He thought about breathing this smoke, which had been in the lungs of another man and now entered his own, a shared smoke that he'd not wanted, but which he shared anyway. It seemed like life itself, imposition and then, as he hurried on toward the *Quai des Celestins*, like escape, the thing which made it all bearable. An astonishing anonymity came with his strides along the pavement, the way in which he darted across the street with Parisian savvy, between *Rue Charles V* and *Rue de Petit Musc*, as if he weren't forty year old Chad Newsome, but just anyone, of any age.

He enjoyed this anonymity. He'd choose to live and die anonymously if he could, no one in particular, just a man escaping, continually escaping from all that went with a name, an identity, a history. Being unknown offered safety; recognition offered only danger, demanded knowing the script, required a past as well as a future. Chad wanted the present and nothing more. Appropriately, all things considered, he crossed over the

Quai des Celestin at *Place du Pere Teilhard de Chardin*. This day, his fortieth birthday, the most meaningful day in his life so far was, to borrow from Teilhard de Chardin, whose statue looked mournfully at him from the other side of the *Boulevard Henri IV*, his own cosmogenesis, his omega point. Ending up in *Place Henri de Galli*, he stood beneath the trees and looked at the Ile St. Louis and at the rump of Notre-Dame Cathedral, which bent the Paris skyline to its will. Not a bad place to be, in Paris, as the sun came up on the day of his fortieth birthday. But, he thought, with tangible fear, struggling to come to grips with this omega point, where did he go now?

In the early morning hush of Paris, Roberta was awake, thinking.

She hadn't walked straight home last night. Using her *Penguin Paris Mapguide*, she had made her way along the side of the Cluny, on *rue du Sommerard*, to Simon's – not precisely to Simon's flat, as she didn't even try to go up. That wasn't her mission. Having made her way there was enough. She found a seat outdoors at a café off *rue des Ecoles* and stared at what she knew to be his building. This thing she felt, sitting there surrounded by tourists, sipping a glass of white wine, was a woman's feeling about a man, about her sexuality, about her needs. Sitting at this cobblestoned left bank ulna, amid a pretentious group of American exchange students (pretending, less successfully than they imagined, to be French), had everything to do with the way Simon had made her feel. It had to do with how she felt just *knowing* that he was over there – somewhere – doing whatever Simon did: sit-ups or push-ups or watching old black and white movies. It didn't matter.

She savored her eagerness, felt the moist vortex of desire. She couldn't have been more content just then, sitting with the taste of wine on her tongue and the tingle of lust in her stomach, with her awareness of a man named Simon in a nearby building. She closed her eyes and against the insides of her eyelids saw something like shade and design, something like – it wasn't nameable what she saw. Then she opened her eyes and saw Simon. He had on running shoes, a tank top, and skimpy wide-legged shorts. Peering from behind the student smoke clouds and a young woman's Gidget Goes Berserk hairdo, she watched him jog across the *Place Paul Painleve* and disappear into the crowds on the *rue des Ecoles*. Exhilarated by what she'd seen and thought and felt, she finished her wine and went home.

Now, lying in bed, she listened to the swish of a bicycle on the street below, following the sounds down the street, over the curb, around the corner. Faraway a church bell sounded. Something rustled in the eaves of the building across the street. Rolling on her side, she stared out the open *porte-fenetre* into the splendor of almost-morning, where a violet color painted the sagging predawn sky, and the remains of night rained purply over her desires.

11

"Chad didn't come home last night," Imad said from where he was sprawled on the sofa.

"I know." Roberta crossed the living room to sit opposite him. "I've been lying in there listening half the night – I left my door ajar just so's I could."

"What should I do?" he asked.

"Not much you can do."

"Histrionics to ring the police."

"Histri-*what's its*?"

"Sorry – too dramatic I mean."

"I don't know about that, since if they're anything like the Lubbock police then they live for drama. But I think it's bit early for calling the police, they'll tell you that you have to wait longer. They have it all calculated out, to be sure somebody hasn't just gone off on a binge or something. I remember when our across the street neighbor Victor disappeared, no matter how much his wife Dee Dee squawked, the police wouldn't do *nothing*, and then – sure as shooting – old Victor, greased-up hairdo and all, turned up out in El Paso with his sister Belinda. I never could understand how Dee Dee put up with that hair. My gosh, he must have made one heck of a mess on her pillow cases every night. I also can't for the life of me remember why he went to El Paso. Doesn't seem like much of an improvement over Lubbock, does it?"

"I wouldn't know," Imad said and then, after a moment or two of silence, "today is Chad's birthday."

"He won't have forgotten that. Trust me. This birthday is big on his mind."

"Did he say anything when he left you?" Imad asked

"He asked me if I knew the way home."

"That's *it*?"

"That's it. Sorry."

Imad cradled his head, the effect of his sleepless night discernible in the eclipses beneath his eyes. "Chad has been seeing someone you know," he said. "As in fucking the young thing's lights out, by way of clarification."

She was stunned. After a long and flustered silence, in which she struggled for the right thing to say, ask, or do, she finally came up with, "and how long has this been going on? Oh, *heck*. Pretend I didn't say that — that sounds like some kind of country western song or something. Look, Imad." She tried to sound sensible, womanly, figuring that might be what he needed just then. "I'm sure he'll show up, we have our birthday plans tonight for — what's the name?"

"*Joyeux anniversaire* — it's just French for happy birthday."

"Oh. Well, it sounds a lot prettier in French. And anyway, it's possible he's just been, oh — I don't know — wandering around or something."

"That's what he's probably been doing, Roberta, of course. Why didn't I think of that? Not fucking his pretty French boy but just wandering around, eating ice cream and window shopping. No, he's holed up, if you'll excuse the pun, with Etienne."

"The young thing's name?"

"So the young thing told me."

Roberta gave him a quizzical look.

"He called here for Chad and I took the call. That's another thing. I can't understand why Chad would give out our home phone number. Think about it. That's — well, that's not a trivial thing, is it?"

"I'm real sorry, Imad."

"He's dipped his wick before, but he's always come home, full of apologies and explanations and once even anger. It was supposed to have been my fault those times because I drove him off. But all the same, he's always come home. This is a first, staying out all night. He's never done this. No message, no phone call — nothing."

Words failed her. She shifted away from him and looked across the room. One of his photographs centered a collection of old metro posters, a man in a raincoat and tortoise shell

174

glasses forever rushing along the *Quai d'Orsay* with a swinging briefcase, as if charging into the neighboring 1932 advertisement about taking the metro to the *Bois de Boulogne*. "Like I said, I'm sorry." Then, focusing on a mess on the floor that she'd only noticed peripherally, she asked, "what in the name of everything holy is *that*?"

"It is – *was* – a pair of Chad's shoes, his favorite shoes to be frank, the ones he says are the most comfortable he's ever had. As I think you've noticed, I scissored the sons-of-bitches to pieces. Ever scissor a pair of shoes?"

"No, sir," she said.

"It's a damn hard task, let me tell you."

Hard to refute the lover scorned right of imminent domain. Cheat on somebody and your belongings are subject to rifling or worse. Roberta knew those rules in West Texas, even if she'd never seen them applied in precisely this fashion. Ruby did punch out some trailer windows when she got cheated on, but that was hardly as personal as a pair of shores. Shoes had a certain flair, Roberta thought. After all, it would be hard to replace them when you went to put them on one Monday morning and noticed they were in pieces.

"I felt as if I had to do destroy something of his – you know? Fretting all night long the way I did – I was so angry."

"Getting your own back? Oh heck yes, I understand. Once, when Loreen K. Albrighton was staying with us because her pipes froze up – which was her own darned fault anyway, I even think she might have done it on purpose just to stay with Helen for a couple of days, she's always saying that Aunt Helen's guest room reminds her of a doll's house she saw once down to Nieman Marcus – well, I did a load of laundry with her blouses and pants in it and I washed them on 'whites,' hottest water possible, then I dried those things until even the stitching shrank. Lordy, if they didn't look just like Barbie clothes when I was done with them."

"I'll have to remember that one," Imad said. "And you're welcome to my shoe trick, if you need it."

175

"Thanks, I guess. Wonderful reaction my laundry shenanigans got, by the way. She still tells everybody about how bad I am with laundry. I mean, she's so danged *stupid* that she thinks *I'm* stupid and did it out of ignorance." She stood up, pulled the curtains back, and stepped out on the balcony. Morning sun glinted on rooftops and a bell peeled. A bus passed slowly along *Rue Monge*.

Imad appeared beside her. "I'm frightened, Roberta."

"I know you are, Imad. I would be too. Honest I would."

'Yesterday, when I went to talk to Simon, I was – fuzzy about how I felt about our relationship, I mean my relationship with Chad. Now I'm confused about how *Chad* feels, not how I feel – and I can't even remember how I felt yesterday – or why."

"Is that where you were? When I couldn't find you? You were with Simon?"

"Yes. Pulled our handsome lad out of his aromatherapy bath, not that a hastily arranged towel doesn't look good on him."

"He does a towel justice, I'm sure."

"Aussie insouciance."

"Come again?"

Imad merely shrugged.

"So it looks like both you and Chad are partial to this disappearing thing."

"Apparently."

"And was Simon helpful?"

"Yes." After a small pause, he said, "Roberta, I don't want you to think that this is all about Chad playing out last night. It's – well, there's more to it – and – all right: here it is, I haven't told anyone, not Simon – no one. I've been offered a job in Canada, at a school outside Victoria, in British Columbia."

She seemed to puzzle over this, turning to him and trying to find some understanding in his face. "But why haven't you told anyone?"

He looked away from her.

"Haven't you already signed a contract for next year – I mean here in Paris?"

"Yes. Of course."

"You'd break it?"

"I don't know."

"British Columbia is sure as heck not Paris."

"True."

She considered the many implications of this information. Then, having coming a little closer to solving the puzzle, she said, "look, there's Aksel."

Aksel peered up at them from his open *portes-fenetres*. "Sleepless night upstairs, yes? Someone was pacing."

"That would be me," Imad said.

"What is the matter?"

"Chad didn't come home last night," Roberta told him.

"Oh dear."

"Precisely," Roberta said.

She looked over at Imad and caught something new on his face; she put an arm around his shoulder and pulled him close.

"Sebastian, he is at home," Aksel said.

"Pardon me? Oh – Sebastian, your – uh huh, that's real nice, Aksel." But after an unsettling absorption of this remark, she said, "are you trying to say that Chad and Sebastian might have gone off somewhere *together*?"

"I won't even listen to that, it is only gossip about the two of them. I asked Sebastian point blank and he denied it. So that is old news not worth dignifying. Sebastian has never allowed Chad to have him in that way."

"Oh, Aksel," she peered down at him. "Y'all ought to hush up right now, don't you think?"

"Why, Roberta? There are no secrets, Sebastian said that Chad did not even know his name. He said that Chad calls him 'what's his name.'"

"Why does this not reassure me?" Imad groaned.

"Look, Imad," Roberta said, "let's go get some breakfast. This whole thing is getting crazier by the minute."

He looked uncertain.

"Trust me, if Chad comes home while we're out, then it can all be said when you get home."

"And I'll come too," Aksel declared from below, leaning over his railing, straining to hear their words.

"Get that skinny Scandinavian booty up here, then," Roberta told him.

"It's got that Lucy and Desi sort of spell this *arrondisement*, doesn't it," Galsworthy said up to them suddenly from the street, "all of you neighbors swapping recipes and dishing the sub-letting downstairs white trash."

"I rang him up." Imad responded to Roberta's unasked question. "Woke him up, I suppose I should say – I thought maybe – you know. A bed for the night sort of thing? Chad's been known to do that."

"And Simon?'

"Yes, I rang him too."

She looked down at Galsworthy, his dogs straining toward some intriguing urine mark on the wall. "Does he take them on the metro?"

"The metro? God, no. Galsworthy always does taxis."

"Oh yes, of course."

"Will someone buzz us up?" Galsworthy asked.

"You'll have to leave the dogs, Chad doesn't like dog hair in the house."

"The boys, like young Aksel there, are virtually hairless in their dotage, and we don't even know if Chad will be home again to care about them *or* their hair, do we?"

"Thank you for that, Galsworthy."

Galsworthy waved up at him. "I call it as I see it, dearest."

"If I had half a spine I'd tell you to bugger off. But I don't – so come on up."

Imad and Roberta went inside, Imad pressed the downstairs door open, Roberta pulled open the apartment's front door, and Galsworthy, Alcazar and Alhambra toiled up the stairs.

"Dear abused, Imad," said Galsworthy, on arrival, tossing the dog leashes to Roberta and pulling Imad into a tight hug, "how *are* we bearing up?"

"We still don't know anything."

"*Au contraire*. Beyond knowing that he's been bonking KY jelly up the worn out backside of some slut in the Marais, *qu'est-ce qu'on doit savoir?*"

"I meant we don't know anything more about where he is or why he didn't come home. I know about the bloke in the Marais, and I've told Roberta about him as well."

"And here I've been sitting on the big secret, *mes lèvres ont scellé*, as if it were positively poison to speak the truth and — the beans have already been spilled."

"Inadvertently, but spilled all the same."

"We're going out to breakfast," Roberta said. "Aksel's coming up to go with us. You're welcome to join us."

"I'll stay and man the fort, sound the alarm if he comes back. Aksel has a mobile, though I haven't bothered to note the number. Have him leave the number on the table."

"How did *you* know, by the way?" Imad asked.

"Know?"

"About Etienne, the bloke with the worn-out backside."

"Oh *him*. Caught Chad red handed, I was coming out of the hairdresser — and *poofy poof poof poof*. There he was, bold as brass, the signs of sex visible on him from ten feet away."

"I'm guessing you promised him to keep quiet."

"As one does."

Imad looked at Roberta in a mixture of embarrassment and panic. "Oh, Roberta, I wonder how many others know."

She put a hand on his arm, which seemed to shiver beneath her fingers.

"I've told only a select few," Galsworthy said.

"*God.*"

Aksel knocked on the door and let himself in. The dachshunds skittered joyfully over to him, yipping, yapping, and waiting for him to pet them.

"He says something to them in Norwegian," Galsworthy told them, "drives them around the bend. However, when he tried saying it to me I felt only a kind of nausea."

"How about some coffee and a couple of warm croissants?" Roberta asked, moving her hand to the small of Imad's back. "Though personally I prefer those *pain au chocolat* thingies. Mercy they're good."

"Sure," Imad said. "Since Galsworthy here is manning – if that's not a contradiction in terms – the fort, why the hell not?"

"I take umbrage at that implication," Galsworthy said.

"You do not, you old queen," Imad answered back. "You delight in it."

Chad walked away from the train station, along a street in Bougival, curving down the hill toward the Turgenev Museum and the Seine. He'd come here because he could. He was familiar with the train line from too many school field trips, acquainted with the museum and the long lineage of the artist community. In this town on the Seine, Corot, Renoir, Morisot and Monet painted, the *literati* danced and drank at *La Grenouillere*, Bizet composed his music, Maupassant and Turgenev wrote novels, and Turgenev died. More pleasant, of course, without students traipsing behind him – or not, as the case may be – but he was moved by his many memories of Bougival. The first time he came here, he'd been nervous about finding the museum. He'd lectured his students as they walked about Turgenev, and how he had stalked the opera singer Pauline Viardot, and about "the boaters," the nineteenth-century Bohemians who adopted Bougival and lived on in the pages of literature and on the canvases of painters.

A trenchant thought jarred him this morning, as he came down the hill: that on this, his fortieth birthday, he was neither exile nor alien nor, perhaps, still an expatriate. Was it just a few weeks ago that he was fretting over these questions of identity? Wondering whether he belonged or not, whether he would ever be more than the outside? Today, he answered the questions, because at the age of forty, France felt as much like home to him as any place ever would – or could. Wasn't this how home felt? He stopped in his tracks, looking down on the blue-green Seine, and plumbed this sensation.

Forget his vaguely American accent, his French had better flourishes in it than some Frenchmen, he'd noticed that on the train, when he'd apologized for his watch's poor time-keeping by rattling off, "*je peux vous dire l'heure a cinq minutes pres.*" Who would have thought such a transmogrification possible for a boy from the South Plains? But it happened. Here, he knew his way around, knew which roads to take and which roads never to take, knew the places to see and the places to avoid, knew how to help and how to ask to be helped. He lived in France. Even if he lost his job at the school, he could live in France. He had a life here, and France was his home. How transitory it was – a blink of the eye, a rushing succession of moments. Just yesterday he had been a star student at Lubbock High School and now – well, here he was. Transitory it might be, but this head-long rush brought him a slowly-unfolding morning like this, rich with insight, beautiful with the memory of real sex, acute with self-awareness.

Chad realized that he no longer liked distance, or the life of an émigré. He liked connection; he liked feeling that he belonged, here, in this place, with these people, amid this culture. He stood in the heart of his tornado and savored something indescribable. Like a dish in which the ingredients were unknown – mysterious spices and herbs – he couldn't properly identify the thing he savored. But it was there in the combination of awareness, conclusion, beginning, and end. A sense of peace came over him and he walked on again, toward the museum. His battle to reach forty was over. And although his life as he'd thought he'd known it was in tatters, and although he could see no clear path to the future, for the first time in his life he felt a genuine sense of peace.

Roberta felt timeless. She couldn't take in the day of the week or the hour, couldn't tell if she was in the past or the future. Her identity seemed smudged. Her life had always made sense. There had been rules, which if followed gave life meaning and – well, what? *Value*, perhaps. But the rules had been a ruse, merely an illusion. Today, in this beautiful amalgam of a city, Roberta realized that there were no rules – and her life did not make sense. She wasn't lost, but neither she did not know where she was. Heading uphill from the apartment she had found herself among shops filled with African art objects and Cafés offering food from places she'd either never heard of or couldn't place geographically (*Côte d'Ivoire, Martinique, Bora Bora*). Street entertainers gathered around a square and its radiating side streets. Music wailed from a bar full of young people sporting such extravagances as tongue piercings, multi-colored hair, blonde cornrows and sleekly shaved skulls. Of course, she had not desired this boisterous dissonance, she had in fact desired leafy seclusion – maybe a quiet park bench. Several vendors tried to interest her in what looked like birds whirling on the end of strings.

Heat reached her from where a flame-thrower performed on the lip of a dry fountain. If life did not make sense, then it could certainly not have a plan. If there were no plan – then it might all be senseless, mightn't it? Oddly, she found this thought liberating. A month ago she could not even have imagined thinking such things, and realizing that made her smile. The flame-thrower – misunderstanding a woman's smile

– smiled back. This amused her even more, and gave her a sexual thrill and then she lusted – dear God did she *lust* – after Simon. She felt her body change at the commands of that lust, felt herself moisten and extend and ache. Coming down the hill behind the Pantheon, she quickly recognized her landmarks and found herself back on the steps of the apartment building. For a moment she paused there, exultant.

Looking back up the street, to where the Pantheon glinted in summer sunlight, she knew that however senseless her life might be, she had been alone in Paris and walked its streets with purpose. *That* made sense and pleased her, pleased her as much as the flame thrower's smile and the thought of making love with Simon – Simon who, even now, had within him the masses of wiggling sperm children she wished to bear and raise and send off to college and watch get married.

Imad lay on the bed, staring at the ceiling. The more he stared, the more he saw. He saw constellations and faces and continents. He'd never really looked at the ceiling like this, though once he thought of painting it. In fact, he had an blue scheme in mind. He would have *had* to look at the ceiling then, but as his project never happened, the ceiling remained undiscovered. Had anyone else ever looked like this at the eroding plaster? His discovery of it felt fiercely unprecedented. He missed Chad. Here he'd been toying with his own abandonment, accepting a job in Canada, and now he realized that he could never have done it. He would have panicked somewhere over Saskatchewan and flown back immediately. Hurt as he was by Chad's behavior he was more deeply moved by his discovery of how much he missed him. He hadn't missed him in Barcelona, but of course there was no worry then about real separation.

Yes, he truly missed Chad.

"No good can come from this lying around," Simon said.

"Where'd you come from?"

"I've been sitting out there for an hour. I have your key, remember? When no one answered after I buzzed, I took the liberty. I thought maybe you were sleeping, but I heard you stirring in the last few minutes."

"Roberta?"

"Out somewhere," Simon said, sitting on the edge of the bed and taking one of Imad's hands in his own. "I'm sorry he didn't come home last night, Imad – the bastard."

"I'm thinking about how much I miss him," Imad said. "That's what I've been lying in here doing – thinking about how much I miss him – how much I want him to come home."

"*Hey*?"

"Surprised you, didn't I?"

"Yes."

"The old tale, you don't know what you've got – *blah, blah, blah*."

"You're in a forgiving mood, I see."

"Not really – not forgiving. Something else." Imad rolled on his side and looked at Simon. "I feel sorry for him, Simon. The poor guy."

They looked at one another.

"It's funny how well you can understand someone else," Imad said, "so much more than you can understand yourself. I mean, I can feel all of Chad's needs as if they're right here," and he touched his chest.

"When you love someone their needs become your own. But mind," Simon said, "you weren't so empathetic yesterday."

"What a difference a day makes."

"And absence makes the heart grow fonder?"

"Yes," Imad said, "it does."

Simon put a hand against Imad's cheek. "I think he's a bloody great fool for cheating on you. And if it were me, I wouldn't be so forgiving and forgetting."

"I said I felt sorry. I didn't say anything about forgiving and forgetting."

"Me, well I feel sorry for *you*."

Imad looked at him. "Thanks, Simon."

"No problem. I can see that Aksel's been here, one of his incomprehensible Norwegian newspapers is out there on the table. It looks like somebody wrote English in a mirror."

"Careful now, you're starting to sound like Galsworthy. Aksel went to see if what's-his-name is home."

"Our naughty Sebastian? Probably 'bowling in Meudon' or 'bird watching in the Camargue.' Bloody great piece of Nordic mischief."

"Thanks again, Simon," Imad said. "You've been wonderful."

"It'll be all right," Simon said, "you'll see. It will all be fine in the end."

"I hope so."

185

Simon, as Roberta hoped, was waiting dutifully for her in Chad and Imad's living room. He kissed her with precisely the amount of passion she wanted, and then they went into her room and sat in each other's arms on the sofa.

"The cat house at the *Jardin des Plantes*."

She looked at him open-eyed.

"I wanted to say something that would catch you off guard."

"You did. What the heck's the cat house at the *Jardin des* – whatever?"

"*Des Plantes. The Fauverie*. It's on one of those posters of Imad's out there, my favorite one actually. Always sounds to me like a brothel, whores kicking up their heels amid the scents of gladioli."

She smiled.

"Ah," he pointed, "I have made the pretty girl smile."

She shrugged. "Has Chad told you the story of my great grandma?"

"Many times. Tornado lady."

"That's her. She committed suicide by running into a tornado – the weirdo. They found her spread-eagled about half a mile down the road, buck naked in the middle of somebody's cotton field. Imagine getting that news. Phone rings. 'Hi, it's – whoever the heck it is – grandma Bertha just took off running into that tornado you probably heard about up here to Lubbock, uh huh, she done thought it was God come for her. Yes, they done found her all buck naked down there to Avenue 11 by the railroad tracks.' Can you imagine? How *would* you grieve over that one?"

"Why are you talking to me about Bertha and the tornado?"

"I have my reasons," she said.

He put his arm around her shoulder and pulled her close. She closed her eyes against the smell of him, brittle and scrubbed, and against the masculine gravelly texture of his chin. When she leaned her head against his, it was as if she'd touched one of those electrified glass balls they used to roll out in science class, the sort that made your hair stand on end. They kissed, and then they kissed again, and then they stretched to full extension on the sofa and they continued to kiss.

"You –" she said.

Hands unpeeling her, he said into the hollow at the base of her neck, "– too."

Uncovered, she lay in his embrace, buried amid his chest hair and sweat, while his hand stroked her hair arm. It had of course been her first time and, despite those first sharp snorts of pain, magnificent. She'd never felt more womanly, more beautiful. Realizing how small she was after all, how narrow was the aperture through which he had to push and then ram, and the little bit of bleeding because he was so big and she was not, had – what? Made it all the more wonderful. She liked feeling small and vulnerable. Of course, after it hurt, it stopped hurting, and then it felt amazing, this movement there in her center, this awareness that it was Simon and that he was inside her, this knowledge that she had opened herself up to him completely.

"Whenever you're quiet, you can hear the clock ticking in this room," she said, her voice seeming to her muffled by the beating of Simon's heart.

"Comforting, lovey, like waves at the seashore, isn't it?"

"When I was a real little girl, I had a kitty, and she had to sleep for awhile in the bathtub with a clock wrapped up in a towel – because she thought it was her mama."

He kissed her. "Dogs for me, only dogs, mongrel bloody hounds who scavenged the neighborhood and terrorized Mrs. Ross, our next door neighbor."

"Poor Mrs. Ross."

"The Kaiser, my dad called her. Used to wear men's military trousers and prune her hedges of a Saturday afternoon, curse like a soldier and kick roots and soil into the road."

"And your dogs chasing after her?"

"They didn't bloody dare go into her garden, they watched her from our side until she headed down to the shops and then they set off nipping her heels." Then, changing gears, closing his eyes a moment and saying sleepily, "Here's one good thing to come from Chad's absence."

"What's the good thing?"

"This," he said, "us, together. His disappearance finally gave us our time together." He touched her lips with the gentlest kiss. "Chad going away – it shocked the future right into the present, didn't it? Made me want the present, what we just did, and a future – however we make that work out."

"And do you – want a future – together?" she murmured into his chest hair.

"I do, Roberta. I want you to marry me and have my children."

She pulled back and looked at him closely. "Y'all *do* know what you're saying, don't you? You haven't known me for more than a couple weeks."

"Now, would I resort to these time-honored clichés if I didn't mean what I was saying?"

She felt the warmth of her words come back at her off his skin. "You know it was my first time, don't you?"

"Pretty obvious, I'd say. And you're going to have to wash the sheets quickly or they'll be stained."

She held tighter against her and said his name as if it were an incantation. "*Simon.*"

And again he kissed her.

12

There it was again – the voice of Loreen K. Albrighton:

"Roberta, girl? You up there? Hey, up there? *Roberta*?"

Roberta leapt naked from Simon's arms and stood trembling in the middle of the room.

"Roberta?" Simon wondered.

"Quick, give me something to wear," she said and then, without waiting for his response, she grabbed his shirt from off of the back of the chair. Pulling it on, she ran into the living room, buttoning as she went.

"What on earth?" she heard Simon saying behind her.

"Here I am," Roberta said, coming through the *portes-fenetres* and out on to the balcony.

Looking up at her, Loreen said, "what in the blazes are you wearing?"

Roberta looked at one of the sleeves as if she wasn't quite sure. And then she said, "it's my boyfriend's shirt."

"Say *what*?"

"Where's Aunt Helen?"

189

"What's the matter with you anyway? Your hair's all a mess. Did I just wake you up? Isn't it nearly dinner time?"

"We weren't sleeping. I mean, we were in bed but we weren't asleep."

"Uh *huh*." Loreen's look could only be called slack-jawed. "I can see right up that thing by the way, and you ain't wearing no underwear, Roberta Martin."

"Well, don't look then," Roberta said, pulling the shirt up tight to her pelvis and shrinking back toward the open *porte-fenetre*.

"And what in the name of all that's holy do you mean, *my boyfriend*? Since when did you have a boyfriend?"

"Since for awhile now, his name's Simon. Where's Aunt Helen? You didn't answer me, Loreen." Roberta leaned forward and peered down *Rue des Bernardins*, expecting to see Helen lurking at the corner café or across the street in front of the bank. There was no sign of her, however.

"I'm getting the lay of the land first – checking around to see what's up. Which seems to be plenty, if you ask me. Chad up there with you?"

"We don't exactly know where he is just now."

"What's that mean to those of us who speak English?"

"He left yesterday."

"You mean he disappeared?"

"We're not sure," Roberta said with a sigh, feeling flustered and yet bolder. What did she have to fear anymore from Loreen K. Albrighton? "It's kind of complicated, Loreen."

"I'll just bet it is, missy, though something seems pretty uncomplicated to me and that's the fact that you're standing out here on public display without no underwear on. You ought to be ashamed of yourself, but of course you never are or you wouldn't have allowed yourself to become one of them plus sizes, would you?"

Just then Imad came out on to the balcony. "What on earth is going on out here?" he asked, looking at Roberta standing with one hand now holding the tails of Simon's shirt tight against her waist.

"Sweet merciful Jesus," Loreen said, "is that there your *boyfriend*?"

"No," Roberta said, "he's Chad's boyfriend. Imad, this is Loreen K. Albrighton, my Aunt Helen's friend."

"The K stands for Karlie," Loreen said. Then, as Roberta's words sank in, she brought her hand up to her chest as if she were having a heart attack. "He's Chad's *what*?"

"His boyfriend. Partner, I think you say now."

"Oh good gravy, this is heaps worse than what Helen said, she's no idea, no idea at all how bad it is. Mercy, mercy, *mercy* – get thee *behind me*, satan."

"Aunt Helen knows, Loreen."

"She don't or she would've said."

"Trust me," Roberta said, "she knows."

"We have a PACS," Imad said, "which means Chad and I are more or less married. So I suppose you could say he's my husband. That's probably most accurate."

"You have yourself a *what*?"

"A PACS. It's a French civil ceremony. By the way, pleased to meet you, Loreen Karlie Albrighton."

"Likewise, I guess. Excuse me, but are you a Mexican?"

"Pardon me?"

"Mexican," she repeated.

"I thought that was what you said. How strange. No," he said, "I'm French."

"You look Mexican."

"Well, I'm not. I'm French. I don't speak a word of Spanish."

"I'd ask you up," Roberta said, "but I don't really have Chad's permission."

"You mean to say you're going to leave me out here on the street?"

Roberta thought for a moment, closed her eyes as if to steady herself, opened them and said, "I guess I am. Sorry about that, Loreen. Will you tell Aunt Helen to give me a call before she leaves?"

"Well, if that ain't the sassiest mouth I ever did hear. I sure as heck hope you know what you're doing, Roberta girl, because Lubbock County isn't big enough to hide your shame once I tell people how I seen you with some Mexican homosexual up on a balcony in Paris with no underpants on."

Simon stepped out just then, shirtless, wearing only a pair of jeans. "Roberta?" he asked, taking her hand and bringing it to his lips for a kiss.

"Loreen, this here's my boyfriend Simon and he isn't Mexican either in case you're wondering – he's Australian."

"Hiya," Simon said. "And you'd be?"

"I'd be shocked all to hell and back, that's what I'd be," Loreen said, looking Simon over. Loreen liked men who looked like Simon. She once developed a crush on an usher at church, because she'd seen him in a swimsuit one summer out at the Texas Tech swimming pool and, according to her, his hairy chest and muscles about drove her crazy. In fact, she stalked him every Saturday morning while he did his shopping at the United

Market, and Helen finally had to tell her flat out that if she mentioned Roland Duvall's chest one more time she'd ban her from her house. So Roberta knew Loreen was a good judge of sexy male chests like Simon's. "Y'all can't possibly be Roberta's boyfriend."

"Actually, to clarify, I think I'm her fiancé. Roberta?"

"Yes," Roberta said. "That's right. We're engaged."

"You're engaged to *him*?"

"Yes."

"I'm sorry," Loreen said, "but as I live and die that can't be true. I mean, honest to God, there ain't nobody who looks like that who's going jump your bones back in Lubbock, Roberta Matin."

"Which is at least one reason why I'm glad I'm Paris," Roberta said. "It finally made me a woman."

Loreen gave them a disgusted face and made a little spitting noise, as if against the evil eye.

"Ah, right then," Simon observed. "I see now. You're part of the bring Chad back to Texas contingent."

"But where's Aunt Helen?" Roberta asked again. "Is she at   a   hotel?"

"Never you mind about that. You'll see your Aunt Helen soon enough, and when you do I reckon –"

"Loreen Karlie Albrighton, you wrinkled up old battle-axe," Chad said, coming down the street behind her.

"*Chad*," Roberta exclaimed. Then turning to Imad, "look, Imad, it's Chad."

"I can see that," Imad said.

"So I see you've met everyone," Chad said.

"I sure as heck have. Your Mexican boyfriend and all. And I ain't neither wrinkled up and I'm not the one standing here for all the world to see without no panties on."

"I'm glad to know that, Loreen. You go ahead and keep your panties on, that sounds like a good idea to me. And Imad? Mexican? Hardly. His parents came here from Morocco, although Imad himself is French."

Loreen looked at Chad, then up at the balcony, then back again at Chad. "*Moroccan*? Like those terrorists who hit the twin towers? Oh, my lord – oh, my *God*."

"He's Muslim," Chad said, "but he's not a terrorist. At least not that I know of. I suppose that's the kind of thing you'd keep to yourself. You coming up for coffee, Loreen?"

"I most certainly am not. I'm heading straight back to – well, I'm going back to talk to your mama. And if she's still alive after I've made my report, we'll talk then about whether or not we come up for coffee or if maybe we just come up there and have us an *exorcism*." Then, startled, she nearly shrieked, "oh, land's sake, I didn't see you sneak up like that. What a pretty dog."

"He wishes he could say the same, don't you, Alhambra?" Galsworthy said, "but alas, Dachshunds weren't bred for deceit."

"You one of this gang?" Loreen said, still staring at Alcazar, who had been joined now by Alhambra.

"I suppose I am, like it or not. I see you've returned, you wicked boy."

"Hi, Galsworthy."

With a toss of his head, Galsworthy asked, "and just who are you, *madame*, speaking in a voice that would wake the dead with an accent that would kill them if they weren't already dead."

"Excuse me?"

"I could hear you abusing poor Roberta from down on the Boulevard St. Germain."

"And I could hear her from inside my shower," Aksel said from his balcony, "I thought that someone had been leaving their television on too loud – and I can't even hear the doorbell or Sebastien screaming when I'm in that shower, that's how loud she was talking." He waved and everyone except Loreen waved back.

"I thought the boys detected the smell of herring," Galsworthy said, "they get those perky ears."

"We have no herring," Aksel said.

"Then lumpfish or scrod, the boys don't discriminate between whitefish, I'm afraid."

"Lord, what a nest of something-or-anothers this is," Loreen snapped. She looked back up at Roberta. "You're going to be one sorry fat girl, missy, once Helen gets wind of these shenanigans." Then looking at Galsworthy she said more politely, "Loreen K. Albrighton, the K. stands for Karlie, and I wouldn't mind getting the name of the breeder."

"His name is Simon, he's the only breeder here, darling. Practically the only one left on this pink little street these days. He can give you his own address."

"What are y'all talking about? Lord have mercy. I mean for them, those dogs, I'd like me a pair of those dogs. What are they anyway?"

"German hounds. Long-haired Dachshunds to be exact."

"Beautiful things, aren't they?"

"Yes," Galsworthy said, "they are." Then, "is it my imagination, Roberta my dear, or are you standing there naked except for one of Simon's manly chemises?"

"How can you be naked if you're wearing something?" Roberta asked. "Everybody wants to say I'm naked, but you can't be naked unless – unless you're naked."

"Come on," Chad said to Galsworthy, "you might as well join my birthday party. Provided I'm still having one." He looked up at Imad.

Imad shrugged with prolonged deliberation, "Look, before you come in. I had a phone call from Etienne, so I know – about all that. Everyone knows, in fact."

Another deliberation, as Chad considered this information. "I'm not going to lie about it."

"What's to lie about? I just told you we knew."

"I only meant –"

A breathy gentleness came into Imad's voice. "Look, I felt in fairness that I ought to tell you – that I already knew. That's all. If you want to call it quits, now's the moment, Chad. I'm sure you know the way back to Etienne's."

"I don't, Imad. I don't want to call it quits. That's why I'm here."

Yet another long pause.

"At least you're safe and I don't have to go and look for your body in the morgue, fished out of the Seine all bloated and nasty – that's a relief. Happy birthday, by the way."

"Thanks."

"Yes, sir, *uh huh*," Loreen said, clutching her purse and heading up the street toward the Pantheon, "ain't it just a *big old* relief." Over her shoulder she tossed, "and if it isn't too much trouble for you, Mr. Galsworthy, sir, I'd thank you kindly if you'd write down that name and phone number for me. I'd like to buy me a pair of them long-haired German hounds."

Chad woke up with a start and immediately noticed Imad' absence.

Through the *portes-fenetres* the extinguishing moon-lit sky seemed fretfully eloquent. He got up, put on a t-shirt and shorts and went out to the living room. The note in its envelope was propped on the mantle. He didn't really need to read it; he knew what it would say. But of course he opened it, and while Imad seemed neither accusatory nor angry, he said that he gone to stay with his sister and her husband in the 8th. He'd taken what he thought he would need for awhile. They would talk soon. With a sigh Chad sat down hard on the sofa and stared out into the morning.

Yesterday he had emerged from the tunnel of his pre-birthday misery feeling complete, wanting to turn over new leaves. Although Imad had been aloof at their dinner party last night, he'd given away nothing about leaving. He had either packed in silence or had already packed and his bag had been ready to go. Chad wished now that they'd had a clarifying fight. He wished Imad had hurled a plate at him or pitched the *gâteau* on the floor. They'd gone to bed with chaste kisses, (but kisses all the same), and now he was gone. Admittedly, he had gone only to the 8th arrondissement, and to a place Chad knew, off elegant *rue Montaigne*. Yet his sense of abandonment was as real as if Imad had flown off to somewhere. Chad read Imad' few calm lines gain and then, to stop himself using the note like a tongue on a toothache, he crumpled it up and threw it into the corner of the room.

His eyes filled with tears and he leaned his head back against the wall. What did he gain if he defeated his ghosts and rebuffed his mother but lost Imad? Leaning forward, burying his head in his hands, he sobbed. He sobbed not because he was growing older, and not because of any of the other things which had bedeviled him for too long. He sobbed because Imad was gone and he missed him. He sobbed because he had felt himself to be in control and he was wrong. He sobbed because he had not foreseen this. Coming to grips with his age, his mortality and his sense of identity did not in the least mean that he was in control.

That's why he sobbed.

196

"You look like some stupid fat girl what's gone and lost her virginity, that's exactly what you look like, Roberta Martin, some happy heathen on her way to hell, just like those idiot Democrats when they had that fundraiser down to the South Plains Mall last year and got drunk as skunks and groped that poor salesgirl from Muleshoe – of course, she was uglier than the backside of a horse and probably encouraged them, but that doesn't excuse it. Remember that picture of them in the paper? The one I put up on the refrigerator, so's we wouldn't forget? Well, that's just what you look like sitting here, like someone smirking her way straight to Hades. Yes, ma'am, you are indeed one shameful slut," Helen said.

"I see Loreen K. Albrighton – the K stands for *kook* – has made herself some kind of report."

"Which is more than you did, you hussy, standing around on balconies without no underpants on."

"I figured that would get top billing."

Helen gave her an unyielding stare.

"For crying out loud, Aunt Helen, I wasn't standing around. We were in *bed* and I heard that – that creature calling from out in the middle of the road like some stevedore down to Galveston. Why in the heck can't she just ring the bell like a normal person? Chad's last name is right there by the button. Even in Lubbock she's always opening the front door and screaming her way into the entrance hall, that's how I burned myself so bad that time on my curling iron, hearing her banshee voice when I just came of the shower and was getting ready for work. I liked to jump ten feet."

"No fat woman's going to be jumping ten feet in this lifetime and right now you are just about the last person on God's green earth to be judging *anybody*. And '*we were in bed*' my foot you brazen piece of work, when it was nearly dinner time. Y'all sure as heck weren't sleeping, that's for sure."

"I didn't say we were sleeping, did I? And I wasn't judging, I was asking."

"Sounded like judging to me." Helen said, finally sitting beside Roberta on the bench.

Roberta had been sitting alone for the better part of half an hour in *Place Paul Langevin*, in the park where *rue des Bernardins* terminated at *rue des Ecoles* and the Ministry of Defense. It had in fact occurred to her as she sat there that Helen and Loreen might be staying in any of the two or three star hotels in the vicinity. After all, it made sense that Helen would position herself close to the potential scene of action, and it explained Loreen's quick disappearing act yesterday. Whatever else you might say about Helen, she wasn't stupid. Roberta had learned that lesson all too well over the years. Yet despite those passing thoughts about Helen and Loreen (and Loreen's horrendous visit), Roberta had essentially been

197

thinking about herself and Simon and not about her original mission to bring Chad back to West Texas.

That mission seemed like a life time ago. It seemed as if it involved someone else.

Roberta had never aspired to having sex with a man like Simon, never aspired to such skillful lovemaking, nor – any of it, including his use of a condom (where *did* that thing come from, just like that, out of nowhere?), a device she'd only ever seen advertised discretely and rather ethereally in *Cosmopolitan*. Lubbock wasn't a place where condoms were much talked about and they weren't even demonstrated in sex education classes. Sex education classes were few and far between in West Texas, and when they did occur they were chiefly motivated by a Christian "just say no" abstinence philosophy. This was the same philosophy that had worked so well for Nancy Reagan and drugs, wasn't it? 'Just say no' sure did clear drugs right off the streets, Roberta thought.

More than anything else, Roberta's love for Simon (because it wasn't just about sex, of course) bowled her over utterly. Love was something to which she had (truthfully, cards on the table) aspired even less than sex. She had spent a lifetime wanting love and then, when she was no longer searching for it, not toadying for favor or running errands or blow-drying Helen's rat's nest of a hairdo in the hope of receiving some few affirming words of affection, love found *her*. However much she might now try to persuade Helen of the truth, it would forever *be* the truth that Roberta came to Paris with the intention of bringing Chad home, not having sex and certainly not falling in love. She had not pursued Simon. Love, sex and Simon had pursued her – it was an indisputable fact.

Traffic and pedestrians passed by, including a silly-looking American family from somewhere Roberta imagined must be a lot like Lubbock, with hefty big thigh bulk (which put her to shame), ludicrous backpacks and money belts. They just flat out looked ignorant. No wonder the French turn up their noses at us, she decided, sitting there in the *Place Paul Langevin*, a self-righteous nation of unstylish fat religious people, bibles and guns. What must this civilized culture have thought of that silly performance by Charlton Heston, the one Aunt Helen ordered in a special collector's edition DVD from the NRA, the one where he held up a gun with American flags and other patriotic rigmarole behind him and said something stupid like, "from my cold dead hands." How many times had Helen made her watch that embarrassing thing?

"It's no wonder the French hate us," Roberta said to Helen, "I mean, just look at them," and she gestured toward the passing husband, wife and two daughters, "big old self-righteous country full of unstylish fat people, bibles and guns."

Helen looked as if she'd been slapped. Her mouth seemed almost to hang slack. She stared at Roberta as if at a stranger. It took her several moments to regain her composure and when she did she said sharply, "still with them judgments, I see."

Roberta shrugged. "I guess. So what's your plan now, Helen?"

"My plan? Well now, part of it's getting back the money I gave you, you thief. Talk about false pretenses. You take the cake for false pretenses, missy. Yup, at the moment I figure y'all aren't no better than a thief."

"I'm not a thief."

"Tell that to the judge."

"What judge?"

"The one what's going to put you in shackles and throw you in prison for me."

"And just how are you going to do that? Oh, that's right, y'all are reporting me over to the embassy. I can't remember now what it is y'all are planning to say, Aunt Helen — something to the Marine guard about me being a terrorist? That's it, I remember now. But if I'm sitting down there to jail in Guantanemo Bay, how the heck are you going to collect any money from me?"

"I got me a good attorney back in Lubbock. He'll have your big butt in front of a judge so fast your head will swim, just you wait and see."

"How's this good attorney of yours going to do that if I'm not in Lubbock?"

"Oh you'll be back in Lubbock sure enough, smarty pants. Oh yes you will."

Again Roberta shrugged.

"You think a man what's been using you is going to keep you around? You aren't nothing but a plaything, Roberta, and you'll feel his shoe on your enormous backside all too soon."

"Do I *look* like a plaything, Aunt Helen?"

"You look easy, that's how you look. Which, I point out, you are."

"I am not."

"Well, it seems like you jumped out of them triple extra large panties pretty darned fast. And I've seen in them in my laundry plenty of times, what with you always over there using up my electricity and laundry detergent, so don't tell me they aren't triple extra large either. Yup, desperate and easy, that's what you are. Lord, there isn't nothing like a desperate old virgin when it comes to easy. Men know that, you got *easy* written all over you. That's precisely what happened to that fool Mamie Sue Rogers out to Tahoka, the one who got herself pregnant from the carpet man who came to show her samples? As if she needed special order-it-up fancy carpet in a double-wide trailer anyway. Heck, if that salesman didn't take one look at her and figure, 'this old virgin's just about the easiest thing I ever laid eyes on.' You know, he must have been a Mexican that carpet salesman, because I swear that child of hers has some kind of permanent tan, don't he?"

"He could have been Moroccan?"

"Huh?"

"The carpet salesman."

"I meant More-what-un?"

"Moroccan, like Imad, Chad's boyfriend. He's from Morocco."

"I ought to slap you for that."

"For what? For saying boyfriend or saying Morocco."

Helen glared at her.

200

"And I'd be careful if I was you, Aunt Helen. I might slap back this time."

Once more Helen looked stunned.

But before she could offer any response Roberta said, "just once in my life I wish I could have a conversation with you like I was an equal. And before you say that I'm not your equal, which I can just about hear coming out of your mouth this very minute – well, I *am*, even if I didn't get to go to school or anything, thanks to you and your stinginess. I am your equal and I'm not fat and I'm not butt ugly."

A profoundly awkward moment extended for some minutes. Rather than look at her, Helen looked up into the trees, where there seemed to be an explosion of birdsong. When she did at last turn back to Roberta it seemed as if her eyes were moist. "You probably don't know it, because of the way I am most of the time, but I love you all to pieces, Roberta."

"I don't think you do," Roberta said. "You're just saying it now because you still need me or something, that's all. I used to think you loved me a little bit, or maybe I just hoped it, but I don't do either one anymore – I don't think it and I don't hope for it."

"You think I'm selfish, you think I only care about myself."

Roberta shrugged in acquiescence.

"Well, I know it seems like it," Helen said. "And who knows, I am selfish sometimes and I have learned to look after myself in the best way I know how."

"By being mean and snake mouthed?"

"Who's being mean now?"

"You lied to me about why you wanted Chad back and you knew all kinds of stuff that you never bothered to tell me – about him being gay and living with Imad, about all of it. You made me look like a fool, barging in here without knowing anything." Again Roberta snipped off any possible reply. "Which I am not, whatever you say. I'm not a fool. I may be naïve and I might be prepared to believe stuff I shouldn't, but I'm not a fool, so don't you dare say it."

Helen looked back up into the trees. The birds were eclipsed by the passage of several police cars, their sirens warbling, blue lights flashing. "I couldn't hardly come live in Paris, could I?" Helen said. "And I don't want to grow old without my son around me. It isn't natural. I wanted him to come home — it seemed like a reasonable thing. But I couldn't think how to do it. So I sent you."

"And of course he wouldn't talk to you or answer anything you wrote — and why do you think that is, Aunt Helen? When a grown man doesn't speak to his own mama, it seems like you'd do a heck of a lot of soul searching about it. *Huh*?"

"You don't think I have?"

"Honestly? No, ma'am, I do not think you have."

"You'd be wrong about that, Miss Roberta. I've wrung myself inside out about it."

"So your solution was to tell me some fib about how you were dying of diabetes and try to trick him into coming back? Presumably alone and ready to go into one of those concentration camps where they convert gay people into some kind of no-sex monsters like what we saw that time on *Sixty Minutes*? Those poor pitiful fools looking like goofs and spouting nonsense, that's what you want for Chad?"

"They are not concentration camps, they're re-education programs and they work real good according to our preacher. Why, I know of at least —"

"Save it, Aunt Helen. I don't want to hear it."

"But —"

"No, ma'am, I don't want to hear it."

Helen looked sidewise at her, then she said, "I do have diabetes."

"Maybe," Roberta said, no longer prepared even to cede that ground.

"I was grasping at straws."

"Whatever. Look. Even if we can't be equals, I'd like it very much if you stopped calling me names and all. I'd settle for that, Helen. And if it means so darned much to you, then figure out what you think I owe you and I'll find a way to pay you back a little bit each month — it isn't any problem with your credit card, you can have that back right now, I have it hidden underneath a stack of towels back in Chad's apartment. Just stop calling me names and trying to make me feel bad."

"I don't know why I do that, you know. Maybe I am just a mean old witch."

"Maybe you are," Roberta agreed.

Helen sighed, eyes closed. "You weren't supposed to agree to that."

"I know."

Opening her eyes, Helen said, "I'd miss you something awful, Bertie, if you weren't around. I can't even imagine what it'd be like to go on living in Lubbock without you."

"You and Loreen K. Albrighton would do just fine."

Helen shook her head.

"Think about what it would be like for me now. That hateful old battle-axe Loreen would be calling me down for the rest of my born days. There wouldn't be *nobody* from the hairdresser to the mailman who didn't know I'd been running around over here without my panties on and cavorting with 'all sorts,' you know that. Even if I wanted to, I can't see how I could go back home to Lubbock now."

"Does that mean you don't want to?"

"I don't rightly know what I want just this minute," Roberta said.

"I can handle Loreen if that's really what's worrying you. I got me enough dirt on her to keep her quiet for about six generations."

This time Roberta sighed. "I for sure don't want you blackmailing Loreen so that I can come back and work some stupid part-time job in the library and do your grocery shopping for you and — oh, for crying out loud, whatever," she said, "it doesn't matter. I'd sooner live in Dallas or Detroit or even *Los Angeles* than go back home to Lubbock right now."

"I thought you were planning to marry that Australian y'all have been sleeping with."

"Loreen got that much right I see."

"Well?"

"Well that's my business, isn't it? And I don't want to count any chickens before they hatch, Aunt Helen. Okay, I'm thinking I might marry Simon – he asked me and I said yes, that's true. But there's a long way to go between here and there. Though I am not a shameful slut and I won't have you saying it. I'm in love and whatever the heck it is that sluts do, they don't do it because of being in love."

"I don't think you're a slut."

"I said I won't have you saying it – but I really don't give a hoot what you *think*. What you think is your own business. I just don't want to hear it, that's all."

"Don't leave me all alone, Roberta. Please."

It was quiet a moment or two and even the birdsong seemed suspended. Then with a note of some wonder in her voice, Roberta said, "now that's the most you ever sounded like maybe you was talking to an equal."

Helen nodded. "Of course you're my equal. Goodness, Bert, you're my own flesh and blood. You're as much a daughter as Chad is a son, as God's my witness."

204

"If I'm as much a daughter as he is a son, then I guess I shouldn't be talking to you either."

"Oh," Helen said, with a sharp intake of breath. "Okay then, *touché*."

"*En garde* then too, Helen, because I wouldn't trust you if you said the earth goes round the sun."

"That's not very forgiving."

"You want forgiveness? I can do forgiveness. Heck, forgiving is easy. But trust is something completely different. I can forgive you right now, here on this bench, for every mean and nasty thing you ever said and did, and –"

"*Did*?"

"Oh, for crying out loud, yes, *did*. Lord have mercy, the list is so long it'd be bigger than the entire phone book. Take the time you let the air out of my bicycle tires, and then you said they'd done exploded because I was too fat. You were trying to punish me because I'd taken up being friends with that new girl

Cathy, whose mother didn't invite you to some kind of party over to the club. I heard you on the phone about that to Loreen. You were trying to teach me a lesson, I guess, or maybe you was just being mean – or both, I don't know. But heck, I forgive you for that and every other damn thing you ever done to me."

Helen winced slightly at the 'damn,' but said nothing about it. With a quizzical look, she said, "how'd you know I let the air out of them tires?"

"Cause you forgot to put one of the screw caps back on – and there was fingernail polish on the other one. I didn't have to be Sherlock Holmes to figure that one out."

"So how come you didn't say anything if you knew about it?"

"You would have denied it. And you would have said something else mean to me. It was just flat out better that I said nothing about all the stuff you did – the things of mine you threw away or broke, the stuff you hid, the nasty things you said to my face and the nastier things you said behind my back. You think there are any secrets in Lubbock, Texas? Heck sakes, Helen, you'd tell something ugly about me to Loreen one day and the next day some big-haired fool with too much make-up on down to the library would be repeating it to me word for word." Once again Roberta sighed. "Anyway, I forgive you, Helen. I forgive you everything. But I don't trust you and I never will trust you. Never. Period."

"Somebody's waving at you," Helen said.

"Oh, that's my friend Torvald Aksel, but we just call him Aksel. *Aksel*," Roberta cried out to him, "come on over." As he did she whistled, "that's a real pretty shirt you got on there."

"Thank you. Galsworthy says it will shrink because I bought it at Spontini."

"*Pooh*. What does it matter where you bought it? Cotton's cotton. Cold water wash and then hang it up in a doorway, it'll be right back like that in a jiffy. Cotton only shrinks because people roast the be-jeepers out of it in dryers. Dryers are not kindly to cotton." Since Aksel was now only several feet from them Roberta said, "Aksel, this here is Chad's mother

205

Helen. Helen, this is just about my best friend in all of Paris, his name's Aksel and he's a Norwegian."

For a moment it seemed that Helen might roll her eyes or make some other sort of comment, since she was bound to have an opinion on Norwegians. But she didn't, she bit her tongue, smiled as pleasantly as if she were attending a barbecue at the Lakeridge Country Club and said, "Hi. Are y'all the one with them pretty dogs Loreen was talking about?"

Aksel looked for a moment at his feet, thinking that perhaps she meant his new red shoes, then realizing what she meant he said, "that is a man named Galsworthy, who does not resemble me in the least and I am thankful for that fact."

"Me too," Roberta said, laughing, "me too, Aksel." Then standing up she said to Helen, "you have no business being here, Aunt Helen. This isn't no place for you. Y'all are the one with judgments and – well, where Chad's concerned, you are as wrong as wrong can be."

At that Helen stood up as well, flushed with indignation, no longer cowed into any kind of submission. Something in Roberta's assault had clearly changed her attitude. "Oh no, I'm *not*."

'You are. I don't hold with them bible-thumping beliefs of yours no more. I don't believe for a second that Chad's a sinner or that anything he and Imad do together is wrong."

"Then y'all are a sinner too," Helen said, passionately. "I may be a mean old bitch, but I know the difference between right and wrong, even if you don't. I'll never be convinced that sin is right. And," she said, hitting Roberta with her words as if with bullets, "my only son is a sinner and he's going straight to hell. I was a fool to come over here, I see that now – I wasted all that money and I even paid for Loreen's ticket. What's the use – let him wallow here in his own filth. Why not? If he chooses sin, then let him choose sin." She glared at Roberta.

Roberta looked back at her, saying, "you've no idea how good Imad is, Aunt Helen, how good he is for Chad."

"If you can even breathe that man's name to me, the man who's stolen my son from me into a life of sin, then – well then, I congratulate you on choosing sin over righteousness, Roberta Martin."

"I haven't either done that."

"You have too – you blasphemous old blimp."

Roberta ignored this return to the cruel words she had known for so many long years. "You don't think Chad's even a little bit – *lucky* – to have everything he and Imad have? Don't you think he's a little fortunate?"

"*Fortunate*? I think the whole ever-loving thing is hideous – worse than I could ever have imagined for a child of mine. And by the way, that credit card I gave you? You can just cut it up with scissors, Roberta, because I wouldn't so much as touch the envelope you mailed it back in. Good day," she said to Aksel, clutching her purse and marching off toward the street.

"Good day to you too," Aksel said. He turned to Roberta, "She may be wrong about many things but she is correct when she says that she is a mean old bitch."

"Oh yes," Roberta said softly, "she is – and for all I know she'll turn out to have been correct about more things than I give her credit."

13

"Hello, mom," Chad said. "How are you doing, besides dying of diabetes and all – Roberta's lost some weight and, oh yeah, by the way, I'm not coming home so stop trying." He found them in the hotel lobby with their luggage, Roberta having reported to him where they were staying on the *Boulevard St. Germain*. Apparently Aksel had earlier seen Loreen dart through the doorway in a pair of sunglasses and a scarf on her head.

"Get out of my way," Helen hooted.

Chad looked at her.

"I mean it," Helen said. "That there's our taxi. Come on, Loreen, get a move on."

"You're leaving without talking to me?" Chad asked.

"Looks like it."

"So then why –"

"We all make mistakes – and this was one big old mistake, *that's* why. Every dang bit of it was a mistake, sending that flabby freak Roberta and coming all this way with poor Loreen, trying to eat that shriveled up junk on the airplane and whatever the Hades it is they've been trying to give us over here for breakfast – a mistake, all of it."

He remained speechless.

"You getting out of my way or what?"

He stepped aside, allowing her to wheel her suitcase, with its pink yarn for better identification on the luggage carousel, toward the door. As she was reaching for the handle he said, "my God, you're a horrible woman."

She snapped her head around, eyes venomous. Loreen's hand fluttered bird-like with nervousness before it rested on Helen's upper arm.

"How *dare* you," Helen hissed.

"How dare I what?"

Helen made a clicking noise that reminded Chad of a rattlesnake or scorpion.

"Are you daring me to repeat it?" he asked. "Because I will."

"You ever hear the one about people in glass houses?"

"Meaning I'm living in one?"

"I don't want to have this conversation. I already decided I wasn't having this conversation, didn't I, Loreen? I've made my peace with all this – well, with all this whatever it is – and that's all I'll say by way of describing it. You can call me what you want, you and fatso up there without her panties on. Go ahead, sit around and call me down, Mr. Smarty Pants. I don't give a flying you know what. I'm not concerning myself no more with sinners."

"I don't get it. You spend all of those frigging years trying to lure me back to West Texas with your subterfuge letters and – whatever the hell else you've done – and Roberta tells me you two actually had a moment or two of real bonding yesterday in the park, and now – this. I don't get it."

"*Bonding*?" she said scornfully. "No, sir. I had me a moment of weakness while we were talking, that's what I had. There wasn't any bonding. And I for sure don't want her thinking there was. She managed to get me all confused for a couple of minutes, that's all."

"Well," he shrugged, "I still don't understand."

"Then don't. Big deal. You can add it to the long list of stuff you don't understand – like how to live a decent life."

They stared assessingly at one another for a long time – a lost lifetime perhaps. Meanwhile, Loreen and the hotel staff, some of whom were now translating the drama for others, observed this lengthy assessment.

"Okay. All right," Chad said at last, the one to break eye contact. "Your taxi's waiting. Don't let me keep you, mom."

Helen closed her eyes and tears, real tears, slipped down her cheeks. Again Loreen's hand held her upper arm, but this time Helen pushed it away. "Leave me alone," she said. "I don't want your pity, you numbskull. Go get in the taxi." Loreen scuttled out toward the waiting car, and Helen said. "This is it, Chad. I mean, this is *it*. There's no more," she seemed to search

210

for words and then with a righteous shake of her head, she spat, "*anything* between us – not now. After this, it's over. Don't you ever call me mom again, not even in your dreams. You understand?"

"What's not to understand? Sounded pretty clear to me – but newsflash, you are my mother, even if –"

"Nope – wrong. Newsflash yourself. I am not your mother because I disown you. As far as I'm concerned, I never had any children. I won't even think about you no more – and I'll throw everything away. Fact is, I should have thrown that crap out years ago. All those posters and junk from high school, they're every single one of them going into the dumpster – just as soon as I get home."

This time Chad's eyes teared up, but he didn't say anything.

"If you ever repent and come back to the Lord, then you let me know and we can talk. Failing that, you're dead to me – and that goes for that sneaky fat thief Roberta too. She's deader than a doornail to me."

"How on earth can you –"

"Same way you ignored me all those years. What have I been if not dead to you? *Huh*? Thought you were so damned smart, didn't you? Treating me like dirt? Not answering anything I sent – not so much as a word. Haven't I been dead to you? So I guess I'm just giving you what you wanted all along."

"Okay," he said.

"Okay," she said back.

"Then why are both of us crying?"

"Who the heck knows," she said. "Because the good Lord doesn't want it to be this way, I guess – but it is and that's that."

"And that's that," he echoed. He shrugged and then, when the taxi driver honked his horn, he pointed again out the door. "You want me to tell Roberta she's dead to you."

"I don't care what you tell her. Tell her I said that bad blood will out and her daddy was never anything but white trash, I knew it all along. I told her mama she was marrying into trash right up to the day of her wedding – you tell Roberta *that*."

"Don't think I will, actually."

It was Helen's turn to shrug. "You're going to burn in hell, by the way – say 'howdy' to your Uncle Earl for me when you get there."

"I'm not, mom – going to hell, I mean."

"Think again," she said, opening the door, "because you'll be roasting for all eternity." Over her shoulder, her Parthian shot, she said, "if it were the Christian thing to do, I'd hate you – I'd hate you so hard it cut you all to ribbons like glass – but it isn't, so the best thing I can do is erase you from my life. So you are erased, Chad. *Erased*."

With that she was out the door, pushing her bag at the taxi driver and climbing in beside Loreen, who was this time allowed to put her arm around Helen's quivering shoulder. Getting in behind the wheel, the driver roared down the street and out of sight.

212

"I'm sorry, Imad. You know?"

Imad didn't look at him. Instead, sipping his tea he asked, "Do you remember how we said we'd buy a place in Tuscany? But, then, it seemed like – what? – Tuscany had become too popular, so we played with the idea of Provence, and God knows *it* became like a London garden suburb, and then we thought of Corsica or Sardinia –"

"I remember looking at that place in Sardinia where it was about 40 degrees in the shade."

"And I remember when you still told the temperature in Fahrenheit. But my point, Chad, is that none of our plans bore fruit. They didn't – what? I mean, keeping to the fruit metaphor, they never ripened."

"Sounds like Oscar Wilde," Chad said, "Chasuble and Prism."

"Beginning of Act Two, yes, I know the reference – but I'm being serious," Imad said. "So – *please*?"

"They weren't plans exactly," Chad said.

"No?"

"No."

Chad had gone unannounced to Imad's sister's place in the 8th, where she seemed almost to expect him. Holding a finger to her lips, she led him to the study in which Imad had taken up residence. Amid the brocaded extravagance of his sister's décor, he found Imad sipping tea and staring out the *portes-fenetres*.

"Then what *would* you call them?" Imad asked.

"Musings maybe. Imaginings."

"Imaginings can be plans. You know, I'm sure this will sound precious – but, it's that whole Hamlet thing, we've talked about it before, from the Act III soliloquy, the dreams in life and the dreams in death. Our dreams aren't alive anymore, Chad. They've died. All our dreams have died."

"We were young when we talked about these things; there was more life ahead of us. And, anyway, it's always the young ones who dream."

"If you stop dreaming, you die."

They looked at one another.

"Maybe you do," Chad said. "Maybe it works that way. The young dream and live, the old don't and die."

Imad seemed to shudder. "But *is* that how it works, Chad?" He looked for a moment at the blossoming horizon. "When I found you were cheating on me again, I –"

"Again?"

"Don't make me list them."

Chad turned away, his eyes smarting. "There's no list, Imad."

"More than one makes a list," Imad said, "and I keep good records. Look Chad, I want you to know a few things. First of all, Simon kissed me."

"*Our* Simon?" Chad said, turning back to Imad. After a moment of confused silence he said, "Roberta's Simon?"

"Yes, the one and the same Simon – who apparently belongs to all of us."

"But why? He kissed you? Isn't he –?"

"Straight? Oh yes. I'm sure he's as straight as a Roman road. That's all it was between us, just a kiss, but it was – meaningful. And memorable. I need to come clean, because it was – and will always be – memorable."

They looked intensely at one another. Chad closed his eyes to the idea of Simon and Imad kissing. Yet, the justice in it was inescapable.

"And, while I am on this coming clean campaign," Imad said, "I should tell you that I was offered a job in Canada. In British Columbia."

"When?" Chad asked. "To be offered a job you must have applied for a job – and a long time ago at that."

"Not so long ago."

Chad sat silently.

"I'm sorry," Imad said at last.

"For –?"

"For Simon, for letting him kiss me – or for causing him to kiss me if you will, and wanting more from it, and for – not telling you about Canada."

Ignoring Canada and everything it meant, Chad asked, "Just how much more *did* you want from Simon?"

"I don't know. More – at any rate."

"Okay," Chad said, "so now you've come clean."

"If we're going to – well, it seemed important."

"Sometimes I fall into the ignorance is bliss camp," Chad said.

"Do you? I don't think you do, Chad. You always want to know everything. Remember that song we heard once? I wish I didn't know now what I didn't know then – or something like that?"

"You're right about me, and ignorance doesn't work – you always find out about things sooner or later."

"Better from me than Galsworthy."

"Infinitely."

"I love Paris," Imad said, "I mean I love the life I'm able to live here, the richness, the feel, the light and the dark of it, weather and people and places and things, so many things, my things, our things, a whole complete life full of things."

Chad stood up and walked to the *portes-fenetres*. "Me too — I like what we've made here. But it wasn't something I dreamed of, the way people do, you know, as in, 'I love Paris and hope to live there.' It just happened."

"Not for me. For me, it was deliberate. It was always my dream," Imad said. "All the time I was growing up it was my dream to be an artist in Paris — to fall in love and live there and paint there, make something new of myself in Paris with — a man."

"That's a hell of dream for a Muslim boy from the projects."

"Do you *think*?"

Chad gave a small laugh. "Then your dream came to pass, if not our collective chattering about a place in Tuscany or Provence, at least your own dream of a life in Paris with the man you love, painting pictures. *Huh*?'

"It did, Chad. Yes. That dream came true."

"Whereas for me, well, it was simply an opportunity I seized, and only later, only now in fact, have I understood that I love it." Then, "It sounds like you haven't accepted the Canadian   offer."

"They haven't needed an answer yet."

They stood for a long while, quietly, not touching, several feet apart.

"I saw my mother this morning," Chad said.

"*Ah*."

"Care to guess how it went?"

"Kisses all around and a one-way ticket to Texas? A big high school band playing on your arrival, cheerleaders and pom-poms, the mayor with the key to city? Actually, I don't think you could get a high school band to play for an occasion like that —

though if anyone could, it would be your mother." Imad shook his head, looking rather enigmatically at Chad. "How I really think it went was frigid and – not reconciliatory."

"It certainly wasn't reconciliatory, though I don't know about the frigid part – in fact, I'd say it was on the hot side. She disowned me."

"Really now? That's a twist. Though it's probably for the best, considering you disowned her years ago. Don't you think?"

"That's pretty much what she said."

"Even Satan gets it right sometimes."

They were silent again.

"I used to say I'd write a novel," Chad said, at last, decanting his own great dream.

"You had plots and characters and titles aplenty."

"Oh God, I did – how embarrassing. Some were okay though. *Teddy Bear Graveyard*. That was my best."

"Don't remember that one," Imad said, "I remember a thing about Iceland, though."

"*Shirtless in Iceland*, I think. Or was it *Bare-chested*?"

"Shirtless."

"That's right. I remember now – the idea of shirtless Vikings appealed to me. Should we laugh at these things?" Chad asked.

"You used to laugh at yourself, it's part of what drew me to you. Your story about the crab puff *hors d'oeuvres*, and how you fed them to – well, I don't remember whose cat it was, but the poor thing died, I recall that much."

"Was taken to the vet in pain," Chad clarified, "unlike my Uncle, the cat survived Aunt Lorraine's cooking."

"It had the benefit of those nine lives, didn't it?" Imad said. "I really laughed when you told me that story. It was the night me met."

"At a party," Chad said. "Whose party was that?"

"It's the story I remember, not the party. You hardly spoke French at all then. Do you remember the first thing I ever translated for you from French?" Imad asked.

"Wasn't it on a condom wrapper?"

"You don't remember."

"Actually, I do," Chad said. "It was *mode d'emploi*. And I remember what it means, if I get extra points for that."

"You don't. I read in *Le Monde* today that there's a handbook for Korean Americans in Los Angeles, written by a Korean American in Los Angeles, which says you should never take a freeway with a 0 or a 4 in it because it's bad luck, but apparently that means you can't take any freeway at all since they all have either a 0 or a 4 in them. Maybe it's – what's that called? When numbers and directions and arrangement of furniture matter?"

"The average I.Q. magnified by universal absurdity," Chad said. "Though I think the expression you're searching for is *Feng Shui*, which I don't believe is Korean. But what do I know? I wouldn't have thought there were enough Korean immigrants in Los Angeles to support a book like that. Who knew?"

"Someone, apparently. Okay, here's another one. Do you remember why Margaret Drabble is my favorite writer?"

"Something about chest hair," Chad said.

"*Wow*. Not bad, it was –"

"Wait, wait, don't tell me yet. It was – it was – it was *Jerusalem the Golden*, the novel where the girl, I can't be expected to remember her name since I never read the book, is having sex with the brother of – the sister, her friend, the one she envies and wants to be just like, same name rule applies – here in Paris, right? Or maybe she's remembering having sex with him in Paris – but, at any rate, she talks about feeling his chest hair through his shirt. You loved it. That's why she's your favorite."

"I'd forgotten that bit was in Paris. My god, you remember my memories better than I do," Imad said. "*That's* depressing."

"Shouldn't you change favorite authors after all this time? And, you know, I'm flattered – I guess – but do you have *any* idea how many times I've known you were feeling up my chest hair under my shirt."

"You've got a lot of it, and chest hair is such a designer feature on a man."

"It'll be turning grey soon. You won't like it as much."

"Isn't there a chest hair dye? I think there is chest hair dye – I saw it BHV, in their new cosmetics department."

"Just for Men Chest – or something like that," Chad said. "I'll look into it."

They were quiet together a long while before Imad spoke. "I was different when you met me, wasn't I? Something's happened to me."

"How were you different?"

"I was witty and vibrant."

"I thought of you then as I think of you now."

"What does that mean? Dull as a post? Or did you think I was witty?"

"Clever, Imad, and cute. Sincerely cute. A great butt on an artist. Incredible combination." Then, realizing he should add something other than the physical, Chad said, "I loved it when you came to watch me play soccer and I'd see you standing there and, honestly, Imad, I'd think – what a killer combination, that tiny butt on that brainy guy. I'd chase the field thinking of you dancing – the way you still do sometimes, like that time to *Dirty Vegas*."

"At Queen? Which song?"

"*Lost not Found*," Chad said at once, unchallenged by the question.

"Was sincerely cute better than witty and vibrant?"

"Better in bed," Chad said, and then thinking about what he'd said, added, "look, they're just words. Let's say you were witty and vibrant, then, it hardly matters. Someday I'll have Alzheimer's and I won't even remember who you are, let alone what you were like when we met. You're plenty witty, Imad, and you've always been. You know that."

"Be on the lookout then for vibrant."

Chad turned and met Imad's eye. An unsounded instant passed, some Rubicon speechlessly passed, some promise finally made.

"Should we recommit ourselves to them, to those — what are they, Chad? I mean, what should I call them, if not our dreams?"

"Ideals?"

"All right, those ideals then?"

With enormous clarity, Chad thought: I've become the someone else I always wanted to be. What I felt yesterday was true. I've had my wish. It happened without me knowing about it. "You really know you're getting older when you find yourself putting your life into perspective."

"You're the one just turned forty. I still have some good years ahead of me."

"I suppose you do. So," Chad asked, staring out at the beauty of the morning, as ripe with color as a pre-Raphaelite painting. "What do we make of Roberta and Simon?"

With a shrug and a smile Imad said, "Personally, I'm going to take the romantic high ground and view it is a Cinderella story."

"Simon is a Prince?"

"I was thinking he was the Cinderella, rescued from his life of drudgery — but I've always said he was a prince of a fellow, haven't I?"

"No," Chad said with a laugh, "you haven't."

"Ah, then I meant to."

"Where's Imad now?" Simon asked.

"Still at his sister's — collecting up his things and his thoughts. Where's Roberta?"

"Shopping, so she said."

Chad and Simon were having coffee together at Chad's request. They sat now at a small round table at the place Simon favored on the *rue de Buci* (because it served meteor beer), a street Chad detested because it heaved with tourists any season, any time of the day or night. "You know, it's — shit,

Simon, honestly, it's unbelievable all that's happened in the last few weeks, I guess that's what I'm trying to say."

"And why are you trying to say it?"

"Not sure, really."

"That can't be why you wanted to talk to me."

"Why not? It *is* unbelievable all that's happened."

Simon nodded. "Hard to put events of this magnitude into context — is that what you mean? I suppose it'd be like me suddenly waking up again in Melbourne — with Marlene snoring there beside me, hair in rollers and cream on her face. You know — the most unexpected thing and no way to put it into context."

"For all of us, I suspect the last month has been even more dramatic than you waking up again next to Marlene."

"Nothing could be more dramatic than that, Mate. You don't know Marlene when she got her hair in rollers."

Chad stretched out his hand, and looked at his veins, his fingers. "Is there a steady state?" he asked. "In relations, in marriage — is there ever a time when you can say, this is it, this is how it should be?"

"No."

"No?"

"Because you only recognize the moment after it's gone, don't you?" Simon said. "It's not possible to see it as it happens. Maybe you're all curled up in bed like, and you think, this is as good as it gets, me all cozy and comfy like this. But that's not a bleeding steady state, is it? That's just feeling cozy and comfy."

"Maybe feeling cozy and comfy and being happy in bed is what a marriage is about."

Simon made a doubtful face. "I've only had the one marriage, and it was *always* happy in bed — fiasco that it was — Forster could have written that marriage into *Howard's End*."

"Maybe there are good and bad steady states, then — maybe the steady state for a disastrous marriage is when it's disastrous?"

"That's the nose on your face, isn't it? Which I guess means that I just contradicted myself about being able to say 'this is it' in a relationship. But what the fuck's all this steady state business about, Chad? What do you really want to ask me?"

Chad closed his eyes and leaned back with his face into the sun. "I want to know what I think about my life with Imad."

"And how does asking me all this help you know that?"

"You seem to have answers for things, Simon."

"Right."

"You do."

Simon was quiet a moment, watching some American tourists peer into the front windows of the restaurant across the street as if it were a peep show, ogling the well-accoutered clientele, then he said, "I think you and Imad are bloody well meant for each other, that's what I think — bloody well *meant* for each other."

Chad opened his eyes and looked at Simon; Simon held the look.

"Don't get it wrong, Chad. Get it right."

"Go on," Chad said.

"Me — I wonder sometimes what I would do if I could turn back the hands of time and behave sensibly — because I haven't always behaved like someone who wants things to work. I know I'm not good at balancing two things in the air at one time and I wish now that I'd learned how to do that — my life would have been different."

"See," Chad said, "that's what I mean. You know things, Simon."

"Right, then, grasshopper."

For what seemed like a long time they were quiet, listening to the street and the whine of a jet overhead. Chad said, not at all reluctantly, giving in to Simon and his influence and the many changes swirling around him, "you kissed Imad."

"I did, Chad."

"Why?"

"Because he needed kissing."

Chad tried to get his mind around the thought that his spouse needed kissing by another man.

Seeing his confusion, Simon said, "Because he needed to know that he was loved."

"And you love him?"

"Of course."

"But it's not – a thing?"

"A thing? What does that mean?" Simon said.

"Something romantic. Between the two of you?"

"Are you asking if I'm two-timing your cousin by sleeping with your boyfriend? I'm straight, Chad, and though I've had many chances to choose otherwise, I can assure you that I am and will remain on my own team. All right? I love Imad as a best friend loves his best friend – that's all."

A moment of silence, then Chad said, "All right."

Then Simon smiled, winked at Chad and said, "did you teach him to kiss that well or has he taught you?

"I'll leave you guessing on that one," Chad said – smiling despite himself.

222

"You know what? I miss the little bugger. I haven't seen him in a day or two and I miss him. We should have invited him with us today."

"And who might this little bugger be? I know you're not talking about Imad."

"*Aksel*," Simon said, as if Chad were dense.

"You're joking."

"I'm not. Talk about knowing things. Really – that boy is a veritable Plato of the Norsemen. I damn well miss the little fucker when I don't see him for a day or two. Don't you?"

Chad thought about Aksel – thought about their many conversations. "I suppose he's rather missable."

The continuing quiet between them was curative, even cathartic. Closing his eyes and filling himself with sun, Chad said, "and you know what. Shit, I even miss that goddamned old rhinestoned bird Galsworthy."

"Ah, well, mate. *There*," Simon said emphatically, "I draw the line."

14

In sixth grade she'd been given a speaking role in the school holiday pageant. Of course, it was the same event as when it had been called the Christmas pageant, they just changed the name to look modern. They even added a song about a dreidel, although there was only one Jewish girl in her entire grade, Lisa Weiss, and Lisa Weiss claimed she'd never seen a dreidel and didn't know what they were singing about. Mrs. Rochester, their director, told Lisa to stop yapping (her word exactly) or she'd send Lisa to the Principal so fast her shoes would smoke (also her exact expression). According to Earlene Rochester they *were* going to sing about this little spinning top thingie, whether Lisa Weiss knew about it or not. Roberta knew that Lisa cried after class because she saw her standing alone behind the library sniveling.

That year's dreidel controversy not withstanding, the holiday pageant was the pinnacle of sixth grade and Roberta wanted Helen and Chad to watch her introduce the carol "We Three Kings," by reading a passage from the bible about the wise men and what they brought baby Jesus, and a whole bunch of other stuff that one of their English teachers, Mr. Delgado, wrote for the occasion. Mr. Delgado had a flair for costumes (he did their annual school play too) and since he wasn't married he got to spend a lot of time down to Houston, which seemed to be pretty nearly every weekend from what Roberta could tell. One Monday he came back with a love bite on his neck, though Roberta thought it best not to tell Aunt Helen about her teacher having a love bite – especially since Helen seemed to look askance at Mr. Delgado. Once asked Roberta if it were true that he wore loafers with tassels on them. He did, although Roberta had protectively said she didn't know.

After another of his Houston trips, he brought back some costumes. Most of them were too large for sixth graders, since he had borrowed them from a friend "in the community theater community." Roberta liked the sound of that double-barreled community spirit and unity. However, large though they were, one toga fit Roberta perfectly. Mr. Delgado and Mrs. Rochester agreed that Roberta could wear it when she read the wise men introduction, and Roberta immediately fell in love with her toga with its scarlet satin piping and purple mantle and, therefore, she kept secret the fact that taped behind the bottom hem was a label that said, "Whore of Babylon." The night before the pageant she was allowed to take it home, and she wore it around all evening, sashaying from room to room practicing her lines, until Helen finally said, "take that ridiculous thing off before you get moths in my house and go spray some Lysol on it – it smells like some trucker wore it on a long haul drive in August."

The idea of a trucker (she was partial to truckers, they always seemed so manly) wearing her whore of Babylon toga intrigued Roberta, though she wondered whether or not he'd be wearing underwear underneath it. Nobody would know what you had on beneath a toga, would they? Maybe he could shift gears better without underwear. Maybe that was why he was wearing her whore of Babylon outfit in the first place, so that he could be naked and comfortable and shift gears and wave at his friends without any binding or boxer bunch-up (Chad had taught her that saying)? Of course, none of this excused the fact that he hadn't showered – but Roberta figured showers were hard to find when you were a long-haul trucker on the road in August, with or without your whore of Babylon toga.

Helen was noncommittal about coming to the pageant. She had a gift exchange party at the Tech Terrace house of one of her bible circle friends and she didn't want to be late. It was always "so darned hard to park on Lizzie's street, they ought to be ashamed." Since Lizzie lived a mere two blocks away, Roberta almost suggested walking – but maybe Helen meant she'd be taking the car to Roberta's pageant afterward, and Roberta didn't want to give her a way out of coming. Chad told Roberta privately that he'd try to ditch Chemistry class. Right up until the moment of her entrance Roberta watched the back of the auditorium, waiting for them. Her parents' death was still fresh – still an open, unhealed wound. Having Helen and Chad at the pageant, well, it meant a lot. Maybe it would mean she *had* found a new family – maybe it would mean that things had happened for the best. But she had started her monologue and was well into the bible passage, and there was no sign of them. Just as she reached the part about the gifts for baby Jesus, Chad bounded breathlessly into the packed auditorium, pushing people aside so that she could see him. And she did.

Even though a woman seated in the front row had said in a loud voice, "she's wearing something from one of them Roman orgies, that for sure ain't no bible outfit," causing people to twitter and mutter, Roberta had never been happier. She beamed at Chad when she finished and he led the applause. She bowed and went back to join her classmates for the singing. Afterward, when she'd changed and given her beloved toga back to Mr. Delgado – who said to Mrs. Rochester in a too-loud whisper that Roberta could hear as she went down the stairs, "thank God we had us a big girl in the class who was too dim-witted to notice she had on a whore of Babylon outfit," she found Chad waiting. He hugged her and kissed her and told her she was wonderful. He even took her to J.T. McCord's for a hamburger and fries, since he reckoned that having ditched Chemistry he might just as well ditch Pre-Calculus as well.

That was the Chad she still held near to her heart, like a talisman of family and love – that was the Chad she adored, and whose loss she had felt too keenly over the years since he left Lubbock.

At the moment, Roberta and Aksel were sitting at a corner table in the Open Café. Outside, on crowded *rue des archives*, men on plastic chairs grouped themselves around tables, and watched the sidewalk parade. Roberta marveled at the miscellany of these passing people, ranging from startled American tourists – their guide books *said* this was the old Jewish quarter, but instead they found men kissing other men and putting their hands up one another's shorts – to scowling locals toting *Franprix* grocery sacks to panhandlers of indeterminate nationality to handsome French gendarmes in tight blue shirts. Outside of television programs set in New York, Roberta had never seen so many different people in one place. The only thing they seemed to have in common was their awareness of the watching eyes within and without the Open Café.

"The only thing these people have in common," Roberta said to Aksel, "is the fact they know everybody's looking at them."

"Which we are," he said.

"Which we are," she agreed. "But it's like they're on parade, isn't it? Knowing we're approving or disapproving or ignoring – or maybe it's the other way around – but as if they were, what? On parade."

"Yes, on parade. That's it."

She watched it all for awhile longer, then said with a sigh, "I've spent a lot of my life asleep, Aksel."

"You are making a metaphor?"

"Oh. Am I?" She didn't know what a metaphor was exactly (she always got it confused with a simile), but she thought a metaphor was when you said something indirectly, without using 'like' or 'as,' so she shook her head, "no, I mean really and truly asleep, every chance I could get. I was forever curling up and taking naps – two in the afternoon, ten in the morning, whenever, always thinking that if I could just sleep – the world would – *what*? Go away, I guess."

"Did it?"

"No. Not once." After a moment more of watching the street she said, "But I could have meant it as a metaphor too, couldn't I?"

"For sure. And now you are awake, literally and metaphorically?"

"Yes, and now I'm awake – and trying to decide if I'm in control of my own life." She took a long swig of her beer, wiped her lips, then she drank again, thinking of this beer swigging as an act of defiance – of liberation even. "This is one huge transformation, if it's true. If I *am* in control." Looking around, at the tables full of men and the line of men at the bar, she thought about how each one of them must have gone through a transformation just to be here. Hadn't they taken control of their own lives just walking through the door of this place – or some place like this – the first time? She liked thinking that she was surrounded by people like herself, even if they were unlike her in other ways. "I was in the holiday pageant when I was in sixth grade," she said. "Chad came to see me. He was so – animated and, well – I should have known, shouldn't I?"

"Because of his animation?"

"Partly. I mean he might have been athletic and handsome but it was a dead give-away him admiring the satin piping on my costume and all, huh?"

"Your sexuality does not make you admire satin piping," Aksel said. "That is ridiculous. Sebastien would not know satin from *le velours* – how do you say it? Oh yes, from velvet."

Roberta shrugged at his mention of Sebastien, at how easily he said the man's name, just as if it were – what? Normal. "You know, I'm still not a hundred percent sure what all I think about Chad being gay. You spend your life thinking one way and then, presto-chango, you're trying to think some other way. It isn't easy, despite how much I like Imad." But she was starting to see this as also an act of defiance, but a more measured, a more considered defiance than swigging beer – a real liberation.

"We have the same issue," he said, gesturing around at the men.

"We who?"

"Gay men. You call it internalized homophobia in English."

"I don't understand," she said.

"Usually, gay men are raised to believe that to be straight is to be better than gay – often they are raised like you, to believe that to be gay is sinful. It can take them years to overcome these effects of upbringing – even after a man decides that he *is* gay and has to *be* gay he carries around the beliefs of his youth. Some people never forget their upbringing or the disrespect of the society with which they identify and so they try to kill themselves in blatant – or sometimes in subtle ways."

"Subtle ways?" she asked.

"Oh – alcoholism, for example. Drugs. Sex."

"Alcoholism, drugs and sex aren't all that subtle," she said. Then, "I never thought about it that way." She hadn't.

"Try to imagine how it would feel to hear yourself described on the television as if you were an object – a *thing* – and then you can also imagine how hard it is, even now in this day and age, to accept yourself."

Roberta knew what it felt like to be treated as if she were an object: the fat girl, the orphan. She'd more or less always been labeled like an object. "Can you really not change?"

"Change?"

"You know."

"Oh – and become straight, you mean?"

"Can you?" she asked back, feeling a little insane, but not just for asking this question. "I guess I mean could you – if you wanted?"

"I do not believe that one can change, Roberta. There are gay men who are able to have sex with women and sometimes these men pretend – at least for awhile – that they are straight. But you cannot be what you are not."

Roberta tried to imagine herself having sex with a woman (but the face that loomed toward her as a possible accomplice was – *incredibly* – the grinning, ringlet-shrouded visage of Loreen K. Albrighton). Roberta flushed, defiantly drank more beer and said, "of course not, how silly of me."

"Yes, it is silly, but I admire your honesty," Aksel said. "You are experiencing a transformation."

"I guess I am – I know I've been burning my bridges, that's for darned sure. And, you know, there are some bridges that can't be rebuilt once you've burned them. I guess the rule is don't even try – to rebuild them, I mean." She looked at Aksel, discovering something profound about this turn in her life. "Just let the suckers keep on burning, right down to the waterline.

Huh? Of course, facing any truth about yourself? Geez, that's hard," she said.

"Some truths are more truthful than others," Aksel said.

"Ain't that the truth," she said, with a laugh at using the word truth again. They were quiet awhile. "Aksel?"

"Roberta?"

She put her hand on his. "I'm glad we swore to be friends. Remember – back when I fell on the sidewalk? I'm real glad."

He looked at their hands, piled on one another and said, still with gentleness, "a moment in our lives, Roberta. A moment."

They stood in the *jardin des plantes*, the Botanical Gardens, at the foot of a sloping hillside covered with variegated flowers. "I can't forgive you, Chad" Roberta said, "although I've tried – well, I think I've tried. I've tried to try, I know that." Briefly her face went blank, uncongealed, and then she said less harshly, "but it doesn't matter if I really tried or not, because I can't."

"Forgive me for what?"

She turned to him angrily. She'd been practicing these words, they were important to her, and he had not made the right response; his answer did not signify understanding. Of course, she knew that he knew what she meant. He knew she meant more than the way in which he'd never come back to get her (or even to see her). He knew she also meant his years of general rejection, ignoring the unities of their childhood, denying her his friendship and love – no letters, no phone calls, no jokes, no stories, no hugs, no kisses. That was what she meant. He walked toward the shade by a pond and she followed him. They stood together at the railing and watched ripples on the water.

"I realize you haven't asked for my forgiveness," she said, "so it's probably self-serving for me to just announce it that way. I'm sorry about that part."

"Oh, I knew what you meant," he said, turning so that he could see her profile. He didn't blame her. In some ways he didn't forgive himself either. "The other night you said you had figured out that your world had always been made up of strangers – or something to that effect."

"I was being amusing, Chad – I said I'd realized how I always depended on the kindness of strangers, it's from that Marlon Brando movie."

"*Streetcar Named Desire*."

"That's right. But yes I meant Aunt Helen, sure I did. I see now that she's always been a stranger – she's not family at all."

"And me."

"You didn't have to be a stranger, Chad, you chose to be one – Aunt Helen had to be. She's nothing but a cold hearted old –," but she left the thought incomplete.

"*Are* we strangers, Roberta?"

"I don't know. I don't think we are – not in that way, not in the Helen way. But there's not much family in what we have. My word, can you imagine me trying to make a mother out of Aunt Helen all those years? What a horse's ass I've been. Huh? Can you imagine a more foolish exercise than *that*?"

A fish rose to the surface, poised between greenery. Chad watched it a moment. Then he moved so that his back was against the railing, and he could look down the hill, toward the streets and the buildings. "Do you know why I wanted you to come up here with me this morning, Bert?"

She waited for him to tell her.

"Because it's where I came when I got my job renewed, when I knew I was going to escape for good and that I'd be staying in Paris – staying in Paris forever I guess."

She looked not at the city, but at the pond and the fish. "I *hate* when you use that word."

"Forever?"

"No," she said, "forever doesn't mean anything, it's just a — a meaningless notion. No, I hate that you say 'escape.' Escape isn't meaningless. And it makes me furious to hear you say that, Chad."

"But that's what it was."

"No, sir, that's just how you *made* it be."

"That's how it was, Roberta — for me, for me that's how it was: escape. It's the truth."

"Why, Chad — why's that how it was for you?"

"Because I was a prisoner there and going away — it was my — *escape* — from jail."

"Sometimes I think I hate you," she said. "I know now that I hate Aunt Helen — in fact, I hate her more than I could possibly say."

"You told me you love me."

"And sometimes I think I love you — a lot."

Sunlight glinted off the *Gare d'Austerlitz* and the windscreens of cars on the roundabout between the gardens and the Seine. He turned back around to the pond and with a shrug said, "you're entitled to your feelings, Roberta — they're all — what? Natural. Understandable. So — well, feel what you want to feel, and let's just see how it all evolves. Shall we?"

She was silent.

"Roberta?"

She examined her watch. "Sure," she said, "but to me, that's just another way of saying something like *forever*. So, sure, we can let it *evolve*. Like Monkeys did when they evolved from out of the jungle into Loreen K. Albrighton." She stood up straight. "I have to stop by the bookstore. I want to find something for Simon."

"I wouldn't mind getting a book or two myself. I'll go with you."

"Okay, that's fine, then." Struggle filled her voice, but abstractedly, undetermined, a voice which was exploratory and tentative – and struggling.

"Second thoughts?" he asked.

"About –?"

He watched her before saying, "in French one says, *je deviens moi*. It's not an uncommon expression here. It means, 'I am becoming myself.'"

She held her hair away from her face, but did not look at him directly. "You can't turn back the hands of time."

"Thank God."

"And you can't – undo what's been done."

"I'm not trying to," he said.

Again, she fell silent. There was a loud slurping noise from the pond, and they both turned to look.

"But I *have* been trying to," she said, "and I probably always will be trying to."

"Oh, Bertie, I'm so sorry. Can't you really forgive me? Even a little?"

232

She cracked at that, relented, and came to stand beside him. Their arms went around each other. They stood that way for a long while, not speaking. Chad started to see that things made sense. He saw a pattern. He felt a dawning awareness of something like knowledge. He stepped away from her and breathed deeply. Then, he turned back and stepped into her waiting arms. She held him in her protective embrace and he felt himself cling to her as if in that clinging some definition of his self might emerge, as if he might finally know who he was, as if he might be able to say, *je deviens moi*.

"You don't really hate me, do you?" he asked her.

"No, of course not."

"Does Simon play the guitar?" he asked.

"Yes," she said, "I think he does."

"You are so lucky."

"Yes," she said. "I know."

"And so's he," Chad said.

She smiled at that, and it was not a smile he could remember ever having seen on Roberta's face — it was the grown up smile of someone who had learned to discern the sadness of platitudes. "Remains to be seen, doesn't it? Remains to be seen."

Roberta had left a message on Simon's *messagerie*, letting him know that she would drop by before lunch. He was waiting for her with croissants and pastries. His apartment was so much *him*, she thought as she came through the door, with its masculine simplicity and crisp — something, like masculinity and yet different. His apartment seemed artless; it seemed as genuine as Simon himself.

"I've seen Chad," she told him, nibbling on a croissant and going to the *porte-fenetre*.

"Oh, yeah?"

"Yeah." She looked out on the Cluny ruins and the lines of tourists. "We fought and made up — and I think it was *meaningful*."

"That you fought or that you made up?"

After consideration, she said. "Both."

"You fought about him disappearing the way he did?"

She smiled, taking into account the many vanishing acts of her cousin Chad. "Yes — about him disappearing."

Simon seemed to understand. "It's about time you two dealt with that."

"I must have thought so too, or I wouldn't have provoked the fight. At any rate, I got him pretty worked up, at least for awhile. I think I've made him jittery, that cousin of mine."

"Me too," Simon smiled. "I'm jittery — I'm *conspicuously* jittery."

"But not because of me."

He looked at her with swift deliberation. "Of course, because of you."

"Simon, you were jittery way before I came into the picture," she said, "you've been jittery all your life, I reckon," and then seeming to adjust to the look on his face she smiled, and with a more good-natured heartiness said, "so don't be tellin' fibs. In fact, it seems to me that I've made you a heck of a lot less restless and edgy. That's what I think. But restless or not, either way – you're about as different from Chad as night from day, because – well, because you belong in your world. Chad doesn't, not yet, and I'm don't, but you do – probably you always will."

"Belong in my world?" He thought about that. "Sounds American."

"I am American," she said.

"I know myself, Roberta – sure, I think I do. So if that's what you mean by belonging in my world, then I guess I do."

"It's what I mean by it this morning. It's kind of a silly 234 expression – maybe I should have said harmony, that's better. You're in harmony with your world. And me? I'm just starting to know myself – and I'm not even close to coming to grips. Not even close. I'm every bit as on edge as Chad."

He brooded a moment, his eyes on her keenly, brooding but not gloomy. "You're full of
ideas today, aren't you? Is this what comes from a morning spent fighting with Chad?"

"I think it's what comes from drinking beers with thought-provoking Norwegian boys. And I didn't really fight with Chad – I mean, maybe I told him off a little. I shouldn't have said I fought with him. I tried to be cruel, though – I really did, and I'm kind of ashamed of that. But I couldn't keep it up and, anyway, he's a tough nut." She whistled quietly and shook her head. "Just look how he's treated Imad."

She and Simon looked at one another and Simon nodded in agreement.

"No excuse for being that kind of hard," she said, "no matter what, not even considering – well, *what* a mother he has – still, it doesn't excuse everything. But who could be surprised?"

"A mother like that excuses a *shitload*, Roberta, at least in my crude view." He thought about something with his eyes closed. When they were open again, he turned to her with a new spark. "Do you remember the first time we met?" But before she could say yes, he said quickly, "I remember, crikey, I remember everything – your laugh – your smile, my God, I felt like I'd done some *Alice through the Looking Glass* maneuver. I was incredibly," he searched for what he wanted to say and came up with, "self-aware – that's how I knew it was the real thing, all of that self-awareness – I thought, my life isn't going to be the same, not now that I've met her."

"That's awfully romantic," she said, savoring it, but wondering about its truthfulness all the same. "And in a million years I never thought I'd hear someone say that to me – and mean it. But I wonder if it's good or bad."

"Bad? How could it be bad?"

"I meant bad for you – not bad for me."

"Why would it be bad for me?"

"Of course, I also remember every darned thing about meeting you, Simon – everything. Lord have mercy, I remember every single hair on that chest of yours, in fact I think I counted them." She smiled at him, turned away. "I can see Chad going back to Lubbock – for a visit. I could see it this morning, clear as the day is long. I don't think it will involve Aunt Helen though – I think he's well and truly rid of her. I think it will involve –"

"Himself?" Simon asked, interrupting her.

"Yes. Himself. Him only."

"And you?

"And me?"

"Are you well and truly rid of Aunt Helen? Or are you thinking of trying to patch things up with her?"

"Oh no, there's no patching that whole mess up. Lord have mercy. No, that period of my life is so over. Over for both of us, Helen as well as me. I detest the woman."

"You sure about that?"

"I'm not always sure about stuff, you know that. But oh yes –I am sure about this, Simon. On this subject, I'm as sure as can be. Too much has happened. I'm different for her now, I'm not the Roberta she – I was going to say 'the Roberta she needed,' but even that's stretching the truth, isn't it?"

"And she's different for you now too?"

"She's not, see – that's the thing. No, she's the *same* to me. To be honest, she's more than *ever* the same, the same hateful old bag. If she were different to me, then there might be – *might be* – some chance of patching things up. But she's not, she's the same – and she always will be the same, sad as it is to say it."

Something came clear to him, and he stood up with sudden energy. "You're going back to Lubbock, aren't you, Roberta? Holy shit. That's what you're struggling to tell me today, isn't it?"

236

"Not permanently."

"Why in the bleeding hell do you want to go back there – it's not a home you're going back to, you know that."

"Maybe not," she agreed. "It's about holding my head up high. You have to understand the way Lubbock, Texas works. If I don't go back, there will always be something – what? Something unfinished. Something ugly. I need to do this, Simon, in order to hold my head up high – in order to say goodbye to everything properly."

"Haven't you done that?"

"No – no, not at all. And I really and truly don't want it to look like that harpy drove me off. I want it to look like –," and she thought about what she wanted it to look like, "like it's all my own choice."

"You care that much about what people think?"

"I care what *I* think," she said, "and in Lubbock, Texas, yes, we do care what other people think. That's our way. That's who we are."

"Am I going with you?" he asked.

Her answer was speedy –practiced. She seemed to be waiting for this. "No. I need to do this on my own, Simon. I need to — square it all — make it be — what word did I just use? Oh, yeah — harmonious. Then I'll know I'm myself — maybe even a little bit like you do. I'll belong in my world, and I can say," she concentrated a moment before coming out with, *"je deviens moi."*

"*Whoa* – and then whoa again."

"I've been paying attention."

"I'd say you have."

"And once I know myself, then I'll know that everything," and she gestured at him, and then out the window toward Paris, which seemed gathered up around the Cluny museum, reflected off the windows and tree tops of the square, then back again toward him, her fingers quivering, "is for real."

"You will come back, Roberta? Won't you?"

"I think so," she said.

"There's nothing, you know, really *nothing* that I wouldn't do for you."

"I know that, Simon – I know."

"Nothing in the entire world."

"I know. I know. But all the same I've just got to go back there — and without you, that part's really important. Like — what? Like psychologically? Is that what I mean?"

"Yes, that's what you mean," he said. "You need to do this so that everything will feel right afterward — and not accidental."

"And harmonious," she said, "and purposeful. Yes — I'll need to know that I'm myself and not some make-believe stupid fat girl from out of Aunt Helen's imagination." She sighed. "I can't barely resist you, you know that, Simon – but –"

"But there we are," he said, moving toward her and taking her in his arms. "And you know where I'll be once you have it all squared. Once you're feeling –"

"Harmonious."

"Harmonious," he said, with apprehensive tenderness in his voice. "All right, then, Roberta. You know where I'll be when you find your harmony."

Before the performance, Chad and Imad sat together over coffee. They talked briefly about a recent terrorist outrage, about incinerated innocent people. Genuine, the smell of coffee and a Cimmerian sky through a dirty window. Something about it thundered with memory, like childhood itself. It touched Chad's inner visions. Reminders of things past swirled up with the coffee aroma, tinctures of childhood released through the phantom shapes that played against the glass. But what did Chad see in the dirty window except his own reflection? Yet, it was utterly real, without compromise. He sipped the coffee, hands cupped around the mug. He blew on the surface and felt the moist hot sensation against his eyelids. Then, they went outside and stood together, contemplating the knurly, dazzling vista of Los Angeles.

Around them, people seemed unusually exuberant, as if they were more interested in each other than the play they'd paid so much to see. The terrace atmosphere was vivacious, communal, celebratory – like a party. Of course, the crowd was largely a Hollywood 'networking' set, though Chad and Imad seemed to fit right in. Their Parisian mien passed them off. Chad felt the sundry eyes upon them. He liked thinking of himself as handsome in this Los Angeles crowd. Men in trendy suits and hand-painted ties ogled him; women in glossy evening wear stared flirtatiously. He invited their eyes with a dimpled smile, and a hand firmly placed in the middle of Imad's back. He could tell that Imad liked having his hand there; he sensed that Imad enjoyed, rather than feared, the admiring looks that handsome Chad Newsome drew from strangers.

"It's sensational," Imad said.

"What is?"

Imad laughed. "The view."

"City view or people view?"

"Both, of course."

They nearly kissed, but did not, their cheeks grazed hotly, and then their lips moved away.

"Sorry," Chad said, "I just can't do it in public."

They smiled at one another with restless passion.

"I'm still letting it sink in," Imad said, "all of the flat open space – all of the flat open people."

Chad laughed. "I wish they could have come up with a tornado, and then you'd have had the perfect Lubbock experience."

"I had the perfect Lubbock experience," Imad said. "Trust me. I'll be telling Simon about it for years. Somehow I don't imagine Roberta ever bringing him there. She seems poised for the leap – and I don't think she'll leap backward, do you?"

"No."

"Did I hear you patching things up with her again?"

"Spackling over the holes we've made? Like a punched-in wall?"

Imad didn't respond; he calmly enjoyed the view. Then, he said, "It was a lovely moment, Chad, standing there looking at the Buddy Holly statue, everybody staring at me as if I were – what did they think I was?"

"It was your accent more than anything – let's say, you seemed exotic. They're used to people from other places, the hospitals and university in Lubbock wouldn't have thrived without immigrants – but they don't usually speak British English with a French accent."

"Ah – I'm exotic now. I'll be treated to, 'some of our best friends are ...' next."

They laughed, and then they listened to the conversations around them.

Chad suddenly recalled sitting beside Imad in a cinema. It came back to him now, vivid and evocative. He recalled the film, a mystery with Catherine Deneuve, and he recalled how Imad's hand had wiggled into his own. In the theater that day, he had not thought to cherish this sense of belonging; he'd liked it, even relished it, but he had not cherished it. Now, he knew that such things had to be cherished. Life was frightening and lonesome; it was important to belong to someone, and to belong somewhere. On the way into downtown Los Angeles, driving along the freeway, with the palm-tree urban landscape condensing into a chocolate blur, with billboards advertising underwear and money services in Spanish, the exponentially exploding cars of west coast America, he imagined that he and Imad might just keep on driving forever, at home simply with one another.

Imad *was* his home, and with Imad, well – he could go anywhere, and feel that feeling which had once come to him once in a cinema on the *Champs Elysees*, and which have pervaded his spirit the morning he turned forty and walked the streets of Bougival. Then, he had thought that France was his home (and it was), but not he realized that it was more complex than that. Imad was his home – and they lived in France.

"It's been a great trip," Imad said, "but I'm anxious to get back to Paris."

Thinking then of the vistas from their *portes-fenetres*, and the church bells from St. Nicolas du Chardonnet, and the dome of the Pantheon, and his quotidian journey on the metro from *Maubert-Mutualité* to *Pont de Saint-Cloud*, Chad's hand moved up Imad's back, and lovingly squeezed his neck.

Roberta had been driving around Loop 289, the freeway encircling central Lubbock, for nearly an hour. The South Plains had been under a tornado watch all afternoon, and she'd been keenly scrutinizing the horizon in hopes of spotting one. She kept the radio tuned to the weather station in Amarillo, her ears alert to the first report of a tornado warning for Lubbock County. The milestones of her life had been passing by with dull monotony: elementary school, junior high, high school, stores, the bowling alley where she'd had her sixteenth-birthday party, drive-through restaurants. She was on the way to surrender her car to the dealer at the airport, the one who had first promised her 'top dollar,' but in the end offered her just about what she could have received if she sold it for scrap. Since essentially it *was* scrap, she didn't care – and she was confused about what to do with the car money anyway. She'd already closed out her bank account, that paltry amount now contained within a cashier's check, tucked into the zippered lining of her purse. Considering the amount her car was fetching, perhaps the man would pay her in cash? That seemed a reasonable enough request. Of course, she figured that if she asked for cash, he'd use that as pretext to lower the price – again.

241

She didn't care.

Passing one of the exits for Texas Tech University, a cold recollection came to her of attending a show there last year with Helen. A fading country western actress singer gave the blessing, standing in a rodeo tie and leatherette skirt, saying something like 'you are a wonderful God and your world is so darned beautiful.' This remembrance tingled through to the new and wiser Roberta, who now detested inanity, the Roberta who had become – w ell, whatever she'd become. 'You're wrong, you foolish actress singer,' she thought, 'God's majesty is in the fact that it's *not* always a beautiful world, and by the way, I'd like to poke out your painted-up homophobic eyes with the metal tips of your rodeo tie.' Roberta's emotions quivered. Torn equally between acceptance and rejection of this new Roberta, she wished herself far away, on another planet perhaps. She wished himself to the very ends of the earth, where water thundered in cataracts off the edge of the known world and sea serpents played, and no one could find her or know her or reach out to her.

She'd last seen Helen by chance, although the timing of their encounter made Roberta wonder whether it was fate more than chance. It happened shortly after she dropped Chad and Imad off at the airport, at the conclusion of their week-long visit. She decided to swing by the South Plains mall. Coming through one of the big main entrances near Penny's, she met Helen and Loreen K. Albrighton face-to-face. Of course, the look of flabbergasted dismay on Helen's face more or less made the sighting worth the pain. They stared at one another in soundless fury. In the end, predictably, Helen simply took hold of Loreen's elbow and pulled the two of them away from Roberta – as if from contamination – and out the door into the shimmering West Texas sunlight. Roberta had turned around after them (it was instinct to do that, after all – *wasn't* it?) and watched them scuttle across the parking lot like a pair of over-dressed cockroaches.

Recalling how she had endured the inevitable Helen episode with self-possession (she'd gone off to buy some new tops and a mauve purse, on sale at Dillard's), Roberta felt better – much better, in fact. She wanted then not to be at the ends of the earth, but smack in the middle of everything, where life and people and colors and excitement eddied disproportionately. She wanted to be found, to be known, to be reached out to – to be held. Still no tornado, so this time she took the exit toward the airport. The car dealership loomed up before her. This then must be it – the moment of no return. The car dealer had a shuttle service to the airport, so this must be a tradition of sorts, trading in your car before leaving the South Plains – cotton, dust, relatives, weevils, churches – behind you. She pulled to a stop by a desiccated pine tree. In the rearview mirror she could see the red spots on her cheeks, glowing with anticipation – with life – and on the backseat, her new roller-model suitcase. She got out of the car and stood watching the far-away city skyline and the billows of menacing cloud. No tornado. And if there had been – would she really have run into it? Would it really have been the sign she thought it had to be? She waited patiently. The engine ticked beneath the hood.

Nothing.

So, she thought, glancing at her watch and calculating the time until her flight: this was it.

245

www.ingramcontent.com/pod-product-compliance
Lightning Source LLC
Chambersburg PA
CBHW020757250626
47155CB00003B/1114